W9-BHG-917

Thomas Keith Tindale
South Hanover
November, 1967.

MARIE BEGINNING

Other books by Alfred Grossman

ACROBAT ADMITS

MANY SLIPPERY ERRORS

MARIE BEGINNING

ALFRED GROSSMAN

Doubleday & Company, Inc., Garden City, New York, 1965

All of the characters in this book are fictitious, and any resemblance to actual persons, living or dead, is purely coincidental.

Library of Congress Catalog Card Number 65-14004
Copyright © 1964 by Alfred Grossman
All Rights Reserved
Printed in the United States of America

To George Lieber (1926–1963)

✳ 1 ✳

At nine thirty, on the first Monday in June, Sheldon Friberg drank coffee in his office on the eleventh floor, and pronounced revelation of impending catastrophe. "Or perhaps," he said, "catastrophe is not exact, perhaps the word for it should be the word for whatever was about to happen to the Incas the morning before they sighted the sails of the Conquistadores. True, it was to bring ruin and desolation, death for many and cultural destruction for all, but to call that catastrophe is shortsighted. Look at that continent now, rich in exciting history, proud and hungry on the threshold of the last century, bursting with the Western ethos, Christianized to the starving dogs that scavenge the villages. No, I as a time-bound creature feel catastrophe, but my great-grandchildren may have other words for it. Nevertheless, my intestines are being marinated in a bitter brew, my spine is a reed thrumming in a wind called doom and my ribs are a cage for the rancid pitiless crows."

"Nonsense," Kennan said. "You don't have the slightest idea what you're talking about. South America's in fine shape. Needs more priests, of course, but I remember reading that a Vatican commission has been set up to see to it, so don't worry."

"I am talking," Friberg said, "about life, not some mythical inverted continent."

"Right," Kennan said. "So let's leave the Church out of it. Now, do I gather you've heard some news about the office that I haven't? I thought things were settling, for God's sake."

"I have heard nothing," Friberg said, "nothing but a faint distant shuffle as something, somewhere, picks up the strings that move us and prepares to make us dance, to twitch our limbs in an alien and incredible parody of free will."

"Good," Kennan said, "so it's nothing that will affect me. Fine. You've been fighting with Sheila."

"Ours is a fabulous marital adjustment," Friberg said; "everybody knows that."

"Well," Kennan said, "I can't say I really want to journey down to the muck and slime of your true self, but I'd say it's one of two things. Either it's a hangover from reading the Sunday *Times* and finding out more about how the world is going than it's prudent to know. Or more likely, you're all crumpled up with guilt and fear about Sheila, guilt that you're so unworthy of her, fear that she's going to find it out and do the sensible thing. It must be tough, being unworthy like that."

Sheldon drained his cardboard cup and crumpled it into the wastebasket. "Fine," he said, "keep it up. Go on reveling in adolescent erotic fantasies of women forever unavailable to you, crippled as you are by the murderous puritanism of an outworn faith. Go on. But I tell you I feel it, I feel it, there is a power moving to pick us up and fling us like dice in a box. We stand, my friend, at the crater's lip, and you for one will regret your awful levity when you are howling and tossing in the maelstrom below. Don't ask me what it is or how I know. Only believe."

"I believe," Kennan said, stretching, "I will go and do some work. Vernon wants to see some ideas for the September show. If you remember the bomb's name before it goes off, send me a memo."

"You're right," Sheldon said, "helpless as we are we'd best absorb ourselves in the trivia of the day."

⌘ 2 ⌘

A few minutes before ten o'clock, on the tenth floor, three young women sat side by side on the couch in the personnel office reception room. This was not comfortable, but the leather chair was occupied by the hat and coat of a friend of the director of personnel. The girl in the middle got up and stepped over to lean against the wall. "Please be seated," the motherly receptionist said, "Miss Ferrucci will be with you shortly."

"The couch is too little," the girl against the wall said, "their legs press on me."

The two seated girls moved sideways. The receptionist resumed typing. From the wall behind her came sounds of other busy typewriters, the hump-clunk of desk calculating machines and the deep artillery of an IBM complex. There was no sound of street traffic and it was too early in the year for air-conditioning.

The machines' sounds grew louder as the inner door opened and Miss Ferrucci came out, smiling graciously through her headache. Briefly: Lydia Ferrucci, twenty-eight, Syracuse College, personnel secretary, executive personnel secretary, for a year now assistant personnel director, hungover. Very striking: long meticulous black hair, sallow but smooth skin. On the small side. But a figure, a figure, a neat bottom, narrow waist, blossoming into enormous articulated breasts straining her modest cashmere, breasts that sang like Excalibur of high endeavor and triumph, breasts that astonished you as the discoverer of the giraffe was astonished, and whispered piously, "Can such things be? Oh, Lord, thy powers."

"Who first, please?" Miss Ferrucci said, focusing her eyes against the morning haze. The girl at the wall stooped to pick her purse and personnel form from the floor. "Follow me, please," Miss Ferrucci said.

Down the corridor, Marie Betty Svobodna saw the men at the desks behind the glass partitions lift their heads and watch Miss Ferrucci's breasts go past. Their expressions were solemn, thoughtful. The heads raised and the eyes moved as a wave rolls over the sea.

Miss Ferrucci held open the door of her cubicle, motioned Marie to sit, sat herself behind the desk and held out her hand for the personnel form. Giving it to her, Marie said, "I'll bet if I had been naked walking behind you they wouldn't have noticed." Miss Ferrucci glanced at her, said mmm, and examined the form, resting brow on finger tips.

"Well," she said when done. "Now I don't think the agency has been very fair to you, Miss Svobodna."

"You pronounce that just right," Marie said. "Most people get it wrong, a lot of times it comes out slob-under, you know? I used to have trouble at school, they made Slobby my nickname. Well, one of them. They used to call me Goosy sometimes because of something that happened in my sophomore year. I'm sorry I'm talking so much, I'm nervous."

Miss Ferrucci flexed her scalp muscles and smiled; this made her eyes water and she dabbed at them delicately with a tissue.

"Unfair to take up your time like this," she said. "In the first place, we wanted a girl with at least one year's experience. You haven't worked in an office at all, I see."

"No," Marie said, "in the summer I clerked in my uncle's fruit store. He paid me practically nothing but my mother said I had to help out, he has a bad heart."

"Funny," Miss Ferrucci said, "I distinctly told the agency what I wanted."

"That's all right," Marie said, "I said I had three years' experience in an office. I made up a name. But I didn't want to lie to you."

"Oh," Miss Ferrucci said. "And I told them I preferred a girl with a college degree, we like to promote from within the organization if there is a suitable higher opening."

"That's right," Marie said, "I told them I went to college in Chicago, Chicago University."

Miss Ferrucci sat up and began to feel better. "Four plus three," she said, "seven; so you must have told them you were?"

"Uh-huh," Marie said, nodding and smiling, "I told them I was twenty-six, I counted too, but I thought I'd better put in another year just in case. But don't be fooled by all that, I really can type, I'm really very good at it, sixty-five words a minute easy. I did a test for the agency. My shorthand isn't as good, but it's good enough, and with practice."

"Yes, well," Miss Ferrucci said. "But tell me something, why did you go so far out of your way to get a job here? Is there anything about this organization that fascinated you, that made you want to get a job here at any cost? After all, typist jobs aren't hard to get, and the salary is only standard."

"Cost?" Marie said. "Oh no. It was just the first one I looked at in the papers that looked halfway decent, and I got, to tell you the truth, bored with looking at them, most of them sounded about the same, so I decided it might as well be the first one, that's all. Though now that you mention it, it's true, you do something with department stores, isn't it? I always was interested in department stores."

Examining Marie, Miss Ferrucci saw: middle height, sturdy figure; pale blond hair in ringlets; wide face, very light brown eyes; cheaply dressed without much care. Aura: very young, younger even than the eighteen announced in the form.

"Well," Miss Ferrucci said, standing, "you won't have any trouble getting a job if your typing is that good. But I'm afraid we did want a girl with some experience, and preferably a college degree."

Marie didn't move. She said, "You mean, no?"

"I'm afraid so," Miss Ferrucci said. "I'll keep you in the files, of course, and if anything suitable comes up. But I'm sure you won't have any difficulties. Thank you for coming in."

"Those things," Marie said, "they're not real. They're, what do you call them, falsies. If you don't give me the job, I'll tell you what I'll do, I'll come in and put a notice on the bulletin board that says they aren't real, they're falsies. I swear I will. Everybody will talk about it."

Miss Ferrucci sat down, her expression puzzled.

"I know they're not real," Marie said, "because my aunt is the saleslady in the department store you bought them and she told me your name from the charge account."

Miss Ferrucci took out a tissue, blew her nose daintily, dropped the tissue squarely in the wastebasket. She removed a bit of fluff from the upper foothills of her left breast and carefully blew it away. She settled herself more firmly in her chair, folded her hands on the desk and looked at the top of Marie's head. "I don't buy them in a department store," she said, "and where I do buy them I don't use a charge account. Now what on earth do you think you're doing?"

Marie sighed and looked at her hands. "Yes, you're right," she said. "I'm sorry. After all, I don't know you, it could have been something you're very sensitive about, something that would have really hurt you when I mentioned it like that. I'm sorry. But I got excited, that business about the college degree, I guess, I had a big fight with my whole family, well, except my father, they wanted me to go to college, I could have had a good scholarship to a couple of places at least, but I didn't want to but we had terrible long fights, and when you said, you know?"

Miss Ferrucci frowned. Certain unhappy self-doubts that had nagged her last night bobbed up into her attention. To evade them, she looked into Marie's eyes. There came to Miss Ferrucci, faint but sure, for the first time in her life, a sincere longing for motherhood.

"Well, that's all right," Miss Ferrucci said. "I appreciate your honesty in apologizing and explaining."

"But one thing," Marie said, leaning forward, "tell me; why do you wear them so big? I mean, my goodness, they're enormous. I know boys are always making remarks about girls in magazines and movies and all, but still, that's different from real people they know, isn't it? I mean, don't you find a lot of times it kind of scares them off, they think with an unbelievable shape like that you must be so experienced, have an awful lot of men after you, and be, you know, demanding, and they get kind of shy about it? And then, there must be a lot of problems, well. What I'm trying to say is, you could have them big, of course, but why do you need them so big?"

Miss Ferrucci, eyes thoughtful, examined her well-manicured nails. "It's pretty dull around here," she said, "like most offices. I wonder, maybe it might be interesting to see what happens to you. It might. An insignificant job like that, you couldn't do anything terrible and I wouldn't get in a jam. It might. I could say you seemed eager, had personal qualities, if anybody asked. Yes, it might. I'll tell you what, you go home now and lie down or something and don't make up any background and don't threaten anybody and don't advise anybody, you just wait. Unless I find someone today or tomorrow I can't pass over, I'll call you. Is that acceptable, do you think?"

Marie stood up and smiled. "That's fine," she said, "just fine. Thanks a lot. I'm glad I won't have to bother going anyplace else."

"Good," Miss Ferrucci said, "and I'm glad you're glad. Now go home, will you please?"

Alone, waiting for the elevator, Marie Betty Svobodna let a big breath out her nose. Then she smiled. "Poor kid," she said softly aloud, "poor, poor kid."

The upper portion of the page contains faded, illegible ghost text (offset from an adjacent page).

⚹ 3 ⚹

Marie Betty took the subway to Brooklyn and then walked home. A quiet time in a fine spring day, storekeepers were lounging in the sun at their doorways; many of them grunted greetings or flapped a hand. Marie nodded.

Leaning against the stop light on the corner of her street, in front of the Ace Dry Cleaner, was a husky youth in jeans, unbuttoned denim jacket over T-shirt, cowboy boots, and a curly brimmed cowboy hat tilted over his eyes. As Marie came to pass him he stepped in front of her, jerked an open clasp-knife out of his waistband and held the point at her navel, hidden from view by his jacket. "You know what I'm going to do to you, baby," he said, without separating his teeth, "you know? Going to cut you just a little piece at a time so you go screaming all the way. You going to like that, baby?"

"Hello, Henry," Marie said.

"Marie," the youth said, putting the knife carefully back in his waistband. "What you doing?"

"I just got a job," Marie said. "Over in New York. The first place I went, too."

"Hey, that's great," Henry said. "No kid, the first place? Job doing what?"

"You know, an office, typing, that's all."

"Well jeest, first time, what you expect? Big place?"

"I think it's pretty big. They've got two floors in a big building on Thirty-fourth Street, over near Sixth."

"Great, Marie," Henry said, "big place, meet lots of people, lots of opportunity. Hey, that's pretty good, congratulations, lots of luck. Hey, you want to celebrate tonight, buy you a beer?"

"Thanks, Henry, my sister is coming over after supper with her husband."

"Some other time," Henry said, "any time you say. And luck, kid." He touched her lightly on the shoulder. "I always knew you were one of the smartest in the class, even if you didn't get so good marks, you just wasn't trying, is all. That right? I mean, why bother? But I always knew you had brains anyway, I could tell. You going to move away from here?"

"I'm not sure how I'm going to do it, Henry," Marie said.

"Yeah, well, whatever you do, Marie, it'll be the right thing. See you around, huh?" Henry moved back to the stop light and leaned his head against it so the cowboy hatbrim almost covered his nose.

Marie walked up two dark flights, sniffed at the hall, unlocked her door and followed the sound of television to the living room. Her mother was ironing in front of the screen. "You give up looking already?" her mother said.

"I got a job, Ma," Marie said.

"You're a liar," her mother said. "You just went out a couple of hours ago."

"I know, Ma, but I got a job. There's a lot of jobs and I got one the first place."

"What kind of a crummy place?" her mother said.

"The company is Superior Services. I don't know much about it. It's big. They've got nice offices, what I saw. Carpet on the floor in the waiting room."

"I never heard of it," her mother said. "How much they pay you?"

"Seventy-one fifty," Marie said.

"Yah, sure," her mother said. "That's what they tell you, sucker. The time they take the taxes and social security and everything out of it, you won't have hardly pennies."

"You got to pay taxes, Ma," Marie said.

"You weren't so stupid you could have gone to Brooklyn College and learned how you don't have to pay no taxes. Or you was decent," her mother said, putting down the iron, her eyes softening, "you could have gone into the nuns. The nuns don't pay no taxes either. But no, not you. Got to do everything your own stupid way."

"I didn't want to go to college, Ma," Marie said. "I didn't want to be a nun. Please, Ma, no fighting."

"No fighting, no fighting," her mother said, picking up the iron. "Always trying to make it look like somebody else is wrong. You know something? Your papa, he isn't so smart, you must take after him in that department, though I got to admit since he got made foreman he brings home good money from the ice-cream plant, just last night he says to me, it's funny, he says, two kids should be so different, Dorrie, even when she was little, oh she raised some hell like all kids raise, but you always felt she respected you, but Marie, I don't know, from the time she could talk, you remember she practically started to talk right away, you couldn't get her to shut up a minute, she always tried to make you feel she knew better, everything she knew better, a little kid like that, he says. And you know what I say, I say snotty, snotty and spoiled. And look what happens, your sister does the right thing, she goes to college like we tell her, she meets a nice guy with a father who owns his own business, she's married, she's got things she wants. And you, you."

"Ma," Marie said, "I just got to be eighteen, you want me to be married?"

"Snotty," her mother said, "she knows best. Just because she got some lousy job. Ahh, go make yourself something to eat before I throw up. And take your good dress off, you want to slob all over it?"

Marie went to the small bedroom she used to share with her older sister and kicked her shoes off. She listened a moment, then padded down the hall to her parents' bedroom, went to the closet, reached up and brought down a half-full quart bottle of blended rye whiskey. She stepped quickly into the bathroom and closed the door. She looked at herself in the discolored mirror, opened the bottle, raised it in salute, and took a long, long drink. She choked her coughs, dribbled water from the faucet into the bottle, padded back, replaced it in the closet and went to her room. She sat on the edge of her cot, in an awkward position, shoulders slumped, knees apart, hands clasped between her thighs. Then she smiled, straightened up, put her knees together and her hands flat on top of her head and said, speaking softly but not whispering, "Goodbye, goodbye, goodbye."

Tuesday afternoon the telephone call came from Miss Ferrucci. Marie was instructed to report to the personnel office at nine sharp the next morning.

After waiting, alone but for the receptionist, until ten, she was sent into Miss Ferrucci's office, given a form and told to fill it out. She looked at it and said, "But these are practically all the same questions I filled out on the other one. How come you have to have it twice? You lose it so soon?"

Miss Ferrucci, going through a card file in a cloud of smoke, said, "You are not going to work for me, thank God, so don't give me a hard time. Do as I told you." Marie glanced at Miss Ferrucci, who was wearing a suit which partially concealed the scope of her chest. "And don't look at me like that," Miss Ferrucci said, "you just keep your nose down and fill that out. Accurately."

"Yes, ma'am," Marie said, and flicked away at the typewriter. When she had finished and signed it, Miss Ferrucci looked it over. "Betty is your full middle name?" she said.

"My parents went to a Betty Hutton picture the night they got pregnant," Marie said. "She always said it was a mistake, she thought it was just a war picture, she didn't realize there would be so much romance with Betty Hutton, but there was. After that she gave up and let him use contraceptive devices, even if the Church is against. She always said it wasn't her fault if he was a bad Catholic and she couldn't help what he did, but I don't think she told the priest. Then a year later."

"All right, all right," Miss Ferrucci said, "all right. God. I just asked." She frowned. "But you put down None for religion."

"Uh-huh," Marie said.

"Well, the question doesn't mean how often you go to church, whether you're practicing, or anything, it just means, what are you. Here, put in Catholic. Neatly."

"I'd rather leave it," Marie said.

Miss Ferrucci frowned at her. "I don't care myself," she said, "but it will look better."

"I'd rather leave it," Marie said.

Miss Ferrucci put the form down and leaned across the desk. "You really don't believe any more?" she said. "Ever? Any part of it? Even the worst times?"

"No," Marie said, "and I never did since I could think."

"I see," Miss Ferrucci said. She took a pen and, in the space marked For Office Use Only, filled in the simple code on Marie's race and color that the Fair Employment Act made illegal. Then she leaned back and in her lecturing voice told Marie of the hospitalization, insurance, and other benefits Superior Services provided its employees.

✕ 4 ✕

At about the same time, James McCue Connor, president of Superior Services, was surprised and perturbed to receive a telephone call from Mrs. Wheeler. She asked carefully after his well-being, then remarked that she and her brother happened to be in the neighborhood, or quite near it, and thought they might drop up for a brief visit if, of course, it would in no way inconvenience Mr. Connor who was, she realized as well as anyone, certainly, a very busy man. Mr. Connor urged them to come at once.

Mrs. Wheeler, and her brother Alexander Forbes, owned, among other things, all of the stock of Superior Services. Waiting for them, Connor smoothed his heavy gray hair, cleaned under his clean nails with a paper clip, and reflected sadly that the truism which had struck him strongly almost forty years ago was still, however trite, true: there was always someone, rise to what eminence and power you will, who could if he wished crawl up your back, and even if he didn't wish the latent ability was unpleasant. Ah well, said Connor to Connor, a few more years and you can be done with it, boy, annuities and fishing and no nervous decisions and nobody to climb up your back. He made a puking face at the thought. He hated fishing and loved his work. To be at the center, to manage, to make men and things move. Fishing, ech! Oh well. He threw the paper clip away and practiced a firm and incisive executive expression, grinned, and resumed reading the letters in front of him. One of the qualities which had carried Connor up the rungs was his ability to put out of his mind what couldn't be helped. If it can't be helped, he had once told his wife, then it can't be important. Yes, dear, she had said, like death. The exchange had stuck in his memory; his wife had died scarcely six months later.

When his secretary opened the door for Mrs. Wheeler and her brother, Connor was as usual struck with their lack of resemblance. Mrs. Wheeler was a small brisk woman in her late forties with reddish-brown hair and a deeply tanned and lined face. She must have, in her youth, been vibrant, if not pretty; she was still attractive, Connor thought, if you could ignore the impression that she might at some moment sink poisoned fangs into your thigh. Alexander, a little younger, was tall, slope-shouldered; a bulbous head with long light hair. He seemed to Connor, who had disliked him on sight and never weakened that emotion, always to be telling himself he must try to charm, and always adding that he had succeeded.

Connor seated the pair and returned, hoping he did not look as he felt, retiring to a fortified position, to his desk.

"Well, my dear Mr. Connor," Mrs. Wheeler said, "let me apologize again for bursting in on you this way, but when Alexander remarked that we happened to be quite near it occurred to both of us that we hadn't seen you in some time and it might be nice for us if we dropped by for a quick visit."

"Fact of the matter is, Connor," said Alexander, who had for a year in his childhood attended an English school and had carefully retained alien intonations, "it always does us good to see you here in the midst of battle, you give such a reassuring feeling of quiet competence, rather like a dynamo, you know, not much noise but heaps of power."

Connor cleared his throat and set his elbows carefully on his desk.

"That's very true, Alexander," Mrs. Wheeler said. "And it's so rare. So seldom you find people who really inspire you with confidence in their abilities. Dr. Wheeler is always remarking the same thing among his colleagues."

"And how is the good doctor?" Connor said, forcing himself to be breezy; he disliked being made uncomfortable by these two, a generation his junior. But with power.

"Hard-working as ever, poor man," Mrs. Wheeler said, "they give him no peace. I had almost literally to use force to drag him off to Nassau for a few weeks this spring, and for the first few days down there he fretted and fussed so that it was worse than if we hadn't come. But when I pointed out to him that we're all made but of flesh and blood, and he as a doctor should be the first to realize it, and we must respect our systems and not demand from them more than they can give, why he thoroughly agreed with me and had a nice relaxing time. And you, my dear Mr. Connor, I know you're of the same mold, I hope you're planning a re-invigorating rest this summer."

"Why," Connor said, "I really haven't stopped to give it any thought, yet. This hasn't been our most peaceful season, you know."

"But then," Mrs. Wheeler said, "you are quite a good few years older than Dr. Wheeler, it's even more important for you to get clear away from the cares and the fret."

"Nonsense, Molly," Alexander said, "why look at him, Mr. Connor is as robust and youthful as a man half his age."

"Oh, I'm quite aware of Mr. Connor's remarkable vitality, Alexander," Mrs. Wheeler said, "it positively awes me every time I see him. But it's no good trying to get away from the plain facts, the years do take their toll. And remember; you, lazy creature, simply can't imagine the effort it must cost some dedicated soul like Mr. Connor to run a complicated merciless machine like this."

"Wouldn't dream of denying that, my dear," Alexander said, "all I say is that Connor here is as fit, no, fitter, than any man his age."

"I'm sure of that, Alexander," Mrs. Wheeler said, "that's why I want to urge him to take the proper and necessary precautions to retain his splendid health."

Battling the feeling that he was growing invisible as they discussed him, Connor said, "Yes, yes of course, Mrs. Wheeler, I intend to get away from it all for a while pretty soon, go up to Canada maybe and get some fishing in."

"And while you're there, my dear Mr. Connor," Mrs. Wheeler said, "I want you to promise me to remember, relax, relax. Now, there was one thing I wanted to mention, something I wanted to thank you for. What was it? Do you remember, Alexander? Of course, thank you so much for sending over that little half-year statement so quickly. I know it was a terrible bother and out of the ordinary, and I'm very grateful to you."

"Not at all, not at all," Connor said.

"But you see, and it fits in very nicely with what I was just saying, Judge Harper, and he's an older man than you, of course, but still, not all those many years older, has decided to take things a little more easily and is having one of those bright young men of his assume more responsibility on advising us. A very nice young man by the name of Merton."

"Eager," Alexander said, "damned eager."

"And naturally we wanted to bring him right up to date on Superior."

"Put him in the picture," Alexander said.

"Well I hope Mr. Merton was pleased with the picture," Connor said heartily, hiding, he hoped, his strangling annoyance.

"Indeed yes," Mrs. Wheeler said. "He remarked immediately that it was just the model of what such a statement should be. What did he call it, Alexander?"

"Why, said it was a position paper, I believe, Molly. Odd expression. New to me." Alexander giggled.

"That's it, a position paper, he said, a real position paper. Yes indeed."

"Well, good," Connor said.

"Indeed yes," Mrs. Wheeler said.

"Seen a few out-of-the-way books in my time, that I'd properly call position papers," Alexander said. "But not that. Excuse me, Molly."

"There was just one thing that seemed to perturb Mr. Merton," Mrs. Wheeler said. "Now what was it? Yes, the growth rate. He seemed a little upset by the growth rate."

"I wouldn't say upset, Molly," Alexander said. "Just a touch concerned, perhaps."

"The growth rate?" Connor said.

"I'm almost positive that was the expression he used," Mrs. Wheeler said.

"Positively," Alexander said. "I distinctly recall it made me think of a door in the pantry of the old house when I was a boy, every six months father would stand me up against it and mark off my height and write the date next to it. Hadn't thought of it in years. You remember, Molly?"

"Why that's preposterous," Connor said, "both our net and gross in both divisions are absolutely commensurate with."

"Mr. Connor, my dear Mr. Connor," Mrs. Wheeler said, "please, you know perfectly well it's no use going into these details with me. And certainly not with Alexander. I just idly mentioned one of that nice young Mr. Merton's reactions. He said he'd get in touch with you in a few days, I'm sure you'll get along splendidly, and you two can talk it out between you to everyone's satisfaction, I'm certain. Now, I don't think we can justify taking up any more of Mr. Connor's time, Alexander. Thank you for letting us intrude on you, Mr. Connor, we are always so delighted to have a few of your precious minutes."

"Absolutely," Alexander said.

When they had gone, Connor said, "God." Prissy old Judge Harper had been an annoyance, but some smart eager young bastard, damn. It occurred to Connor, as it occurred every time he saw Mrs. Wheeler and Alexander, and as he forgot in between, that some people didn't have anyone to crawl up their backs. But then, he added, they didn't have the fun of the game, either. Heavily, he went to lunch.

"And what," Mrs. Wheeler asked Alexander at lunch, "have you to occupy yourself with this afternoon?"

"Well, there's a board meeting of the silly philly at five," Alexander said, "I really suppose I'd better attend."

"Grown men fussing about little pieces of paper," Mrs. Wheeler said.

"Oh quite, I know it," Alexander said, "foolish, really. But still, once you get into it, there is a fascination in the stamps. Although I must admit I'm nowhere as keen these days as I used to be. Still, I'm on the club board, and noblesse oblige. And then before that I'd better drop into the little flat, make sure everything's hunky-dory. I've been out in the country since Saturday, you know."

"Yes I do know," Mrs. Wheeler said, "and I'll bet that poor thing is half-starved by now."

"Oh well," Alexander said, "I left a lot of those Italian sausages and some chocolate. She's all right."

"It's not a balanced diet," Mrs. Wheeler said.

"Besides," Alexander said, "makes her almost glad to see me again, knowing that, whatever, I'll have some proper food sent up."

"Well, I still think the least you can do, considering you keep the poor little thing locked up in that one room all the time, is to see that she has enough to eat."

"Little thing," Alexander said, laughing. "Why, she'd make two of you, Molly my dear. She's a very big girl."

"That's right, you always did like your girls big," Mrs. Wheeler said.

"I don't know about that," Alexander said. "One I had before this was quite tiny, actually. Remember that old knapsack I had? Used to be able to get her into that with a little thought. My, she didn't care for it. No, I find a variety is most pleasing, short and tall, dark and fair, although I will admit I can't abide really thin girls."

"But tell me, Alexander, don't the poor little things, after a while, become, oh, sullen? I mean, there they are, away from the world, and you playing perfectly nasty and horrid tricks with them, I'm sure. Don't they become, well, withdrawn?"

"Indeed they do, Molly, and it's a tribute to your keen sense of psychology that you see it. Oh yes, it's quite a regular affair, first, you know, when they realize you're serious and they simply can't get out and they can make all the noise they wish, there's all that expensive soundproofing, they're furious, and then after a bit, with one thing and another, they're quite subdued and helpful, and then, just as you say, they begin to go sullen. Oh, they'll do what you tell them, of course, no question of that, but there's a sulkiness. But I don't let that go on, I promise you."

"Well now don't tell me what you do, I'm sure it's perfectly frightful."

"Oh, no one thing, my dear, sometimes it's this, sometimes that, all depends on the girl. There's always one thing she likes least of all, and if you take the trouble to make it perfectly clear to her that she simply must not sulk, or, as the saying goes, else, why then everything clears right up. Oh, of course, in the long run they can't help themselves, they get fainting spells or crying spells or some such nonsense, and there's nothing to be done but get rid of them and start afresh. But by that time usually I'd just as soon have a bit of change myself, so that's all right."

"Tell me, Alexander," Mrs. Wheeler said, "what do you do to this one, that she likes least of all?"

Alexander laughed. "Oh, Molly, Molly, I knew for all your protestations you'd get around to asking me that."

"Very well, Alexander," Mrs. Wheeler said, "if you're going to jeer at me like that."

"Molly, Molly, I'm sorry," Alexander said, "I wasn't jeering at you, honestly I wasn't. No, it's quite simple, really. I have this chest of drawers in the room, a fine solid piece of furniture, and if necessary I simply stuff great handfuls of her in the top drawer and then close it. Not close it actually, of course, but I try."

"Handfuls?" Mrs. Wheeler said.

"Oh Molly, use your imagination. I've even made a joke of it, don't you see, chest of drawers?"

"Goodness," Mrs. Wheeler said, "I can imagine she wouldn't like that. But isn't it difficult for you, I mean, I should imagine she would be so upset she would simply lash out regardless."

"Now Molly, be reasonable," Alexander said. "Of course I have her quite tied up. You needn't talk as if I were a fool."

"I see," Mrs. Wheeler said. "It does sound complicated."

"Yes," Alexander said, "in a way it is. You'd really be surprised at the number of details one has to think through if everything is to go properly. If you consider it, you'll see it really isn't all that easy to keep an active young girl for a couple of months while making sure she doesn't do any harm to oneself, even in one's least guarded moments, and then get rid of her, without doing her any lasting harm, you understand, that would be very unfortunate, and without the possibility of unpleasant consequences. And then the smaller but still important details, how to enjoy one's privileged position of, you might say, temporary ownership to the fullest, without boring repetition. Oh, it demands ingenuity. Psychological subtlety too, you mustn't think I spend all my time simply bashing the poor things about. Far from it. Yes, it's a challenge, but then if it weren't a challenge it wouldn't be worth the bother, would it?"

"I suppose not, Alexander," Mrs. Wheeler said.

✵ 5 ✵

Friberg's wife Sheila was short, plump, and juicy; black hair, sweet mouth. (They were both just thirty, married four years, had one child, a girl named Rebecca, nine months old.)

When Friberg got home, bringing with him for dinner the bachelor, older Kennan, he found his wife laughing. "I was backing out of the Grand Union," she said, "and I had Rebecca under one arm and I was dragging the cart full of stuff with the other and an old lady with a dog was passing and the dog got me like in the funnies and I went backward across the sidewalk and slammed against a parked car, clutching Rebecca, and the cart went sailing off and hit a man who was reading a newspaper and turned over and everything came bursting out and two eggs broke. And Rebecca looked bored, I thought she was going to tell me it's a good trick but she bets I can't do it again. And oh wait until you see the bruise on my bottom. I've been thinking how the whole thing must have looked."

"God almighty," Friberg said. "I get home after a peaceful day at the office and what do I get, reports of carnage, bloodshed, and catastrophe. I feel like a pay corps soldier who wandered into the front lines. You're all right?"

"With a bottom my size it takes more than a parked car to do any harm," she said.

"Spare our celibate guest the grosser domestic familiarities," Friberg said and went to see his daughter.

Sheila got Kennan a drink, ginger ale for herself and her husband. "Good thing it didn't turn out worse, could have been a nasty accident," Kennan said, who found conversation with Sheila not easy. "What with holding the child, and then if the car hadn't been there you could have fallen off the curb, or," Kennan went on, with a feeling familiar from New Guinea, imagination helplessly compiling the permutations of disaster, "there could have been a car coming along and," Kennan shook his head.

"Nuts," Sheila said, "real accidents only happen in the newspapers, you know that. Besides, my infant child clutched to my motherly breast, a kindly God wouldn't permit such a thing." Kennan shuddered. The terrible pitfalls of love. He could see himself in Friberg's office, the telephone ringing, Friberg's choked cry at the news. Desolation. Horror. And although he knew Sheila's God was a flippancy, He was not a flippancy for Kennan, and kindness was not among His leading attributes. Kennan shook his head again and took a pull at his drink.

"The little one," said Friberg, sitting, "seems to have survived your acrobatics."

"She's fine," Sheila said. "A horse. Nothing bothers her."

"I know it," Friberg said, "her mother's child. I tell you, Kennan, I spend all day at the office among sensitive people, exquisitely sensitive people whose nerve ends are fronds crushed by a touch, delicate to the very blow of air, then I come home to these two healthy animals who wouldn't mind if a mountain fell on them. Happy animals. Sometimes I think by mistake I've wandered into the zoo of heaven."

"That's all right, like me," Sheila said, "like me is fine, she can be as much like me as she wants, only once she stops being a baby she's not going to be fat, not if I have to put a muzzle on her."

"You deny your heritage?" Friberg said. "A mother in Zion, my mother, your mother, her highest aim is the children should put on some good healthy flesh. A little more chicken soup? Another plateful noodles? A second portion cake? A nice rotund child, cheeks like mounds of red marzipan, haunches that spurt succulent juice if you touch them with a fork, why that's the outer visible manifestation of inward grace. If I may borrow a phrase."

"Mock on, mock on," Kennan said, "with your lions and your human torches and your old men who think mercy is a sin, you wait a thousand years. Boy, will things be different."

"Aren't you prey to a certain historical confusion?" Friberg said.

"It's no joke," Sheila said. "It's bad enough for any kid, I hate to see it, but for a girl, and when she gets to adolescence. Oh no, not Rebecca. I went through it in my time, and that's enough."

"We're at adolescence now?" Friberg said.

"It may be funny to somebody else," Sheila said, "but I remember what I went through. Did I hate myself and that big ass of mine. I used to make bargains, I don't know who with, just bargains, that if in a week I could be slim and sparkling I'd sacrifice things, I'd be bald, I could always get a wig, or I'd have a disease on the skin of my left hand, I would always wear one black silk glove, mysterious and romantic." She giggled. "Adolescence."

"Yes," Friberg said, "you've mentioned it. But, and I'm not sure I can word this with just the proper delicacy, it has occurred to me that the ass of which you are so scornful has stood you in good stead, remarkably good stead. I don't say it was your whole army or even your main base, but it was a considerable part of the battle."

"Yes, well I was lucky, that's all," Sheila said, "and I didn't know I was going to be, could I?"

"Hah," Friberg said. "Lucky, that's all. In the mock-heroic tradition. Grant takes Richmond, Tenzing conquers Everest, Khrushchev lands on the moon, she gets me, and she was lucky, that's all."

"And of course," Sheila said, "I'm talking about my virginal period. I thought that if I wasn't the same shape as the girls in the movies I couldn't do what they were supposed to do. I didn't know till you came along that a fat ass could function just as well as the boniest model in Harper's. Better I bet."

"Yes," Friberg said. He did not know whether Sheila did this direct sexual referral, as she always did with Kennan, purposely to embarrass him or not. Friberg had never mentioned it; he did not want her to be self-conscious if it were something of which she was unaware.

Kennan, as always, was embarrassed, and as usual fumbled to cover it with a reference to the office. "Yes, well, speaking of adolescence, I see you're going in for child labor in your shop. That new girl of yours, where Mrs. Passanante used to be, looks as if a truant officer will be coming in the door any minute."

"Did she strike you as looking that young?" Friberg said. "Odd, she didn't me. She's eighteen, as a matter of fact, but I thought she might be older."

"What have we here," Sheila said, "all things to all men? Who's the new slave?"

"Name of Svobodna," Friberg said. "The Bulge brought her up today. She seems capable enough from the few words I had with her, Mary said her typing was all right."

"Attractive," Kennan said, "very attractive, a kind of smoldering innocence, rather fragile."

"My dear Kennan," Friberg said, "the apparitions of faith are very well in their place, at Lourdes, if you wish, or some primitive Sicilian pesthole, but not, I plead with you, on the eleventh floor of the Leventritt Building. Smoldering innocence indeed. A pleasant enough girl from what I could tell," he said to Sheila, "a touch of tough worldly wisdom earned in the slums from which she no doubt sprang, probably early experienced in life's warmer passions."

"My," Sheila said.

"As usual," Kennan said, "you impose the rational grid of spurious sociology on the universe and insist that it conform to your preconceptions. A striking example. You only have to gather from her speech and position that she is lower class, and at once reality vanishes and you see nothing but some kind of stereotype out of Studs Lonigan. She is," he said to Sheila, "a very pretty girl with a curious and rather appealing hesitance about her, a soft unsureness and, I repeat, an innocence."

"Smoldering," Sheila said.

"Oh yes," Kennan said, "definitely smoldering."

"Tell me," Friberg said, "did you step out of Plato's cave long enough to say two words to the girl? Or are we operating with your usual scorn for mere evidence?"

"Well, no," Kennan said, "I didn't talk to her. But there is evidence and evidence, there are sights for those who can only see and sounds for those who can only hear, and there are deeper and surer signs for those who perceive more deeply and more surely."

"How about feels for those who can feel," Friberg said, "or by God don't tell me that's what you're talking about, you didn't start copping grabs off her smolder, not the kid's first day in the office for pete's sake."

"I pity you," Kennan said, "self-damned to live in a world of gross simplicities, all things reduced to their basest metal. There is so much you miss."

Friberg, who did pity Kennan, smiled and said, "Good, I've got just about as much as I can handle right now."

"I'll have to meet the creature," Sheila said, "and apply my sure womanly instincts. You're probably both wrong, of course. Is she a virgin?"

"She would assume you had a diseased mind to think it possible," Friberg said.

"Probably," Kennan said, "and if not technically so, certainly in spirit."

"I'm a man who has a daughter," Friberg said. "Would you tell me how you do that? It could be a useful trick."

"None of your business," Sheila said. "Rebecca will live her own life without a father sniffing around what she's doing."

"Great," Friberg said, "my daughter is nine months old and I'm not allowed to wonder if she's a virgin. But I suppose she'll have a mother to whom she will naturally confide the physical and emotional details."

"Naturally," Sheila said.

"Great," Friberg said. "It makes me feel all in-groupy. Do you think you could get your great warm womanly duff into the kitchen, I'm hungry."

"Whenever you say, dear," Sheila said, rising.

Kennan sucked the ice in his glass, which had long been empty. He liked an evening with the Fribergs, but they had the curious habit of replenishing his glass only after dinner. Not to do it on an empty stomach, he supposed, or some other odd piece of non-drinkers' superstition.

When Kennan had gone, Sheila said, "He drinks too much."

"Quite controlled," Friberg said. "And he needs some pleasure. I know, you don't much like him, and he does drink a lot and he does have a somewhat sexless aura, but the poor guy is quite bright and is someone to talk to in the office and I feel sorry for him and I find him amusing."

"Yes, you know, men his age who never married and live alone, and all that spiritual business, he's kidding but he really means it, but, no, I like him all right. Let's go to bed. I'll go check on Rebecca."

When Sheila came out of the bathroom she stood with her back to the mirror and looked over her shoulder at her bottom. "Boy," she said, "look at those colors. What a bump."

"Well, it was a waste," Friberg said from bed, "all that empty space. Nature abhorred it. Does it hurt?"

"Nah," Sheila said. She came to the bed and knelt between his legs.

"Horse," Friberg said, folding his legs around her. "Big old horse. Indestructible."

"A good thing for you," Sheila said, "you need me." They made love.

Kennan lived in the upper Thirties, a short walk from the Fribergs'. When he got home he hung up his coat and tie, emptied the kitchenette ashtray of his morning cigarette, rinsed the cup and saucer in the sink and went into the one large room that was the apartment. He had had a pleasant enough evening, but was glad to be alone again. He rolled up his sleeves, then knelt facing the wall in front of the small wooden crucifix. He lowered his head and closed his eyes. Very quickly, the certainty, happy, warm, possessing, reached into and around him. He moved in it slowly, deliciously, his mind turning and rolling in languorous delight.

He got up a little stiffly, took the bottle of bourbon and a glass out of the cabinet, and stretched out in the big chair. He yawned. Only two drinks, maybe three, and sleep, he thought.

He took four. Then he pulled off his clothes and went to sleep. But he awoke in a few hours, still in the dark of night, and when he awoke he was crying.

✖ 6 ✖

Lydia Ferrucci got on the elevator, said, "Hello, Mr. Vernon," smiled at Marie and pulled in her chest so the door could close. Moving out on the ground floor she glanced behind her, stepped to the side and smiled more brilliantly at Marie. "All right, let's go," she said, and set out briskly. Marie came along. "Miss Ferrucci," Vernon called.

"I swear every time I tell myself I have to leave the office early something happens to make me late," Miss Ferrucci said to Marie, "come on, let's run."

Around the corner Miss Ferrucci slowed. "What are you running away from him for?" Marie said.

"Vernon? He's our company professional. He's been working on me for months, telephone calls I don't need, visits I don't need, every time he sees me I can hear the cloth tearing. I'm not boasting, it happens to everyone, he'll get to you."

"Why don't you?" Marie said.

"No thanks, he's married," Miss Ferrucci said.

"Gee," Marie said.

Miss Ferrucci stopped. "You going somewhere? Otherwise I'll buy you a drink or a Coke or whatever you take. I want a drink, myself."

"If you're going to drink straight whiskey, at least you ought to order Scotch or Irish," Miss Ferrucci said, "but that's just cheap blended rye, gah."

"I like the taste," Marie said.

Miss Ferrucci laughed. "Boy, I'll bet you're a shock to one of those liquor snobs, you know, that have only the one brand of Scotch that anybody civilized could drink, they only put out a hundred bottles a year, they pay a PR man to keep their name out of the papers."

"What's a PR man?" Marie said. "What does Mr. Vernon do?"

"He's your boss's boss. Head of the publications division. Makes a lot of money and take my advice, don't mess. I've heard too many mean stories about him."

"I was just curious," Marie said.

"I must say," Miss Ferrucci said, "you're a disappointment to me. You've been here, what is it, two weeks now, and I haven't heard a thing, you haven't made any trouble or got into any trouble or anything. Could I have made a mistake?"

"I don't know," Marie said. "And I've been busy. I found a place to live in New York, and moved. And I've been watching and listening to the other girls, they dress differently than I did, smarter, and they sound smarter, too. Not the typists like me so much, but the secretaries."

"Oh? Where did you move to?" Miss Ferrucci said.

"It's near First Avenue, on Tenth Street. Boy, it's crummy down there, but I don't care."

"Crummy?" Miss Ferrucci said, "you mean all those Puerto Ricans that do nothing but knife white people and have illegitimate babies and go on relief and ought to be sent back to Cuba where they came from?"

"There are a lot of them," Marie said, "but the place must have been crummy before they got there, it couldn't have happened so fast. A lot of the old people are Italian, there are a lot of Italian stores around."

"Thanks," Miss Ferrucci said.

"Oh stop it," Marie said. "What do you think the place I used to live in was? Crummy. Where most people live, it's crummy. Who said it's because they're Italian or Slovaks or anything? It just is."

"All right," Miss Ferrucci said, "all right. Let's have another drink. Now, how do you like it up there?"

"It's fine," Marie said, "I like it fine. I mean, it's not very interesting, typing all day, almost all about shoes, shoes, shoes. But there are people and I listen to them, and it's interesting."

"What do you think about Friberg?"

"Oh, he's the most interesting to listen to. He sounds like he'd rather be a teacher, or something, than writing about shoes, shoes, shoes. And there's Mr. Kennan who keeps looking at me, but I'm not sure I know what he's talking about when I hear him. And there's Mary, she's nice."

"Yeah, poor kid, she's been trying to have a baby for two years now. Well, I'm glad you like it, but so far you've been a disappointment. Maybe when you settle down you can make a little trouble, once you get over the novelty of it all and apply your mind."

"Yes, well," Marie said, "it depends. I notice you haven't taken any of my advice."

"And you were so right," Miss Ferrucci said, arching her back. "Whether you knew it or not. It's not me they want; it's them. I'm never loved for myself alone. Look at those," she said, indicating two men some tables away whose mouths moved in speech but whose eyes stayed fixed on her thorax, "they've been like that for half an hour. I'm just the launching platform they don't even see. And really; it's not even them they want, not any real way, it's just the idea of them, the idea of so much of them, the idea that what they daydream about all the time, that they exaggerate in their daydreams all the time, is really there with the exaggeration exaggerated. That's what fascinates, anyway it fascinates the sick types, they come out of their holes and elbow everybody else away. The stories."

"God almighty," Marie said, "you don't mean to say you're real?"

"Hah," Miss Ferrucci said.

"Wow," Marie said. She laughed. "And that's why I got the job."

"Not really," Miss Ferrucci said. "Oh, hell. Have you got anything going? I don't, let's go home and I'll fix us some dinner."

"This is really some nice place," Marie said.

"I put a lot of work into it," Miss Ferrucci said.

"A rug. A fireplace. Boy, I knew my place was crummy before, but," Marie said.

The telephone rang. "Hello Norman," Miss Ferrucci said. Pause. "No, Norman, it's impossible." Pause. "Norman, I don't want to, I told you last time was the last time, I'm sorry about your nerves but I don't want to. Anyway, I've got somebody here." Pause. "Norman, stop it, get hold of yourself. It's not a man, it's a friend, a girl from the office." Pause. "Norman, I'm sorry, good-bye."

"Like I said," Miss Ferrucci said, "sick types, I tell you."

"I could easy go away, you want to call him back," Marie said.

"No, I don't want to," Miss Ferrucci said, "and don't get any ideas this is a cat-house, it isn't that he wanted. It isn't even that, maybe I should say. He wanted to take pictures of me. Pictures."

"What kind of pictures?" Marie said.

"Pictures," Miss Ferrucci said. "He was good to me when I needed help once, and I did him a favor back, and he certainly needs help, but I'm fed up with it, it's too much."

"Oh, that kind of picture," Marie said. "He sell them?"

"No," Miss Ferrucci said, "not that kind of picture. Well, pictures of them, of course, what else, but I don't take anything else off like they do in art studios all the time and usually he doesn't even take my head, just them. Naturally."

The doorbell rang. "Oh, no," Miss Ferrucci said, and opened it. Norman was younger than Marie had imagined, and very thin and very nervous. He had a camera hung around his neck, a meter stuffed in a side pocket, he carried a bulging leather case, and his knees moved, his shoulders moved, his head moved. Miss Ferrucci closed the door behind him. He said, "Lydia, for pete's sake, Lydia, have a little mercy. For the last time if you want it to be, but just this time."

"I've heard that," Miss Ferrucci said.

"Lydia," Norman said, "what do you want me to do? You want me to cry for it? You want me to fall down on my knees and beg you? Lydia, you don't know what it's been, these last two days. I called you all yesterday evening, all evening until midnight I called, but you didn't answer. I was nearly out of my skull. And then again today, this horrible job I did, Lydia. Lydia?"

"Oh for God's sake," Miss Ferrucci said, "all right, Norman, this once."

"Wheeew," Norman said, putting down the satchel, taking the camera from his neck, "Lydia, thanks, thanks. You don't know. Look at that." He held out his hands. They trembled. He fell into a chair, breathed deeply and shook his head.

Marie stood up. "Well, I'll leave you two," she said.

"Oh, hi," Norman said, "I didn't see you."

"No," Miss Ferrucci said, "you stay, you might as well. We're in the other room; the bedroom; with the door open. And we're going to be very quick, aren't we, Norman, very very quick. You can help me throw him out if he tries to make a production out of it." Marie sat down.

"Sure, Lydia," Norman said, "quick, no production. But some shots, I got to have some shots. What I've been through. This job, for two days, I don't know, I've done it before and it's been bad, but never so bad as this. This fall collection, two days now I been shooting this bunch, stirring them up, kidding them along, making them look alive, you know, not the same old dead jazz, for two days, and I'm good, I'm really good, you know, you don't get the money I get if you're not good, but the thing is, for two days I been looking at those models, ten, twelve of them, and I got sicker and sicker, I thought I couldn't get through. I kept thinking, my God, have you ever seen anything so ugly, ever in your whole life? No flesh on them, not an ounce, not anywhere, it's like they're like a lobster all bone on the outside, imagine it, a five-foot-ten lobster dressed up in woman's clothes, posing the way they're taught to pose, they can't help themselves, even if I don't want them posed. No flesh, and these enormous inhuman eyes, and poses that are supposed to show off women, I couldn't stand it, I never thought I'd make it through. Lydia, hey, how about it, you get ready?"

"All right, Norman," Miss Ferrucci said, "just take it easy." She went into the adjoining room.

"Look at them, look at them," Norman said as Miss Ferrucci passed. "Don't get me wrong," he said to Marie, leaning forward, "I'm not like a lot of guys with women, they don't mean the same to me, I admit it, I'm not ashamed of it. I'm not proud, I admit it. And I don't mean I'm a faggot either, I'm not much of anything that way, it's the way I am, I admit it, Lydia will tell you. But like today, when I get real shook up, real shook up bad, the only thing does me any good is to shoot that pair of Lydia's. Boy, aren't they something? You ever seen anything like them? I been in camera work since I was nineteen, I never seen anything like them, not on models, not in shots. Oh, sure, big ones, there are lots of big ones, but not big like that, not, not." He held his hands out in attempted definition; they shook, his whole arms shook.

"How can you take pictures," Marie said, "shaking like that?"

Norman picked up the camera, held it to his eye and pointed it at her. It held steady. "A pro, kid, a pro," he said. He got up, took the satchel and went into the adjoining room.

There were floods of light coming out the half-closed door as Norman arranged his illumination, and Marie caught phrases of instruction, "A little more to me, some left turn, no, back a little, now the other side, way over, way, way over." In ten minutes Norman came out grinning. "Great," he said, "nobody would believe how great. Okay, let me wash up and I'll take off home for the darkroom." He put the camera down and turned into the bathroom.

Miss Ferrucci came in, attired, adjusting her hair, and sat across from Marie. She looked away. She shook her head. "No," she said, "that's it, never. I've said it before, but I mean it. The first time, I admit it, there was a little something, a little kick. But no, no more, it's, it's."

"Degrading," Marie said.

"Yes," Miss Ferrucci said.

"Sure, you said no before," Marie said, "so you'll say no again and do it again. How come you said no on the phone and then he comes you let him in, I bet that happened before."

"Never again," Miss Ferrucci said.

"Sure, sure," Marie said. "You say. You really want to stop it, make him stop?"

"Of course I do, I said it, I said so," Miss Ferrucci said.

"One way," Marie said. She rose, picked up the camera and smashed it into the stone of the fireplace. It made a noise.

Norman came out. He howled. He lunged, knocked over a

table, fell to his knees by the fireplace. He picked up the camera with his finger tips and moved it. It tinkled. "No," he said, "oh no, you can't, you can't ever do a thing like that. Not a camera. My God almighty," he said, looking up to Marie standing above him, "not a camera, you just can't do a thing like that to a camera. Don't you know anything? Don't you know what a camera can do that nothing else there is can do? Don't you know how many years it took to learn how to make a camera that can do what this could do? Don't you know what it takes to make a camera? If you know anything, how can you do a thing like that?"

"Now you'll stop it, taking pictures like that of her. It's ridiculous."

Norman looked at Miss Ferrucci. "How could you let her do a thing like that?" Miss Ferrucci gestured.

Norman moved the camera again. It tinkled. He rose carefully, tucked the camera under his jacket against his chest. "Maybe I can save some of the shots," he said. "What a thing to happen, what a thing." He left.

"It's insured," Marie said.

"I don't know, now," Miss Ferrucci said. "That was a pretty awful thing to do. I wouldn't have let you do it if I'd known. He's really not a bad guy, and it's his whole life, cameras."

"It sure is," Marie said. "Wow."

"Well all right," Miss Ferrucci said, "I know he's queer about it, but he is, that's the way he is. He's not mean or vicious or doesn't want to hurt, it's the way he is. You can't judge like that, right and wrong, wrong, bang, break it up. You can't."

"You said you didn't want him taking the pictures any more. Now he won't," Marie said.

"Even that," Miss Ferrucci said. "Sure I said it and I meant it, but you can't say black, white, you saw yourself how I told him no, but I let him come, how do you know I didn't partly want to take the pictures and go on taking them, I didn't, but how can you know?"

"Sure," Marie said, "and how can I know you didn't keep me here on the chance I'd do what I did, what you really wanted? No, you got to stop that somewhere. Sure, of course, no black, no white, no simple, blah, blah, sure, who doesn't know it? But you can do that the rest of your life and never make anything happen.

You got to stop somewhere and when you stop you got to judge. You got to say, yes, sure, there's this reason and that reason, there's this behind it and that in front of it, there's all kinds of people and all kinds of causes, and yes there is, and yes there is, but finally you got to stop and judge. You got to say, all right, there's everything, but I'm going to judge, I'm going to say it's good, or it's bad. And then you do something about it. If you can."

"You God?" Miss Ferrucci said.

"No, and neither is He," Marie said. "I'm a person, and a person has to stop and judge or he's not a person, he's a blob. That's how it is. You got to be honest about it as you can and fair as you can, but you judge."

"All right, all right," Miss Ferrucci said. "You sure did. Look, all this, I have a headache. You mind if I don't make us dinner?"

"Sure," Marie said. She picked up her purse and stepped behind Miss Ferrucci. She patted her once on the head, and went to the door. "Don't you worry," she said, "I know what I'm doing."

✻ 7 ✻

"I know what we do," Marie said, "but what are we for?"

"Come on now," Friberg said, "don't ask foolish questions."

"You know what I mean."

"It is problematically in the interest of those who make and sell shoes to purchase, at nominal fee, a weekly periodical giving them information on all current aspects of interest in their trade. It is problematically profitable for those who make and sell objects, materials, and services to those who make and sell shoes to advertise in that periodical. We provide such a periodical and such an opportunity. It is almost certainly profitable for us to do so."

"Is it?" Marie said. "You wouldn't have thought so."

"When I say us, I must specify that I employ two meanings. One us, which does not include us, is the stockholders in this organization, who hold the stock and receive profits therefrom. The other us, that is, us, is those who are thereby provided employment in, and emolument from, the enterprise. Clear?"

"Yes, yes," Marie said, "I know that."

"In like manner, other segments of this organization provide like service and make like profit from other aspects of the manufacturing and commercial world. There are further opportunities for service and profit in various forms of merchandising into which I will not now delve. Got it?"

"So people sell more things and make more money, and we make more money from helping them."

"Very well put. It makes us sound so jolly."

"Aren't we?"

"We certainly are," Friberg said.

This in August, just after Marie became, on provisional trial, Friberg's secretary, Mary having conceived.

"But still, it isn't what I meant."

"That is, you don't know what you meant."

"That's right. Oh, I don't mean what is it all for, like what are we on earth for or anything ridiculous like that. I mean, it just doesn't sound likely, when I think about it, that there could be all this"—Marie waved an arm to indicate the stretch of desks and machines and people on the floor outside Friberg's office—"so many people, so busy all the time, and living off, you know, even to eat and to sleep inside, and thinking about, from me all the way to you and Mr. Vernon."

"Oh, nice, nice," Friberg said.

"Because you've got to think about something you do all day every day, except weekends and holidays and vacations, but add it up, thinking and doing, why Mrs. Helmer told me in the can she's been here twenty-two years."

"Our oldest employee, matter of fact," Friberg said, "honor her."

"Twenty-two years, and even if Mrs. Helmer doesn't happen to be anybody who thinks so much, even so, all the effort and everything. I mean you have a wife and kid, and even I, even I have a cat. And all of it, all of it, from what we do like you said. It doesn't seem possible."

"It needn't," Friberg said, "it is."

"So strange," Marie said.

"Dreamlike? Irrational? Unreal? Hah. If you're a good girl and get my coffee promptly and remember where you put things, I'll let you go to the convention in September. That'll peel your pensive little scalp. When did you get a cat?"

"Sunday. The man upstairs gave him to me, he got tired of him."

"Very sweet of you," Friberg said.

"He's not much fun," Marie said.

"The cat or the man upstairs?"

"Him?" Marie regarded Friberg and made up her mind. "He's all right, but he's got a girl. What a beast, terrible. But he says, he knows she's maybe not the prettiest girl in the world but not only will she do anything he wants but she knows things to do he never even thought of. He says," she said, expanding rapidly, "it's because she lived for a year in Singapore with a Chinaman, and they're so old. Lots of times after she goes he comes down and has a beer with me and tells me about what they did, boy, I thought I had heard everything you can hear about it, you know, you grow up in the streets, but some things." Marie shook her head.

"Indeed?" Friberg said.

"I couldn't imagine," Marie said. "Nobody could, you'd have thought. And complicated, wow."

"Well," Friberg said.

"Yeah, I know," Marie said, moving out to her desk, "back to helping." Friberg looked after her.

The doorbell rang in Friberg's apartment, Marie opened it. Kennan stood on the mat. He said, "Who? Isn't this? Marie? The office?"

"Hi, Mr. Kennan," Marie said.

"What are you doing here?" Kennan said, and colored. "That is, my God, I didn't."

"Baby-sitting," Marie said. "The girl they had at the last minute couldn't make it, so I said I would. You want to come in, but there's nobody here but me and the kid sleeping good."

"No, no," Kennan said, "no, I was passing and thought I'd drop in, see the Fribergs, thank you, well, good night."

"You're here, you might as well come in," Marie said flatly, and stood aside. Kennan wavered a moment and went in.

He sat folded over on the chair edge, his hands on his knees. "I live quite nearby," he said. "I just thought I'd drop in for a moment."

"I'd get you something to drink," Marie said, "but I don't know where they keep it."

"Oh no, no," Kennan said. "It's not that, I had a drink, it's all right, I."

"What's the matter?" Marie said.

"Nothing," Kennan said. "The Fribergs, they're nice people,

you've met Mrs. Friberg. Of course, of course, you must have, wouldn't let anyone she hadn't met sit with the baby, no. Jewish, take good care of the children, yes. Well, thank you, I'd better be going along." He gripped his knees harder. "Could I have a cup of tea, do you think?" he said.

"What's the matter?" Marie said.

"A cup of tea? If not too much trouble?"

"What's the matter?" Marie said.

"Just a little bad news this evening, it wouldn't surprise me if I'm a little upset, that's all."

"Somebody die?" Marie said.

"That's it, exactly," Kennan said, "how did you know? Somebody died. Not a surprise, really, an old man, a priest. Have you ever been to Europe, traveled?"

"No," Marie said.

"No, of course not, lived all your life in the city, certainly. When I was a boy, the summer I was fourteen, Father Francis took a party of us, five or six young fellows, on a trip. France, Italy, Austria, Germany, six weeks. It was quite glorious, it really was. Never been away from home before, all the different cities, beautiful cities, beautiful churches, I remember it all as quite glowing. He must have been in his late forties then, a long time ago, so it's no surprise. It was important to me, I'll tell you why, it really was. It wasn't that I had a very bad war, not at all, but I was wounded pretty quick, New Guinea, and spent a lot of time in the hospital and then when I went back up north I got sick, you know, some kind of jungle rot like everybody, but I had it bad enough, and back to the hospital. Most of the time in the hospital, it seems to me just about all the time, I passed thinking about that trip with Father Francis. I believe I wouldn't have been able to stand all that time in the hospital, it was hot and I wasn't comfortable, not at all comfortable, worse sick than wounded, to tell the truth, if I hadn't had that trip with Father Francis to think about, how beautiful it was, I honestly believe that. But he was an old man, now, of course, God rest his soul."

Marie laughed. "That's pretty funny," she said.

Kennan frowned.

"When you were in the hospital, when was it . . . 1941, '42?"

Kennan nodded. "That's pretty funny," she said. "You lying there in the hospital all the other side of the world, thinking about those places over in Europe, how nice they were, and right then, what was there? Boy, there was war there, and people getting killed there and people starving and ones like the Fribergs shoveled into furnaces and everything you could think of. And it made you happy, that's funny."

"Oh, now don't say that," Kennan said. "It was a memory of another time." Marie laughed.

"Well, yes, you're right, of course," Kennan said. "I mean, I suppose I knew, of course I knew, that terrible things were happening in Europe then, certainly. But it wasn't then I was thinking of, it was what had been, that's no sin, surely. Is it?" Marie shrugged. "Well it isn't, is it now?" Kennan said. "Is it?"

"I suppose not," Marie said.

"Could I have some tea, a little hot tea?" Kennan said.

"So Father what's-his-name died?" Marie said.

"Francis, Father Francis."

"I don't like priests," Marie said.

"Well, yes, I know," Kennan said. "There's a bit of anti-clerical in most of us, I suppose. For one thing, I think we tend to transpose the hierarchic principle into political terms, and naturally we resent it then. And then a lot of the clergy, especially the American clergy, aren't really very well educated, well, when I say American what I really mean is Irish-American, I don't know how many times I've been embarrassed, I'm Irish, of course, by some priest who was nothing better than a half-educated Philistine. But you have to understand that given their background they're really doing very well, and besides, one can't impose one's own standards, it's perfectly possible that a man of more education, wider culture, wouldn't in many cases have the necessary rapport with his flock. It's all very well for us to ask for philosophers, but that isn't what everybody asks for in a priest. And also, perhaps a little, we're really envious of them, that they have a vocation and we don't, and because we're envious we get hypercritical of them, trying to show that they're not really worthy of their vocation. You see what I mean?"

"There was one that always used to try to finger me," Marie said. "And the other one that used to try to finger my little brother."

"That's terrible," Kennan said. "I know things like that happen, but how terrible for you."

"Well, it wasn't all that bad," Marie said. "I'll get you your tea."

"Thank you," Kennan said, "I'd appreciate that."

When Marie came back with the tea she said, "I knew a man once who wanted to be a priest, well, he was a kid when I knew him at first, he was sure he had a vocation. The day before he went off go the seminary he said to me, Pony, he called me Pony, I don't pretend it's going to be easy, it isn't, I know myself, and it isn't. I'm not the smartest brain in the world but I know I'm going to be a lot smarter than most of my teachers and superiors, and it's going to be hard not to fall into despising them for their ignorance, and then falling into doubt of what they represent because of it. And then, my blood is as hot as most, I suppose, and it will be a fight, sometimes a terrible fight, away from the sins of flesh. And worst of all, of course, at the bottom of it all, is going to be the struggle to hold faith, no, not hold it, that's the wrong word, it sounds as if it were something trying to get away from me, no, the struggle to keep myself open to the faith, to let the grace come into me and fill me and make and keep me sure. Oh, I know it's all going to be tough in various ways, from basic things right down to the trivialities, like the look of mocking amusement I'll see in the eyes of people, people whose minds I can in very many ways respect and admire, the mocking look when they hear I'm bound to be a priest, just, to them who have not had the grace, another superstitious fool, or worse, another dull-minded hypocrite out for a safe life. Well, the Lord knows I'm not a saint and never will be, but Pony, however hard it is, I'm going to fight it through. There are other important things in life, sure, but for me this one thing is so much, so overwhelmingly the most important that everything else is reduced right down to nothing. I believe, I was meant to believe, I will sustain and be sustained in my belief, and I will act my life through and in accordance with my belief.

"What he said to me. Well, I guess you know what happened, next time I saw him, maybe less than a year later, he said, Pony, he still remembered to call me Pony, I'm a fool, the worst God damned kind of self-hypnotizing fool there can be, no, I'm worse than that, if I had really been able to hypnotize myself into that

nonsense, if I could have succeeded in glazing my eyes and dull-
ing my ears and stunning my mind and so swallow the whole
imbecilic vicious mess, well I would have been fine, just fine,
probably get myself canonized when the Kennedys take over in
Rome, but no, I couldn't even do that. I'm a self-hypnotizing fool
who can't hypnotize. Well, anyway, that's over with now, thank
Christ or Fu Manchu or whatever I've got it out of my system.

"And you know what I'm going to do to celebrate, Pony my girl,
my duck, my darling? I've got a little money in the bank that
Granddaddy left, I'm going to take that money and get my ass on
a plane for Paris, France, a city where you've never been and I've
never been, and I am going to have myself the most prolonged
and indisciplined orgy since the first fur-legged Goth came rip-
ping into the plump white-fleshed west, dirty, smelly, itchy-assed,
a hard-on a yard long and twenty years of kill or die scrabbling
to make up for. I don't know because I've not been there, but I'm
told where I'm going there are houses full as plum tarts with
young girls, lovely girls, juicy girls, girls tumbling one over the
other for the chance to make you a happy man, I'm told there are
streets where they stand shoulder to shoulder for block after
block, tall and short, dark and fair, each with her special way
about her, all of them calling out please, let it be me, let it be me
this time. That's where I'm going, Pony, and when you see me
next you'll be looking at one very tired prematurely aged man.
My hair may be white and my hand may be palsied, but I'll have
a beautiful smile in my eyes from looking at my memories.

"He said. Well, I guess it wasn't hardly three months later I
saw him again, and he sure did look terrible, but there wasn't
any smile in his eyes or anywhere else on him. Pony, he said to
me, Pony. And he sat down bang. I thought he was going to cry,
but he said to me, Pony, I can't tell you how bad it's been, I can't,
but oh Pony, it's been terrible. Yes, it was true, there are a lot of
girls around for the taking, but I couldn't take them, couldn't do
it. I don't know, I don't know why, but I couldn't, no matter what
they did. Oh, once or twice I was all right, but even then there
was no pleasure in it, I was so worried that I could, and then it
was so mechanical and the girls were so plainly putting on they
didn't mind what they were doing and I kept thinking that I'd
forced this girl, this human creature, to degrade herself, forced

her with the fear of poverty and the club of money, and then I thought of all the other men before me and after me doing it with her, and, it was terrible, Pony, terrible.

"But I've put that behind me now, and I know what I'm going to do, I've sneered a lot at the world's way and the common sense way and the practical down-to-earth way, but in the end it's the only way. I'm going to settle down into a job and work hard and earn a decent living and I'm going to find a nice girl whom I can love and who'll love me and we'll get married and have children and raise them up decently and pleasantly and that's the life there'll be."

"Yes," Kennan said.

"Well of course," Marie said, "that's what he did, pretty soon he had a good job and he met a girl and they got married and had a couple of kids and they had a house. But then his wife ran away with a colored man and the children fell sick and died and his house burned down from a busted heater and he got canned from his job on account of with all this he wasn't paying attention so good."

"I can understand," Kennan said.

"Then," Marie said, "he took to drink. Or he tried, I saw him try a lot of times, but he just wasn't meant to be a drinker, he'd get two or the most three drinks inside him and blooie, it all comes up again. So he shot himself. In the head."

"That's too bad," Kennan said.

"Yes," Marie said, "I guess there are some people who just can't do anything, who just don't have anything at all in their whole lives. Empty, all the way empty and empty all through."

"Yes, well," Kennan said. He stood up and knocked his teacup and saucer off the arm of the chair. "Sorry," he said, "but I'd better be going along. Thank you for, thank you."

Kennan walked home, entered his apartment, emptied the ashtray and put the morning coffee cup in the sink. Then he went and sat in the living room for some time, without drinking. Once he went to his knees in front of the crucifix, but he rose again almost immediately, back to his chair. After an hour he went to the bathroom, took a half-full bottle of red sleeping pills out of the cabinet, ran a glass of water and came back to sit on the couch which converted into a bed. Sipping the water he swallowed all the pills. Almost immediately he felt drowsy. He went to the desk and brought a pen and pad to the couch. He wrote the date on top, then *"Dear,"* but could not immediately think of anyone to address. While thinking, he passed out.

When Friberg learned, the next morning, that Kennan had not come to the office he telephoned to see if there was anything he could do. There was no answer. He had Marie telephone several times in the afternoon, but there was no answer. "Odd," Friberg said, "a man of regular habits, and while not exactly abstemious, not one for carrying over into the sunlight the excesses of the dark. Probably got a cold or something and shoved the phone into a drawer. However, think I'll drop by on the way home, see that all is well and nothing needed. Why don't you come along, the poor guy may need a woman's ministrations, the pillow smoothed, the ashtray emptied, the cup of hot tea."

"All right," Marie said.

"Why the fearful look? Don't tell me you're afraid of sickrooms, a healthy bundle like you? Or is it that you fear the sight of a man in bed will flake away the last vestige of your self-control?"

"Let's go," Marie said, "come on, let's go."

"You really take a dare to heart, don't you?" Friberg said. "I've got a couple things to finish up. What's the matter, got an early date?"

"Yes," Marie said. "Come on, let's go now."

"All right, all right," Friberg said. "Far be it from me to let my labors interfere with your erotic campaigns."

When there was no answer to Kennan's bell, Friberg said, "Well, he could have been called away somewhere in the night, I suppose, and not had a chance to phone the office today. Maybe I'll slip a note under the door, telling him to get in touch when and if he decides to resume normal civilian life."

"Get the supe to open the door," Marie said.

"You think so?" Friberg said. "I'll feel an awful idiot if there's no reason. If he's away or just doesn't want company. For all we know he has two gypsy girls packed around him."

"Get the supe," Marie said. "Quick."

Friberg frowned. "You know anything about this?" he said.

"Get the supe," Marie said.

Kennan was obviously alive; on his back on the floor, breath quick if shallow, bubbles rising and breaking at his mouth's corners. He had thrown up on the couch and rug. Marie wanted to clean up while they waited for the ambulance, but the superintendent, a young Negro, insisted that nothing be touched. "I'll clean up myself after, if need be," he said, "but the police don't like nobody to mess around before themselves."

The ambulance and police came and went efficiently. The intern assured Friberg that Kennan would be perfectly all right. "A circus," he said, "if he's kicking now, it's a circus."

Friberg sat and watched Marie on her knees sponge the couch and rug. When she returned from throwing the rags in the hall incinerator, he watched her. She nodded. "Sure," she said, "it's my fault. I got no excuses. Didn't even have a reason, was just playing with him. But boy, I want to tell you, this is one good lesson for me."

"Playing around? With Kennan?" Friberg said. "You don't mean last night at my house?"

"Yes," Marie said. "Oh for God's sake, not playing around like that. I talked to him. But I tell you, it's a lesson to me. The long run, maybe it doesn't matter what you do, even changes you make maybe are bad, well, you never can tell, people can a lot of times twist bad changes into good changes or at least fix it so it doesn't make much difference. But you got to stop short of death. Death, and there's no chance of anything. Death, and even luck won't help, or a visit from the flying saucers, or some invention you never thought of, or whatever. No, anything goes, maybe, if you get pushed far enough or, hell, I'll admit it, sometimes because I think I'm right and sometimes just because I want to, that's all. But no, you got to stop short of death. It doesn't give you any chance at all."

"What do you mean, talked to him?" Friberg said. Marie shrugged. "All right now," Friberg said, "you sit down. Now listen to me. I guess this is your first contact with something like this, and it's upset you, perfectly natural. And in your upset state to put together the fact that you happened to talk to Kennan last night and the fact of what he did later and you feel guilt about it. The way you insisted on cleaning up. Well, that's natural too, maybe, but it's not rational. It's nonsense, you understand that. Just because you happened to see him before, you are not responsible. Now come on out of your shock and I'll take you home. Or do you think you better lie down here a little first?"

"All I can say is, I was sure lucky," Marie said, standing up. "This time. Next time maybe not. I'll just have to watch it, that's all. But this time, I sure was lucky."

⚸ 8 ⚸

Coming out of Friberg's office, Vernon, for the first time, stopped at Marie's desk. "Well now," he said, "we've seen each other around but I don't think we've been properly introduced. I'm Rupert Vernon."

"Yes, sir, I know who you are, of course," Marie said. "My name is Marie Svobodna."

"Good, very good," Vernon said. "And I hope you're finding life happy here with us? Everybody treating you right?"

"Oh yes, sir," Marie said. "I find it a very pleasant place to work."

"Good," Vernon said. "You're lucky, Shel Friberg's a great man to work for."

"Indeed he is, sir," Marie said.

"Good, good," Vernon said. "And anything I can do for you, don't be shy, come ask me, my door's always open."

"Thank you, sir," Marie said, "I appreciate that."

"Good," Vernon said.

Friberg, who had been listening, called Marie in. "Oh yes sir?" he said. "Indeed he is? I appreciate that? What's got into you this morning?"

"I have decided," Marie said, "that my speech is too often careless. In the future I will attempt to speak with greater precision."

"No," Friberg said.

"Besides," Marie said, "I have heard that Mr. Vernon is a man of great charm and possesses many sterling qualities, and I naturally wished to make as pleasing an impression upon him as possible."

"Vernon?" Friberg said. "Charm? Qualities? Why the one single and solitary quality Vernon has or ever had is the reputation of being the major ass-chaser in this organization, and frankly I doubt if it's a reputation he deserves."

"It is possible, is it not," Marie said, "that such was the quality I had foremost in mind?"

"You're kidding," Friberg said. "Come on now, you're kidding."

"I fail to see," Marie began, but decided to stop. "Sure," she said. "Miss Ferrucci told me he was always chasing, he's a terrible toad, is all I know about him."

"That's it," Friberg said. "A toad. And, I repeat, a reputation doubtless much exaggerated. No, I certainly wish for you as active and healthy a social life as possible, but not Vernon or the likes of him."

"No," Marie said.

"My fatherly instincts rebel," Friberg said.

"No," Marie said.

"I must say, Alexander," Mrs. Wheeler said, "I am pleased with that Mr. Merton. One is accustomed to a professional manner, of course, but even beneath that he does seem so much to care, to have our interests deeply at heart. So refreshing."

"True, Molly, quite true," Alexander said. "But then in all fairness I must say that you always did have the habit of commanding loyalty. I suppose it's because you are so thoroughly patrician that you bring out the best in servants. Now don't scold me, Molly, for calling that nice young man a servant, whose grasp and acumen I admire just as much as you do. It's only on the foolish leveling ear that the word falls harshly. Facts, after all, are facts. Most relationships are in one way or another of master and servant, and I don't mean a shred more of honor to the one or to the other. If I were in the position of servant I would be proud to carry out my allotted tasks to the very best of my ability."

"And I really do believe," Mrs. Wheeler said, "we ought to fol-

low his advice about letting poor dear Mr. Connor step into
retirement. Not immediately, of course, but I'm glad I decided to
let Mr. Merton commence discreet inquiries. Are you thinking of
going into politics, Alexander?"

"Politics, my dear?"

"You made me a speech."

"Why no, my dear, it had not particularly occurred to me. Although as a matter of fact I have been thinking more than usual
these days. Fact of the matter is, Molly my dear, lately I've found
myself getting a bit on the bored side, you know? The stamps
seem to mean less and less to me, and the country, well, it doesn't
speak to me as much as it used, and even my little domestic arrangements. Well, perhaps especially my little domestic arrangements. Seem to have gone a bit flat. Funny, really. Got a new girl
last week, you know."

"Why no, I didn't," Mrs. Wheeler said. "Is she nice?"

"Oh yes, quite nice, a bit on the fragile side for a change. Well,
there we were, I'd gotten her, and you know it's not all that
simple, not without its difficulties and its problems, getting them
so there's no danger of fuss and bother afterward."

"Yes, dear, I realize it," Mrs. Wheeler said.

"But I'd done all that, and there we were, I'd finished explaining to her just what was what, and I leaned back and lighted up
a cigarette to give her time to quiet down a bit, and you know,
the thought came into my head, well, there I was, having gone
to considerable trouble and expense so that this very attractive
young woman would be available to me for any little fun and
games I wished, and there she was, but. Damnit, I just wasn't as
eager as I'd been. Any little fun and games I could think of, why,
I'd done it before, you know? A touch jaded, that's what it was.
Well, nothing very serious, to be sure, and I passed it off after a
bit and I set about things, but then later it occurred to me that
in this craving for novelty there was the very real danger that I
might go just that little bit too far and have a very embarrassing
situation on my hands."

"Oh Alexander, you didn't," Mrs. Wheeler said.

"No, no, my dear, quite caught myself in time. But it did occur
to me. And then, in the last few days, I've been having, oh fleeting, of course, fleeting, but really rather abnormal thoughts, you

know, girls with quite impossibly long legs, or quite impossible figures, or quite impossibly young, that sort of thing. Ah, well, I expect it's partially the weather to blame. Will this summer never pass?"

"Now, Alexander, I want you to take care. Fun and games, as you call it, is all very well, although I'm sure it's horrid, but we can't have anything serious happen. I don't know, perhaps a new hobby would amuse you. Photography, for example."

"Oh, Molly," Alexander said, laughing. "I passed through that long ago. I have album after album. Although they're not the sort of thing I would want to show you. No, something will pop up, I'm sure. For one thing, I think I'll part with this one already, yes, I know, it's little more than a week, but I really think I will, and get someone quite unusual, quite different."

"Perhaps that will answer," Mrs. Wheeler said. "Now, what could it be? Let's put our thinking caps on. A Negress, perhaps?"

"Oh, Molly," Alexander said.

"Yes, I suppose you've done that. Well, now. A Chinese? A Turk? An Australian? No. I'm afraid I'm not being very helpful."

"My dear," Alexander said.

"Alexander," Mrs. Wheeler said. "Alexander, I do believe I have hit upon it. Your young women, they've all been very attractive, if I know you."

"Yes, Molly, if I do say so myself, I have a fairly keen eye."

"Well then, there you are. Next time, get an ugly one. Oh, not hideous, to be sure, but not glamorous, either. Think how surprised she'll be."

Alexander thought for a moment, then rose and kissed his sister on the forehead. "Molly," he said, "I can't thank you enough. You've given me a simply wonderful idea. I won't tell you what it is until I've tried it, but bless you, my dear."

"Oh, you're quite welcome, Alexander," Mrs. Wheeler said.

Miss Ferrucci said, "I heard about poor Kennan. I know he hangs around with Friberg. Did you have anything to do with that?"

"Don't ask me," Marie said, "because I won't talk about it. But don't you worry. If I did, nothing like that is ever going to happen again. Cross my heart."

"All right," Miss Ferrucci said, "you just be sure."

56

"I'm sure," Marie said.

"Okay. Now, a guy is taking me down to the Gate Theater tonight, that's near where you are. You want to meet us for a drink afterward, with a date or without?"

"I'd like to, fine," Marie said. "Is this another one of your crazy ones?"

"I don't know, I just met him," Miss Ferrucci said. "I've got hopes."

"I'd like to, fine," Marie said, "but I guess I better not. I got a date."

"Well, I said bring him along."

"I don't know," Marie said. "He isn't anybody particular. You might be embarrassed in front of your friend."

"What has he got, scabs all over?"

"No," Marie said; "just a guy I met on the subway a couple of weeks ago. He's in love with me. He wants to marry me. Funny."

"Mother of God," Miss Ferrucci said. "Bring him. I want to see."

Miss Ferrucci and her escort sat in the corner. Miss Ferrucci wore a white cocktail dress; her breasts loomed and glimmered in the half light. Her escort was tall, broad-shouldered, black-haired, sunburned, white-toothed, dark-suited, white-shirted, white-tied. Miss Ferrucci's escort leaned over Miss Ferrucci and murmured, "Not complaining, baby doll, but let's cut it short with these buddies of yours and go off somewhere by ourselves, hey?" Miss Ferrucci smiled.

Marie came peering through the dark. She was wearing red pants to her knees, sandals, and an orange blouse which slanted to leave one shoulder bare. When close enough to see Miss Ferrucci's expression she said, "No, huh?" Miss Ferrucci shook her head no. "That's what I thought," Marie said, "but then I'd done it and it was too much bother. Maybe next time I better bother, huh?" Miss Ferrucci nodded yes.

A thin young man in a short-sleeved striped shirt shambled up behind Marie. "This is Art," she said, "Miss Ferrucci, Lydia." "Johnny Bergen," Miss Ferrucci's escort said, half-rising and shaking hands. "Sit down, sit down, make a party." They sat down.

"What'll you kids have?" Johnny said. "Coke? Beer? Booze? Or," he said, leaning forward elaborately, "you really want to put on a blast, I got friends here, can get you the stuff straight and strong, right into the old veinola, pow." He struck his bent arm. Marie and Art looked at him. He leaned back. "Joke," he said.

"A rye for her and a beer for me," Art said. "I never use narcotics, they make me sleepy."

"How was the play you saw?" Marie said.

"We didn't think much of it, did we, honey?" Johnny said. "Just some more of the old jazz about like how everybody's alone and nobody gets to anybody and you got to love, you know, all the same old pizza pie."

"There was one good scene," Miss Ferrucci said, "where a man, he's in the flower business, gets orders from his boss to breed flowers without any smell, his boss is also going into the perfume business, you see, and he wants to be able to sell the perfume to put on the flowers, but the man has this long struggle with himself and at the end he can't make himself do it, 'I must abstain,' he keeps on saying, 'I must abstain.'"

"Sure," Johnny said, "that was pretty funny, but I keep telling you, honey, it wasn't meant to be funny."

"Perhaps not," Miss Ferrucci said, "but it was."

"It was, it was," Johnny said, "but you know, when a bit is funny and I'm pretty sure it wasn't supposed to be, it always makes me kind of jumpy, like I'm not sure if I should go ahead and laugh or try not. Anyway, it was extra funny because I'm in the flower business myself, more or less, and I kept thinking what a lousy idea, yeah, I know, it was symbolical, but still what a lousy idea. No perfume, I don't care what, is going to smell like a flower."

"Flower business?" Art said.

"Well kind of," Johnny said, "I sell seeds."

"Who for?" Art said.

"Turin and Raskob," Johnny said. "Why, you in the business?"

"My father is," Art said. "He's got a nursery."

"Yeah? Where's it at?"

"Out near Hydesville."

"Sure, there's a lot of nurseries out there, some big ones. What's the name of yours, I heard of it?"

"Crete, Crete Nurseries," Art said.

"You're kidding," Johnny said.

"No," Art said.

"Jesus, that's one of the biggest operations in the trade."

"It's pretty big."

"That what you do, work for your old man?"

"No, I've got two older brothers, they're in the business. But I don't do much of anything."

"What do you mean," Miss Ferrucci said. "You don't work at all?"

"No," Art said, "I guess I don't. My father, he doesn't care, he says if I want to I'm welcome, but I know with my brothers in it there really isn't any need. But if I don't want to, he says it's all right with him. So I don't."

"Now wait a minute," Johnny said. "You mean you just live off your old man?"

"That's right," Art said. "Fundamentally. He's made over a share of the business to me, like to my brothers, and I live off that."

"How about that," Johnny said, "how about that. Nothing to do but lie around and the money rolls in. That's some set-up you've got there, kid. Just a playboy, hey?"

"That's right," Art said. "Just a playboy. If your next question is what kind of a car do I have, it's a Triumph T-3. I live with my parents on the island but any time I feel like it I take off for New York and stay at a hotel, where I'm known as a generous tipper. You mind all this?"

"Take it easy," Johnny said, "cool down, no offense, don't be so sensitive. I was just curious, it's not so many times you meet a young guy who doesn't have to work for the old living, you know?"

"I'm sorry," Art said.

"That's quite a deal," Johnny said. "But how come you don't, you know, how come you're not, I don't know, out in Las Vegas or down in Miami, living it up, sun, sand, music, show girls, the whole bit? Especially the girls, huh, how about that?"

"You trying to be offensive, or are you asking?" Art said.

"He's just asking," Miss Ferrucci said.

"You ever tried living like that?" Art said. "You ever know any of the girls out there? Come on, I'm just asking."

"No," Johnny said, "not yet."

"Save your trouble," Art said. "Is it dull, are they dull. That's why I'm not, all right with you?"

"Art," Marie said. "Enough."

"Well it's not only that," Art said, "but it's an aspersion on you, that if I have some money and time I could do better, that's what it meant."

"Maybe," Marie said, "but that's what most people would think, you don't, fine, but they would. He didn't mean any harm."

"Hell no," Johnny said. "I just envy you, kid, that's all. What I wouldn't give. Jesus. I mean, I'd go places, but I'd take Lydia with me, hey, baby?"

Miss Ferrucci, thinking she would not willingly go to Staten Island with him, said nothing. Marie asked for another drink; a round was ordered. Miss Ferrucci said, "But dull, don't you find it dull, doing nothing, no regular activity?"

"You'd be surprised how many times people ask me that," Art said. "You know, I don't. I like to walk out there, on the island, I was brought up there and I know the country out there as well as anybody does, and I like walking around it. And I read a little and I play the flute a little, I'm not good but not bad. And when I feel like it I come into the city, I've got a lot of friends here. And then recently, of course, there's Marie, nobody could be dull with her. No, I like my life. Of course," he fell to a mumble, looking at Marie.

Marie said, "My sister had a friend who played the bass fiddle until the mice ate holes in it."

"Lord almighty," Johnny said, "what I would do."

"We'd better be going," Art said, "Marie?" She nodded, finished her drink, they rose and left.

Johnny sat silent, then he shook his head. "You never saw the nurseries, his old man's. Jesus, it's beautiful. They got everything there, annuals, perennials, flowering shrubs, exotics, everything the soil will grow. And what a job they do. Jesus, to think, having a place like that to work for that was your own." Miss Ferrucci, for the first time since Marie and Art had come in, smiled.

Two hours later, Johnny left Miss Ferrucci's apartment, smiling. He'd not scored, of course, he had not expected to this first time, but she had let him unfasten her brassiere, and had gotten a lot of feeling and impassioned kissing. Next time sure. He thumped a rhythm on the banister going down. Miss Ferrucci bleakly prepared for bed, Johnny crossed off like a flattop in her mind.

In Marie's room, after their second intercourse, Art lay on his back and again asked Marie at some length to marry him. She put one hand lightly on his mouth and fell asleep.

"Now before you gape your false-naïve eyes at me," Friberg said, "and ask me what it's for, I will explain. You may sit down. You have too much make-up on."

"Possible," Marie said. "I'm experimenting. Too much, too little, too formal, too casual, too loose, too tight, I'm trying things out. Today I'm, let's see, too much, too loose, too casual. It's a funny combination, makes me look like a shy girl trying to go on the make. Yesterday I was too tight, too formal and too little make-up, didn't you notice, I looked like a whore on a holiday."

"I suppose you keep charts of all this," Friberg said. "To prevent duplication as the weeks go by."

"Sure, I made a chart," Marie said, "but it's not weeks, I mean it's less than two, there are only eight combinations, I figured it out. This is the third day, so watch this space. It's interesting."

"I see, self-improvement through self-experiment. Laudable, very. But my dear child, what of the real you?"

"A naked old woman," Marie said.

"Yes," Friberg said. "To return to the matter. But, by the way, how do you gauge impact and reaction of these various costume changes? Do you have a preselected test audience? Do you give depth interviews to random selections on the public street? Or are you seeking that arrow best able to strike a specific target?"

"Mostly the mirror and how I feel," Marie said. "But people notice. Yesterday I met Mr. Vernon on the elevator, he said whoo-hah at me. I was his type, I guess."

"And a whoo-hah from Vernon is a whoo-hah indeed, hey? I'm surprised you so much as washed your face after the triumph if you think you really had him on the hook." Marie smiled. "Vernon," Friberg said, "that castrato Don Juan." Marie smiled. "But I suppose you know him better than I do, by now?" Friberg said. "Tell me, am I right or wrong?"

"You were going to tell me about the show," Marie said.

"Now just one moment, little friend," Friberg said.

"Just whoo-hah," Marie said.

"All right," Friberg said. "Now the function of this monster biannual folk gathering is to bring together in warm and sympathetic jollity all those of us, of station high and low, privileged to help keep this nation shod. If you knew German I might say it is an occasion of Schadenfreude, as you do not I will say it is one reeking mess. Buyers, sellers, makers, takers, and seven hundred and forty kinds of go-between parasites, all gather in jocund expectation of learning something to their profit, getting to know someone to their advantage, imparting misdirection to their competitors and, by no means least, getting the hell out of whatever hole they live in and away from whatever slattern they live with for a week of tax deductible revel. Clear enough?"

"But what does our kind of parasite do there?"

"Ah, as always, our singleminded aim is to ease burdens, to smooth paths. We will have a booth where the lost and puzzled may come to find their way, a room where the weary may rest, the discouraged may take alcoholic heart. We will put out daily, which means I will have to write and you will have to type like hell every afternoon, a scratch sheet giving the latest and most precious poop on the course of events, we get the mimeograph room to run overtime. In addition, our Sussman, that demon salesman, will be smearing himself against every ad prospect he can push into a corner with his chicken-fat belly. And in addition I will spend much time passing from comrade to old comrade, increasing, if it is at all possible, the love, and what is more, the respect in which I, and through me this organization, am held in the trade."

"I got it," Marie said. "What do I do, in the booth or in the room?"

"No, not exactly. You'll have to spend most of the day here, coping while I'm gone. With my usual cunning I have this year again obtained the services of Lydia Ferrucci to command our booth."

"Miss Ferrucci? Why her?"

"Why, because her training in personnel work has given her a smooth and gracious mien in dealing with all assortments, and the fact that being in personnel she has nothing to do anyway."

"What else," Marie said.

"True, the fact that Lydia has what are doubtless the best developed mammaries this side of the Urals was a minor influence in my generalship."

"What's on the other side?"

"The model state farm Lactopetrovsk where Socialist science working on Marxist-Leninist principles along lines first described by Academician Lysenko has succeeded in the serial production of women all and exclusively tit. You're a good straight man, little sister. No, there may be calls on you during the day, at lunchtime to relieve Lydia, but your major expenditure will be after five, overtime, of course, in the booth and to help out Sussman in the room. Oh, you'll see. Every moment will be golden."

Marie at noon stood on the sidewalk in front of the great commercial hotel, looking up at it. So standing, she impeded brisk traffic, which cursed her. Owners of flower shops, teletype operators, buttonhole finishers, the speeding loiterer, all cursed her; tourist, they said, bumping. When she had looked enough, she went inside.

She stood in the enormous lobby, looking at the Stonehenge of pillars, each imbedded in a clump of men moving their hands, the fat chairs and couches, each bearing its load of agitated rump, the tracer cross-patterns of men and women looking for somebody. She stood there until a bell captain asked what she wanted; she mutely showed him the paper on which she had written the formal title of the show; he directed her to the elevator.

She stood inside the entrance to the one-block-length room that held the show booths. From there she had full vision of only a few, ten, perhaps, or fifty, of the displays, but between and around these there were patches of more, and between and around the patches there were glimpses of further. "Wow," she said.

Easily following the efficient identification system (even numbers that side, odd this; aisles lettered) she slowly pushed her way past displays and through people. She came at last to where Miss Ferrucci stood, in a brightly lettered and patterned plywood alcove decorated with covers of the magazine superimposed on stylized shoe patterns (the work of poor Kennan, all but the finishing touches). Miss Ferrucci said, "Am I glad to see you."

"There's so much of it," Marie said.

"There certainly is," Miss Ferrucci said, "and I'm tired of all of it. I'm tired of sitting and tired of standing and tired of talking to these idiots. Sussman's out of the room now, I'm going to go up and lie down for a while, then I'll go eat."

"And the room upstairs too," Marie said.

"Things will quiet down now for a while. I'll be back, if anything comes up you can't handle tell them in an hour," Miss Ferrucci said, took her purse and left.

Marie sat down and watched the crowd, hoping the questions would not all be too difficult.

When Miss Ferrucci came back she asked if Marie had had any trouble.

"It was silly," Marie said. "Six of them wanted to know where booths were, they all had the listing booklet, so I showed them the names in the list and the numbers and explained how easy it was to find everything. Two of them came back and I had to explain again. Then three wanted to know where the men's room was, I showed them the sign pointing. Two wanted to know could they buy a copy of the magazine, standing right where it says free copy. And one said he was from Chicago, did I know anybody else here from Chicago. I told him to try booth 102, that's the Detroit Chamber of Commerce, the nearest I could find. It was silly, so easy."

"Certainly," Miss Ferrucci said. "What did you expect, problems?"

"And there was one lady who asked if I'd seen her fiancé, she was a little old for a fiancé, you'd think, she said he said he was going to the men's room and she should wait for him but that was two hours ago, I guess he was one of the smart ones who could read the signs going but couldn't find any signs back. I told her to go to the lost and found. And one man asked me to have lunch with him, said he hated to eat alone. I told him I had lunch. He was ugly."

"You see any that weren't?" Miss Ferrucci said.

"No," Marie said. "Well, I better get back. I thought it would be more interesting. I hope it's better tonight." Miss Ferrucci shrugged.

That evening, at six, Marie got off the hotel elevator at the twenty-sixth floor, where the company had its room. Up the long,

carpeted corridor there came enormous noise: bellowing, laughter, breaking glasses, bursting music. The long corridor was
empty, but all the doors on either side of it were open and Marie
could see a foot, a hand, a buttock flash out of door after door and
then wink back. She started down the corridor.

She passed the first room, stopped, and went back to look inside. A cheap phonograph spattered the furniture with the
nauseating grease of Hawaiian music. A thin elderly woman with
a black hat was sitting in a plain chair. In front of her danced a
stout middle-aged man. He wore flowered shorts and around his
neck heavy ropes of red and blue artificial flowers. The thick hair
on his chest was gray. His head was bald. His feet were clotted
with bunions. He moved his hips with the music, floated his short
arms before him and behind, teetered a few steps to the left, a
few to the right. He was smiling and humming. His flesh wobbled
and shone with sweat. By the door a young man sat, chewing his
thumbnail.

When the record ended the elderly woman nodded, got up and
came out of the room, brushing by Marie at the door. The dancing
man sighed, pulled a brocaded bathrobe over his shoulders and
came over to Marie. He was still smiling a little. He took her by
the arm, his palm wet, and pulled her into the room. The young
man stood up and said, "Papa."

"Sure," the man said to Marie, kneading her arm, "it's not
dignified, you don't have to tell me it's not dignified, I promise I
know that. So? Just answer me one little thing. You know a better
way to sell? No, don't answer me, you know a better way I don't
want to hear it, at my age you don't change so easy. But forty
years in the business, I don't know a better way to sell. So why
sell, you ask me? Why not, a man my age, lie back, take it easy, let
the younger ones do it? I'll tell you why." He put his arm around
the shoulders of the young man. The young man said, "Papa,
please." "I'll tell you," the man said, "it's for him I do it, it's for him
I work. My son. He should have something to be proud of from
his old father. Also my daughter, a lovely girl, she shouldn't God
forbid have to marry a man for his money but for love. Also my
wife, nice things she likes, nice things I like to give her. It's a
beautiful home. That's why. Is it wrong, a man should want to do
things for his family, his own? No, tell me anything, but don't tell

me it's wrong. And also, you know, I'll tell you something I don't tell everybody. I like to dance. Like it? I love it. When I get up there, the wonderful music going through my head, I feel, I feel, who can say how I feel? A poet I'm not, but I can tell you I love it. So, I better go to the bathroom. You know I got a bladder condition."

The young man looked after him. "The creep," he said, "the stupid disgusting creep. God."

"Does he really sell anything like that?" Marie said.

"Sell?" the young man said. "Sell? Sell what? He got rid of the business four years ago for half a million bucks. Sell, for God's sake."

"Well who was the lady?" Marie said.

"How the hell should I know," the young man said. "Some bag I found in the lobby and gave five dollars to come up. Papa," he called, "rub yourself good all over, you'll get a cold from the sweat. You hear me, Papa?" He moved to the bathroom door. Marie backed out.

Peeping into the next room, Marie had time to see only a blur of partylike animation, couples and groups standing, gesticulating with glass and cigarette, before her eye was caught by the honest blue gaze of a tall man leaning against the wall. He immediately came over and, hand on elbow, guided her inside. "You don't drink, not like these tarts," he said. "Come in, I can talk to you, not like these floozies."

"Are they?" Marie said.

"Look at them," he said, "my co-workers, my colleagues, my professional equals. Look at them, listen to the volume of sound they produce. Incredible. That's all they are, mouths, big wet flapping mouths, mouths and anuses, and the information value of the sounds they produce at the lower orifice is probably the higher. Incredible."

"I mean the girls," Marie said.

"We won't discuss them, it would soil you," he said. "The usual riffraff you find at these gatherings. Disgusting. Models, salesroom types, secretaries, that kind of thing. Secretaries. Would you believe it, last year when I moved up to head design and production, it was actually hinted to me that I might want to exchange my good old Miss Marbury for someone younger and more photogenic, yes, that is the precise word that was used to me, photogenic. Unbelievable. As if we were going to circulate pictures of the office staff to keep up production. And as if I didn't get the work of three out of my Miss Marbury.

"But speaking of photographs, I'll show you something that illustrates what I mean. For a few years now, in what little spare time I have, I've been fooling around with infrared photography. Oh, I'm no basement wizard or anything of the sort, but I have gotten some pretty fair results. I brought my rig here with me and last night I amused myself by a little prowling. Here, look at this, if you will." He picked up a tan leather dispatch case, riffled quickly through it and handed Marie a photograph. It was dim and gravy-colored, but it was clear enough to show a man and woman, fully clothed, embracing. "What do you say to that?" he said. "Taken right out there on the twenty-fifth floor of this hotel, in a little cul-de-sac near the service area."

"Twenty-sixth floor we're on," Marie said.

"I always refuse to truckle to the absurd superstition that omits the thirteenth floor," he said.

"What do you tell the elevator man?" Marie said.

"Now you may say, no, pardon me, there are those who may say, this is harmless enough, even if they didn't know. But I happen to know. The man caught in that charming little scene, I won't tell you his name, of course, just happens to be married and have three children. A fact of which the woman was perfectly well aware." He shrugged and put the picture carefully back into the dispatch case. "Well. It gives you some further idea of the quality of the people I have to work with. Blow-hards, emptyheads, the morals of a gutter cat. I suppose I should be inured to it by now, but I'm not, and frankly I'll be bitterly regretful if there ever comes the day when I am."

"You don't like your job, why don't you change?" Marie said.

"Oh no," he said, "but you're quite wrong, I'm sorry to have misled you. I do like my job. Like it? I find it fascinating. Certainly the people I work with are a perpetual annoyance, but the job itself, oh no, absolutely fascinating. And right now I'm working out the biggest problem I've ever tackled. More than that, it's going to be the biggest step forward in the shoe industry." He stopped and frowned. "I'm sorry, that was inadvertent. It sounded worthy of one of my colleagues. The biggest advance in the shoe industry since the introduction of automatic machinery. Come over here by the window where it's a bit quieter and I'll tell you about it." He opened his dispatch case and took out a heavy sheaf of paper. "Here it is, the whole project detailed, broken down, step-by-step, every aspect; design, production, merchandising, extrapolations of probable sales, everything. It's really all finished, I admit, but I brought it along with me for some last-minute tinkering before I make my presentation to the board. Look, here are the production layouts, prints of necessary machinery changes, with costs. Here, breakdown of labor costs. You'll notice here that although labor goes up slightly at the frame stage the over-all increase is minimally significant. A result of some pretty clever design work. Now, here, the new patterns, all laid out, right from scratch. Here, baby shoes, you see in this blow-up where the insert is, there, the series, one two three four. Then children, then, here we are, right through early and late teens, you see, the insert formed to expand right along, there, there, and there, until there, the permanent adult shoe, you see how it's come right along, you see?"

"No," Marie said.

"Well, of course, foolish of me. I let myself get lost in the details which you can hardly be expected to follow. I must remember that for my board presentation. No, the essential insight is perfectly simple. We start with the infant shoe with the invisible built-in insert. This commences the modification, do you understand, the progressive modification of the foot, which as growth proceeds leads inexorably to the use of our successive models, each of which continues and adds to the modification until the final stage. You see what that means, don't you, it means that every child started on Em-Jay shoes will of necessity, I repeat, of necessity, spend the rest of his life in a pair of Em-Jay shoes. Of necessity. Exhaustive tests conclusively prove that point. Once the foot modification has begun, any other last will be so painful as to be useless. Yes, yes, surgery, you're going to say, but after all, everybody knows what medical attention costs these days."

"I see," Marie said. "You cripple the kids so they have to use your shoes."

"Cripple, exactly," he said, "yes, just exactly. And take my word for it, it will be five years before the competition can come out with an answer, five solid years at the most pessimistic forecast. Now, what do you think of that?"

"Well, it's logical," Marie said, "but I'm not sure it's reasonable."

"Have a cigarette," he said. "I don't use them myself but I like to carry them for those who do."

Marie accepted a cigarette and excused herself. She looked into the room across the hall but there seemed to be little action, a group of five rather young men sitting talking. She was about to pass on when one of them called, "Hey, now don't run away like that, come on in and sit with us a spell." He got up and grasping Marie's shoulder led her into the room. "Drink?" he said. "We're just sitting around talking about our wives. You know, it's a laugh, really. You hear some of the older men talk, why when they come to a show, get away from home and all, it's nothing but one long crazy party, you know what I mean, girls and so on. But maybe it's me, every time I get away I end up, mostly with the same bunch of fellows, talking about our wives."

"Now I don't agree with Will at all about this thing," a young man with short red hair said. "This routine of just leaving the money on the bed, it's not, don't laugh, it's not romantic, it just isn't, and everybody knows you've got to keep romance in your relationship."

"What do you do," Will said, "dress up in a costume with a cape before you hand it over?"

"Now I'll tell you what we do, and I think it's a pretty good arrangement, a pretty successful one. When we decide that we want to, that we both want to, when we decide, then we give a call to this couple we know that live just down the street, wonderful kids, just our age, and they drop whatever it is and come on over. Then I give the money to them and my wife and I go stand out in the yard while they hide it someplace in the house. Then when they give the word, we come inside and I have to find the money. I'll tell you, you wouldn't believe the laughs we've had, my wife and I, looking for the money before we can go ahead. Of course we do the same for them whenever they decide they want to."

"Well," a stout young man said, "if that's a successful arrangement for you, then more power to you. But I've put on too much weight to go racing around the house like that. Although I agree with you that just leaving the money on the bed, like Will says, well, it leaves something out. No, what we do, I'll tell you, Sears has these gizmoes, they run on regular house current, all you have to do is bolt them to the floor, and you feed the bills into the hopper, there's a safety guard with fail-safe cut-off, and out comes the prettiest green flower you'd ever want to see. There's a two-year guarantee against damaging any of the bills and a four-year warranty on faulty connections. Safe as can be, and when I hand my wife that lovely green flower, why, I feel I'm really doing things right." He chuckled. "Green flower, that's got to be kind of a password in our house. Once on the television somebody was talking about gardens and said green flower, my wife and I, believe me, we laughed."

A young man with a bow tie, slightly younger looking than the others, said, "I don't know what you fellows are making all this fuss over, on the bed, hunting, flowers. Maybe it's because my wife and I haven't been married as long as you fellows and your wives have, but we just do it in the plain ordinary simple way. She just lies down on her back and I just shove the money into her until we're both tired. I don't see what you need all this fancy stuff for."

"If I can ask a question," Marie said, "aren't there times, I mean, maybe one day you leave your wallet at the office, or maybe you don't have any change, or something like that. Aren't there times when you just go ahead and sock it into her, go now and maybe pay later?"

"Boy oh boy," the first young man said. "I had no idea, I thought she was just somebody in the trade, like us. You know, she's the first one I've seen at the show this year, but they usually don't start hanging around until late at night. All right now, come on, run along, there's nothing doing for you here."

"Can I finish my drink?" Marie said.

"Take the glass with you," the young man said.

In the next room they were not talking about their wives, they were talking about the statuesque blonde girl who stood before them in a model's pose, feet angled, head turned to show profile. "She might do," one of them said, "at least in street clothes."

"Do, what do you mean do?" a man with a clipboard said. He

stepped up and pulled the girl's face around toward the group. "Look at that, it's exactly A.B.'s type, but exactly, hell, don't you remember this summer in Fort Worth the way he glanced at that waitress? Same type, exactly the same type. What are you talking about?"

"I said she might do. At least so far, in street clothes. What did you say those figures were?"

"Thirty-eight, twenty-seven, thirty-seven," the man read from his clipboard, "five-nine in heels, twenty-four years old."

"Uh-huh, what else?"

"I told you, I didn't have time to get anything more. Jesus, Roger, you know how rushed we've been."

"I'm not blaming you," Roger said, "I'm just trying to get the facts, do the job right."

"Let's get on with it," a third man said, "all right, you're not a virgin?"

"No, sir," the girl said.

"How many times have you had intercourse?"

"Approximately sixty-three," the girl said.

The man deftly manipulated a slide rule, and grunted. The clipboard man said, "Just about perfect, I'd say. A.B. likes them experienced, all right, but not too experienced."

"Of which, orgasm achieved in?" the slide rule man said.

"Sixty-two," the girl said.

"Fair enough, fair enough," the clipboard man said.

"Fair enough," the first man said, "but it's A.B. we're thinking about. How about your partners, were they satisfied? You got any testimonial material, letters, memoranda, anything down in black and white?"

"I didn't think to bring them, sir," the girl said, "but I've got a drawerful at home. All my friends said they were very satisfied."

"Hmm," he said. "Don't like taking her word for it, guess we'll have to. Right, now, you have any peculiarities, any prejudices, anything you won't do?"

"No, sir," the girl said.

"Sure now? Where's that list, Harvey?" The clipboard man handed him a piece of paper which he gave to the girl. "Anything there you have any objections to?"

The girl glanced down the list. "No, sir," she said, "but what does W.O.O.M.O.G. stand for? It's something I never heard of."

"With one or more other girls, what do you think it means?"

"Yes, sir. No, sir, I do any of those."

"We don't have too much time, Roger," the clipboard man said.

"Going just as fast as I can," Roger said, "but we don't want any bad mistakes, now do we? All right, let's have a look at you." The girl quickly took her clothes off and assumed another pose, her hands behind her head and her pelvis stuck out. Roger frowned. "Hold it," he said, "those thighs, up on top, there looks to be a difference there. Bert?"

The slide rule man whipped out a tape measure and knelt in front of the girl. "Nope," he said, "both the same, to the quarter inch."

The telephone rang. The clipboard man answered it, said, "Right, right. Right," and hung up. "He's downstairs now, on the way up. Got to decide now, do we use her or not."

"I hate to do it without more time to decide," Roger said, "but I guess we better. All right, you get in the other room like you were told. You did tell her, Harvey?"

"Sure, I told her, I told her everything," Harvey said.

"And when you hear the door close, it means we've gone and A.B. is here. Then you come out like you were told."

"I had her do that for me, Harvey," the clipboard man said. "She's good, honest, she's really good."

"Let's hope A.B. thinks so," Roger said. The girl took her clothes into the other room.

The door opened and A.B. came in. He was tall with heavy black-rimmed glasses. "Hello, boys," he said. The others stood up.

"A.B.," Roger said, "we were just on our way out. Got things to do, contacts to see. You've been working twice as hard as all of us put together. If I can offer a piece of advice, I'd suggest you take it easy here for a while, sit down, have a drink or so, forget the burdens you bear."

"Why, that's very thoughtful of you, Roger, boys. I think I'll accept that piece of advice and do exactly that. See you men later, I hope?"

"Yes, sir," Roger said. The group went out; Roger, last, closed the door sharply. Marie jumped and looked toward the other room.

The girl came out, dressed again, combing her long hair. "Hello, honey," she said to A.B.

"Hello, baby," he said. "Look, did I remember to put that package for the Simsons in with my dinner clothes, it struck me I didn't have it at the apartment."

"No," the girl said. "You forgot. I remembered. Big old important shot can't remember anything."

A.B. laughed and kissed her on top of the head. "Thank you, Carol honey, thank you," he said. "I've never once known you to forget anything."

"Now wait a minute," Marie said. "You know her?"

A.B. had a jolly laugh. He put his arm around Carol's waist. "Yes," he said, "we've been pretty well acquainted for some time now. By the way, things go all right? Wasn't too much of a bore for you?"

"Same as always," Carol said, shrugging. "That bald one gets more grouchy every year."

"Old Roger, yes," A.B. said, "a heart type. Going to find himself face down on his desk one of these days, he doesn't relax. I've told him so."

"Not every year?" Marie said.

"You know how it is," A.B. said, "the boys like to do something for me, they like to think they're arranging a happy surprise. A shame to spoil their fun. Be bad for morale, too; this kind of thing really pulls them together, makes a team. Sure, Carol just wears a different dress, they don't notice."

"But," Marie said, "how about her? How about the poor kid?"

A.B. frowned. "Anything happen?" he said to Carol. "None of them tried anything with you?"

"No," Carol said. "Just the usual."

"But," Marie said, "the usual's terrible. Like she was a half pound of hamburger."

A.B. frowned. "Terrible? Carol, honey, you don't mind the old routine, do you? You never said you minded."

Carol thought. "You know," she said, "now that I think about it, I don't like it. I don't really like it at all. Like a half pound of hamburger that's probably got sawdust."

A.B. sat down, took off his glasses and rubbed his nose. "My God," he said, "this is terrible. It never occurred to me. Baby, why didn't you say something?" Carol shrugged. "You could have given a hint. God, all these years. I feel awful about this, awful, I feel a real bastard about this. What can I do? What can I say?"

Carol patted his cheek. "Don't take on," she said, "it isn't that bad."

"Yes it is," Marie said.

"And what about next year," A.B. said. "I can't let you go through it again if that's the way you feel. What will I tell the boys?"

"It'll be all right," Carol said.

"No," A.B. said, "absolutely not. Now wait, I've got it. What we'll do is, get married, and next year I'll bring you with me. They'll understand there can't be any fooling around then. How about that, baby, how about it?"

"Get married?" Carol said.

"Right," A.B. said.

Carol put away her comb and rummaged in her purse. "If you want," she said. "I believe you're as good to me not married or married but I suppose we might as well."

"Wonderful," A.B. said.

"There's still something not right," Marie said.

"I want to thank you a lot for bringing this business to my attention," A.B. said, "a whole lot. Can I get you a drink?"

"Might as well," Marie said.

The next door was closed, but as Marie stood before it listening for an indication of inner activity she placed her hand on the wood and the door swung open with a squeal. Four startled men turned in their chairs. A young one of them, his shaggy black hair, ill-cut dark suit and air of spiritual intensity demonstrating that he was a Great Russian Communist functionary, said, "That was to be locked. Hah, American efficiency, American competence, hah."

"Vanushka, Vanushka, where are your manners?" said an older man, rising. He had a pompadour of graying hair, a gray mustache, and pointed beard; a Soviet Communist functionary of the previous generation. "Since you are in, young woman, we invite you in. Please lock the door behind you and do not, for the moment, distract our serious discussions." Marie locked the door and sat down.

A young American, wearing a Yale Glee Club tie and half-moon glasses peered over the rims at Marie before turning back to the low table around which they sat. "Interesting," he said.

A middle-aged American with the tooth of a Rotarian on his vested belly said, "Let's cut out the cackle. All I've heard so far is a lot of generalizations about peace and friendship and mutual benefits. I'm not here for a United Nations chin-chin. You have any hard proposals, I suggest you lay them on the line."

"With that at least I can agree," the young Russian said. "*Mir i druzhba, mir i druzhba,* until there is no room for cabbage in the cabbage soup."

"Images from peasant life," the young American said. "Charming."

The older Communist chuckled, glancing at the young American, then became sober. "Very well," he said, "you are right, of course. Practical matters. Simple. You are in the business of selling shoemaking machinery. We wish to buy shoemaking machinery. Specifically, of the following types, but you had better speak, Vanushka."

"Yes," the younger Communist said, smoothing a sheet of paper. "We are interested in the following models: October Forever Marks IV and V, Heartland Preserved Marks I and III and the Artillery Hub to Hub, all Marks."

"You handle that, Jay?" the older American said.

"That would correspond," the young American said, smoothing his sheet of paper, "to our Bulldog Dyna-Feed Special, both models, the heavy duty Champion Whirlaway Maxi-Fab and the, ah, Streamlane Auto-Stab Triple-Fac Producto Chief."

"That is accurate according to my information also," the younger Communist said.

"Excellent," the older Communist said. "It is pleasing to see that the young men of both our nations speak the same technical language. Encouraging. Now, as I have said, we are here today simply for an agreement on principle. We will obtain machines so that our ever-more-prosperous-people can have shoes, you in turn will not only earn a handsome profit but provide wages for your starving workers."

"Listen, Commie, our workers are fat as hell," the older American said.

"A witticism, pardon," the older Communist said. "But details of payment, delivery dates and so forth can easily be negotiated, once we have agreed among us."

"One moment," the younger Communist said. "There is the further essential matter of safeguards. What arrangement are you willing to put forth to guarantee that the machines you furnish will not have been sabotaged to break down in use, after payment? Perhaps the money can be paid into a fund supervised by a neutral power. The Czechs are very knowing about shoe machinery, I believe."

"Now wait a minute," the older American said, "talk about guarantees, and I'll ignore that dirty smear of yours for now, what guarantee can your people give us that you'll use these machines for what they're supposed to be, not convert them to producing war material. I think something along the lines of an inspector stationed in each factory of installation. We can work out a cost-sharing arrangement."

"Inspector," the younger Communist said, "why say inspector when you mean spy? An inspector like your man Powers?"

"Gentlemen," the young American said, "technically speaking."

"Not now, Jay," the older American said, "this isn't a drawing-board matter. You can't give a thing away with these birds."

"Vanushka," the older Communist said. "The logic of the situation."

"As I warned you," the younger Communist said, "they wish to sell us inferior machines and commit espionage into the bargain. We must never sleep."

There were three hard knocks at the door. The younger Communist dropped his paper. The older Communist said, "I outlasted Stalin." The older American said, "If the Fair Trade boys find out about this." The younger American looked nervously at Marie and said, "Pull your skirt down."

The knocks were repeated. The younger American got up slowly, went to the door and opened it an inch. He was immediately pushed back into the room by a waiter with an enormous cart containing bottles, glasses, ice buckets, sandwiches, small frankfurters, and bowls of potato chips. "For Christ's sake," the waiter said, "you're on the phone every five minutes getting my ass in a sling with room service and now you don't even open the door." Marie slipped out behind him.

When she got to the room at the end of the corridor, Marie found Sussman alone with his feet on a chair, reading the financial page of the *World-Telegram*. She asked what she could do to help. "Empty the ashtrays, I guess," he said. "And open the windows. This place stinks."

In the morning Friberg asked Marie what she'd thought of the show. "Revolting," she said. "Dull but revolting."

"Don't sound so surprised. That's what I told you," Friberg said.

"But there's one thing. The room, our room. Mr. Sussman says nobody uses it at night, after everything's over."

"Nobody does, unless Sussman sneaks back with a bellboy, which is unlikely, his wife would raise hell. Why, did you want to give a party?"

"I'd like to sleep there. If it could be arranged. Without any trouble."

"Sleep there? In the middle of all the empty bottles and dirty glasses and butts? With Sussman's oily patter dripping off the walls? In heaven's name why?"

"I'd clean up a little, it would be all right. I never slept in a hotel before. I'd like to, if nobody would mind."

"I see," Friberg said. "I don't see why not, I suppose. I'll check on it."

Marie locked the door. She took off her shoes, stockings, skirt, blouse, and garterbelt, and went to work straightening the room. When she had done enough she went to the bathroom and washed. She came back, took an unopened bottle of bourbon from the half-full case she had shoved under the table and poured a drink into the glass she had washed. Sipping, she wandered the room, admiring the walls, clean, the furniture, whole, the upholstery, untorn, the area, spacious. She bounced a little on the double bed. "Very fine," she said. "The way to live." She got up and opened all the drawers of the dresser, wondering if anything had been left behind, but there was nothing in them except clean white lining paper and an extra blanket in the bottom drawer. She took her things out of the overnight bag she had brought —a clean blouse, underwear, stockings—put them in the middle of the top drawer and closed it. She poured another drink, sat in the big chair with her feet on the coverlet, and made the effort to remember just how it felt to be in her own room. She realized how quiet it was here; no sound of motors, horns, bells, voices from the street. She sniffed; the cigar smoke was gone now, leaving only a hint of the smell of polished wood; no smell of dust and garbage.

The telephone rang. She let it ring four more times, then picked it up. "Hello? Hello?" Mr. Vernon's voice said. Marie made a sound. "Hello there," it said, "this is Rupert Vernon. Heard you were staying the night, Lydia, thought I might come by for a drink and a chat. If you're not busy."

"All right," Marie said, and hung up. She put her blouse on, glanced down, grinned, and decided the tails were long enough and no skirt. She took a full bottle out of the case and put it in the drawer under the extra blanket, in case he got fussy about the company liquor when he found out who was there. She unlocked the door, took her purse into the bathroom and fixed her make-up and hair.

At the knock, she called from the bathroom, "Come in." She waited a few seconds, brushing her hair, and came out, brushing. Rupert Vernon, who had been twirling his hat on one finger, grabbed at the hat with his other hand and took a backward step. "Wrong room," he said, waving the hat, "sorry, Miss."

"Hello, Mr. Vernon," Marie said. "You heard the girl from the booth was staying here and you thought it meant Miss Ferrucci but it meant me. Have a drink."

Vernon stopped waving the hat. "You," he said.

"Me," Marie said. "Have a drink."

Vernon leaned against the dresser and laughed. "A surprise," he said, "quite a little surprise. That's exactly what did happen and you know, I thought her voice sounded funny on the phone. Quite a surprise, but I will say it's a pleasant one, a very pleasant one."

"Have a drink," Marie said.

When, with drinks, they were seated and Marie had modestly crossed her legs, Vernon said, looking at them, "Very nice, very nice indeed."

"Don't be stupid," Marie said.

Vernon raised his eyebrows and said, "No. But I want you to

understand, about Lydia, I just happened, and thought I'd come by for a minute, I mean, she didn't."

"I know, I know," Marie said, "she told me you had been chasing after her for months, she won't cooperate because you're married. But you're supposed to do a lot of chasing around, just about everything you see worth chasing, the word in the office is. How come you do that? The word in the office is something's wrong with you, you know, the jazz about proving your virility and all like that."

"Oh God," Vernon said. "Is that how they talk about me?"

"Uh-huh," Marie said.

"Proving my virility, God," Vernon said. "All right, you want proof, is that what you want? Go ahead get your ass in that bed and I'll give proof, I'm forty-six years old and I'll give you as much proof as you can use, I'll give you proof until it comes out of your ears, go on, you want proof, get over there."

"No," Marie said.

"I'm sorry," Vernon said. "I'm sorry. I shouldn't have talked like that to you. It's not your fault. I guess that's what they do say."

"Yes," Marie said. "But how come you chase so much?"

"So much?" Vernon said. "Do I chase so much? I'm forty-six years old and married and have two children, so I guess it's so much. If I were ten, fifteen years younger and unmarried everybody would take it for granted. Say I was a fairy if I didn't, matter of fact. I guess so."

"But how come?" Marie said.

"Tell me something about yourself," Vernon said. "You a New York girl?"

"I can understand," Marie said, "a man's your age and married, it doesn't mean he can't have a quiet something here or a quiet something there, like they do all the time in stories, or like in that movie, but how come you want to get yourself talked about?"

"That's funny," Vernon said, "that's a big fat laugh. Ha, ha."

"Sure," Marie said, "I see how you could run a very efficient little operation, a set-up not too far from the office for convenience and time-saving, the overhead wouldn't have to run to much and I'm sure there'd be a tax angle in it, have some pretty little thing installed, not a special model, maybe, but young and cute and bouncy, and you could have a turnover period of a couple of months if you wanted diversification, sure, I can see all that. But why chase around the office?"

"You see so much," Vernon said, "you tell me what world you're looking at."

"It isn't like that?" Marie said.

"Hell," Vernon said, "give me another drink. You know it's not like that. Or maybe you don't know, you're young, nobody so young knows how lousy things can get, when you come to the time when your chances run out."

"Chances for what?" Marie said, giving him his glass.

"What do you think you're talking about?" Vernon said. "Look at me. Don't tell me what you see, I'll tell you. A big man a little gone to fat. Chins, plenty of chins." He pulled a thick handful of flesh from under his jaw. "Plenty of skin on top of the head, too." He stroked the meager sideway strands so they fell over his ear. "Nice watery blue eyes under the glasses. See? See?"

"Oh well," Marie said, "the total effect isn't that bad."

"The total effect," Vernon said. "I'll tell you what the total is. The total effect is a successful businessman who's forty-six years old and been married nineteen years and gets up in the morning in his house in Ridgewood and goes to the office and in the evening he goes back to his house in Ridgewood. Sure he does. What else does he have to do? Is any young pretty girl going to bother with him? I'll tell you, she isn't. And she's right, why should she? What can I do for her? If I were rich, sure, but if that's what she wants I'm not rich. Do something for her career? Do what? The kind of jobs I can get she can get without me. Marry her, give her a family? If I were to break up my family and I wouldn't, the girl who would marry me I wouldn't want. But what am I talking about, what girls? What girls do I know? Sure, I see them on the streets and I see them on the subway and I see them in the elevator. But I don't know them, why should they know me? The girls I know are the girls in the office. So you still ask stupid questions about why I chase the girls in the office? I'm going crazy, seeing all the pretty young girls, they're the only ones I can talk to. Sure I chase them, I chase but they run faster. And why not? They're younger."

"You don't do so good, eh?" Marie said.

"A drink, sometimes, sure. Dinner, sometimes, sure. They're curious. What is it with this funny old man? But that's all. I try to suggest, to hint, the possibility we could be intimate, they laugh. Or get insulted. Sure, why not? Once, once in the last two years, anything else happened. She left before your time. Very tall girl, taller even than me. Buck teeth. Terrible looking. But young, at least she was young, and I was so desperate, I kept not looking at her and remembering how young she was, twenty-three, twenty-four. But even that, you can't keep not looking forever. And all the pretty young girls I see."

"Certainly," Marie said, "but there are certain arrangements society makes."

"Sure," Vernon said, "and what do you think I do? Sure, forty, fifty dollars, they come, you screw, they go. Sure, they're pretty and young and they put on a great little act. But it's cold, it's so cold. It's what I do, but I'm dying for something else, as young, as pretty, but warm, just a little warm."

"It's a problem," Marie said. "Your wife and you don't get along much?"

"Sure we get along, we get along fine. She's been a good wife and a good mother. It's not her fault. You know, it's funny, it didn't creep up on me until a couple, maybe three years ago. I'd just gotten a promotion and a big raise, we went out to celebrate, left the kids with a sitter and went out on the town. I don't know exactly when it was that evening, but at a certain point I found I was staring at my wife and saying to myself, Oh my God, she's ugly, she's hideous. Been pretty enough when we got married, but now, now. Always had been a big girl, but now, fat, pig fat, sag fat. And a mustache. And pebbly skin. And thin hair. Horrible. Not her fault, but horrible. That's when it really started, when I began to go crazy looking at all the pretty young girls. I tell you, it's killing me. What do you think I work so hard for, and I don't care what Friberg tells you, I do work hard. To get my mind off. But it's tough, it's terribly tough."

"You want another drink?" Marie said.

"All right," Vernon said. Marie made them drinks.

"You'll excuse me," Marie said, "but you're a liar."

Vernon took a swallow and put his glass in the center of the little table. "What makes you say that?" he said.

"Come on, come on," Marie said. "What do you really do for kicks? Go in drag? Get a girl to beat your ass? Dirty pictures?"

Vernon laughed so hard, throwing his head back and his legs out, that the chair started to tip over. He leaned forward, chortled down, and said, "Well, well, well."

"Uh-huh," Marie said.

"What did I do wrong?" Vernon said. "First time it happened. I'd better know."

"First you tell me then I'll tell you," Marie said.

"Not much choice," Vernon said. "All right. All my life, I liked older women, first I ever had must have been fifteen years older than I was, a kid, and she was the cook in the family next door in Ithaca. And it went on like that, not fifteen years older, of course, but older. Sure, I knew girls my age and younger, but it wasn't nearly as much fun, they were silly or squeamish or ignorant or scared or something. Sure, I got married, a girl younger than I was, but it hadn't yet really occurred to me to make the connection about liking older women, I thought it had just happened that I happened to know women that were older. But six, seven years after I was married, I'd started a little something with a woman who ran the grocery, it occurred to me, that's what I really liked and that's what I really wanted, and what I liked and wanted was to be able to move around. So I got separated and moved around. Of course, as I get older the older women get older, so it's gotten to look pretty silly to anybody else, I suppose. I don't care about that, but it wouldn't look so good to the office, so I work up this reputation as a frustrated old man chasing after the fresh little skirts. That's fine, all the other men figure they can understand it even if they don't feel the same way. It's acceptable. Youth, youth. Meanwhile, I have my fun. You'd really be astonished at how many women of mature age are hot for a good old time. I've got two now, one a Swedish woman in Yorkville, a widow, her husband was a woodcarver, the other is from Colorado, she sells in a department store, they must both be over fifty, and you don't have to believe me about this, but I tell you we have our times. Now, what makes you so smart?"

"It just wasn't right," Marie said. "Nobody gets themselves into a trap that easy. They get in where they feel so trapped, they do something about it. You can always do something about it, this side of being dead. Of course, what they do to do something about it may land them up in something worse, but they try. They don't just sit and suffer, like you were saying."

"You know," Vernon said, "you're a very smart little girl, but you're wrong. Oh, you were right about me and I guess it would be right about you, but for a lot of people, for most people, you're wrong. That's just what they do, get themselves into traps and then do nothing about it but suffer. Hell, they don't have to get themselves in, they just get in, life gets them in or fate or God or whatever. But the point is that they don't get out, even to something maybe worse maybe not, they don't try to get out and they don't and exactly what they do is sit and suffer. All their lives through."

"I don't believe it," Marie said.

"It's true," Vernon said. "Not me and you, but a lot of people, most people."

"You really think so?" Marie said.

"Now," Vernon said, "what am I going to do about you? Can't have you blabbering my little game around the office. Get you fired, maybe."

"Wouldn't do any good," Marie said, "I could still blabber. No, what you'll have to do is make me your secretary, she's an administrative assistant, so that's a promotion and more money, which I could use, and then if I see any nice clean-looking old women in the subway I can be right there to tell you about it."

"I've got an administrative assistant," Vernon said. "Very competent girl."

"Sure you do," Marie said, "and she can be just as competent for somebody else."

"Or else, eh?" Vernon said.

"That's right," Marie said.

"You understand," Vernon said, "my back's not really up against any wall. It wouldn't really do me any harm."

"Whatever you say," Marie said.

"On the other hand, it wouldn't do any good. And, smart and tough, you could probably be useful. All right," Vernon said, "we'll see what we can see."

"Good," Marie said.

Her first step up.

✳ 9 ✳

On the first day she worked for Vernon, Marie came back from the sandwich store with her lunch, a ham sandwich on white, an apple and a carton of milk, and went into Friberg's office. He had his feet on his desk and was reading the *Times*. He looked up and resumed reading. "Please, come on," she said, "cut it out." Friberg put the paper down and looked at her. "Can I sit down and eat my lunch?" she said. Friberg shrugged. She sat down, took out the sandwich, unwrapped it and took a bite. "You're still pretty mad," she said.

"That's right," Friberg said.

Marie sighed, opened the milk carton and took a swallow. "It's silly," she said. "I explained it all over to you once. It's two things, more money and I can learn more. Not from Vernon, from the job, it covers more ground so I can find out more. You act like I was choosing Vernon over you, and it's silly."

"Indeed," Friberg said. "Incidentally, word has filtered through to me that your new buddy was noticed mousing around the hotel the night you stayed. Have a good time, did you?"

"Just silly," Marie said.

"Oh, stop it for God's sake," Friberg said, getting up and slamming the door. "What do you think you are, you mean-eyed little slut, Hera on Olympus reproving the foolish wind? I thought we were friends, that's what I in my unworldly innocence thought, and then you go and do a thing like that, go off screwing with that bounder Vernon for a lousy few more dollars a week. How do you think I feel about it? Delighted in the vindication of my judgment of you? Pleased with my own good taste?"

"Well," Marie said, "in the first place I didn't. And in the second place what if I did? I never heard you say there was anything wrong with screwing."

"Not with Vernon," Friberg said.

"Because he's in the office and he's your boss and you don't like him and if I screwed him why didn't I you, boy, what a reflection on you, is that it?"

"Of course it is, you imbecile, what do you think I've been saying?"

"Ah, Sheldon, Sheldon," Marie said. "Cut it out. You don't want to screw me and you know it. Be honest. You and me, I was a grown-up daughter or a baby sister you could have fun with just walking on the edge of sex, playing with it, making jokes. You know that as well as I do. But it's silly, I'll say it again, mean-eyed or not. I didn't with Vernon and that's that. But look, don't you see the spot I was in? I've been working here for four months now. I learned all I could about what goes on here from this job. No, not from you, I don't mean, but because we are friends I can go on learning from you even if I don't work for you any more. But from the job. Four whole months. It was time, I had to be going on, someplace where I could see more, learn more. Sure it's only a little step up, but it's something, and I've got to get moving. I'm going to be nineteen in February, you know that."

"Moving," Friberg said.

"Sure. One thing I've learned already, I've got no reason to believe anybody, except maybe you and I don't think you want to, can run things better than I could. But I've got to get moving. That's why."

"I suppose," Friberg said, sitting down and putting his feet back on the desk. "I give up. Tell me, this gag about all of four months and going to be all of nineteen and so forth is intended to be amusingly endearing, I take it? Youth's naïve concept of time, and so on, rather charming, et cetera? Is that the point?"

"Now, you know it is," Marie said, eating her apple.

"As long as we both do," Friberg said. "All right, peace. You have your way to make in the world, you feel, and care not whose bones you grind into the cobbles as you tread over. Now, my wife, who seemed to be somewhat put out at our little rift, and who unaccountably tended to take your part, had instructed me to ask you for dinner tonight. Since I seem to have reversed my decision never to sully my tongue in speech with you, do you want to come eat with us stepping stones?"

"First, one thing," Marie said. "You said about us being friends. Well, not that I've had so much experience in things like this, but as far as I go it's not only friends, but I love you and Sheila, you know, in a family way."

"Why?" Friberg said.

"All right, all right," Marie said. "Just let it go like that. Now tonight, I said I would have a drink with Lydia Ferrucci after work, she wants to buy me one for my new job, and that drags on, so if I could come after supper?"

"Dinner," Friberg said. "Sure."

Lydia Ferrucci said, "Have fun working with Vernon?"

"It was fabulous," Marie said, "I never knew it could be like that. And that's what he said too. He never knew it could be like that. Now look, you stop it. I had it out with Friberg once today. I didn't see much of him. That Miss Merlin, she was very nice about showing me things. Is she really quitting because I'm taking her job?"

"She's quitting, but I think she's had an eye out anyway, this just decided her. That's a very nice little raise you're getting."

"I know," Marie said.

"Look, October first, there's going to be an apartment available in my building, on the seventh floor. It's more expensive but it's much bigger, nice view. I was thinking of taking it and getting a room-mate to split the rent. I didn't mention it before because you couldn't have afforded it, but now you can. You want to?"

Marie thought for a moment and said, "Sure. I'd like to. You see that what's his name you were with again?"

"No, thank God, that's just what he was. His trouble is that he's not queer enough. I didn't get a chance to tell you, but I like your boy, Art. He seemed very sincere."

"Oh, he's sincere," Marie said, "the trouble is he doesn't have much to be sincere about."

"He still want to marry you?"

"Sure."

"Why not?" Miss Ferrucci said.

"Why?" Marie said.

❉ 10 ❉

Alexander Forbes stood while the headwaiter seated his sister, then sat down. They ordered martinis. Alexander said, "Well, my dear, in the final analysis, as usual, I leave the decision up to you. Not very manly of me, perhaps, but experience has sufficiently proved that yours is a far better head for these matters than mine."

"I do think," Mrs. Wheeler said, "that Mr. Merton's point of view seems sensible. A younger, more vigorous man than dear Mr. Connor, to cope with the increasingly complex problems of the day, yet one with plenty of mature experience. I do like that combination."

"Have we ever met this Vernon?" Alexander said.

"I don't believe we have," Mrs. Wheeler said, "but of course we will arrange to do so. Although I'm never sure what one brief meeting tells. Perhaps more important, that nice young Mr. Merton has had him thoroughly looked into, and reports that everything is quite in order. Adequate middle class background, somewhere in upper New York State, Wharton School, fine business record, married, two children. Well, we shall see."

"I don't know, Molly," Alexander said. "Merton's reports are fine, as far as they go, and I'm sure that efficient young man did his usual thorough job, but I put a great deal of weight on your infallible instinct for people."

"We shall see, Alexander, what we shall see," Mrs. Wheeler said. "Now, tell me, what mischief have you been getting yourself into, although I must say, you look perfectly well."

"Fit as could be, Molly my dear, fit as could be," Alexander said. "No, I can't say I have any gossip that would be of interest to you. Life just does go on, you know. There was one thing. Man named Peterson, you know the name? Bought the Grevere place after the war? Came to see me one day last week. What he was getting at, terribly long-winded fellow, was to sound me out on the political side with an eye to doing some work on the National Committee. He knew I contribute, of course, but thought I might usefully take a more active part. I didn't say yes, didn't say no, wanted to give it a bit of a think. What do you say, Molly?"

"Come, Alexander," Mrs. Wheeler said, "what on earth do you know about politics?"

"Yes," Alexander said, "that was just my first thought. Perfectly true, I don't know a thing in the world about the grubby side of it all, one hand washing another, favors and patronage and all the sort of thing that comes to your mind when I say politics. It's not the sort of thing people like us would know about or care to. But, you know, it has occurred to me that it's really a rather shallow view. We must remember that behind, overshadowing all that shabbiness, are principles, very real and very significant principles, eternal principles one might very well say, principles of honor, of dignity, of right thought and right action. I know I'm not a bookish man, but I have done some reading in my time and at the odd moment I've thought about what I've read, and it does seem to me that there might be room for a man to do some useful work. Certainly from everything I see about me in this country today it would do no harm at all if a voice were raised in political circles reminding them that there are indeed eternal truths, truths more important than disgusting shallow comfort, indeed, more important than mere brute existence."

"My dear Alexander," Mrs. Wheeler said, "say no more. You've convinced me that you've convinced yourself, and far be it from me to dissuade you from any activity that will keep you from harm's way. But speaking of that, you really must tell me if you found my little suggestion useful."

"Suggestion, Molly?"

"Alexander, how disgusting and ungrateful of you. After I put myself to the fuss and bother of applying my mind to your nasty little habits, you."

"Molly, Molly," Alexander said, holding up his hands, "forgive me, of course I remember, I was simply not thinking. Of course I remember and I assure you I'm very properly grateful. Well, to tell you the truth, although you certainly did give me a very useful idea, I'm sure of it, as it worked out it has been a bit on the disappointing side. What I thought of, with your help, was that it might be amusing to get a particularly attractive girl and pretend that she was ugly, complain to her that she was ugly, rather knock her around a bit for being ugly, make her apologize for being so ugly, and describe in her own words just how ugly she was. Was looking forward, you see, to a bit of enjoyable conflict between a woman's pride in her beauty and apprehension of my little sanctions and so on. Well, I put myself to a little extra trouble and did indeed fetch up with quite a smashingly good-looking girl, Scandinavian in origin, I believe, one of those natural blondes, you know, that always look their best a trifle bruised?"

"Bruised, Alexander?" Mrs. Wheeler said.

"Let me finish, Molly. Well, I had scarcely started out, explaining to her how unattractive she was and how annoyed I was at having to put up with such an unattractive girl when, to my utter astonishment, I must say, it came pouring out of her that she really did think she was ugly, had thought so as a child and always had since, knew that other people said otherwise but never really believed them, thought they were saying so to get something from her. As I say, this came flooding out of the child and I tell you if she had had any clothes on and hadn't been restrained in a rather awkward posture I'd have sworn I was in the office of one of those psychiatrists. I burst out laughing, but of course that was the end of my little game. Funny, really."

"Oh dear," Mrs. Wheeler said, "what an unfortunate chance she should turn out not quite right. Do you have her still?"

"Oh yes," Alexander said. "Indeed, I was hoping at first that since she was so exceptionally attractive I wouldn't be bothered with that annoying boredom. But I'm afraid it was not so. Oh, I'm enjoying her, of course, but it's such a very familiar enjoyment."

"I have another idea, Alexander," Mrs. Wheeler said. "Disturbed persons, such as this poor girl seems to be, are often quite creative. Why don't you ask, although I don't suppose you do much asking with these unfortunate creatures, why don't you instruct her to think of some, oh, I don't know, some novel entertainment or some sort of amusing display. She must by now have an idea of your tastes."

"Of course, Molly, I always do that as a regular thing. But I'm afraid your clever theory about creativity isn't true in this case. She did just what they always do."

"Always?" Mrs. Wheeler said. "What is that, Alexander?"

"Oh Molly," Alexander said, "use your imagination, for heaven's sake."

"Alexander Forbes," Mrs. Wheeler said, "don't you dare speak to me in that tone of voice."

"No, I'm sorry to have sounded exasperated, Molly," Alexander said, "but really, put yourself in their place, what would you do if some big bad man set you down in the middle of the room and told you to do something a bit racy or you jolly well would get some more nasty whipping?"

"I cannot imagine such a thing happening to me, Alexander," Mrs. Wheeler said, "and I think it in extremely poor taste of you to suggest it."

"Molly, I wasn't suggesting it," Alexander said. "Really now, let's not squabble. I'll tell you. They always do a little dance pretending to do you know what, that's what they do."

"Oh, I see," Mrs. Wheeler said.

"And of course, that is what she did. Quite well, too, I feel that by this time I've become quite a connoisseur, she did very well, and even better the second time."

"The second time, Alexander?"

"Why, yes, after I'd punished her for not doing well enough, you know. It's what one does as a regular thing. No, as I say, this one has been quite rewarding, but still, I must keep my ears and eyes open for something special, just for a change."

"Well if you humbly promise not to snap at me again," Mrs. Wheeler said, "I'll tell you if anything pops into my head."

"Molly, my dear," Alexander said, "I hereby humbly promise. I am ever so grateful to you, you know that, for concerning yourself in my silly little pastimes."

"Well, that's all right, Alexander. After all, what are we put in this world for if not to help one another? And now, there has just popped into my head an idea for you, but I won't tell you if you will laugh at me if you have thought of it already. Would it amuse you to find some girl that has been very carefully brought up, a clergyman's daughter perhaps, and then, in the horrid way you have, absolutely force her to say shocking things she would never normally dream of permitting herself to say even if she knew them?"

"It would be amusing, Molly," Alexander said, "you are perfectly right. And I had thought of it, and quite some time ago. But you know, and really, this ties right in with what I was saying earlier on, it's an indication of the decline of standards of the world we live in, I have never yet found a girl, however decently brought up, who had any particular objection to saying anything at all. Why, if they once get it into their heads that using such language is what you are trying to persuade them to do, quick as a flash, before you can hit them a second time, they'll come out with expressions that even I have never heard of, that even I find quite shocking. It wouldn't have happened when we were young, Molly, my dear, but that's the nasty way of the world now."

"I'm sorry, Alexander," Mrs. Wheeler said, "but perhaps one of these fine days I will come up with something for you."

"I'm sure you will, Molly, my dear," Alexander said.

⌘ *11* ⌘

Early one evening, shortly after having moved in with Lydia Ferrucci, Marie was alone in the apartment when the doorbell rang. It was Kennan, thinner, paler. "Mr. Kennan," Marie said, "one sees but credits not."

"Hello," Kennan said. "Can I come in?" He was wearing a green tweed suit, a brown sweater, white shirt and dark tie. Although he was shaved and his light hair brushed he looked badly cared for, as if he had come from a public ward. He entered slowly, sat on the couch, picked up from the floor the book Marie had been reading, a volume of the Morison history of the Navy in the Second World War. "New Guinea," he said, "I was in that."

"Were you? Were you really?" Marie said.

"Twenty years old. Sergeant Francis Kennan, aged twenty. A sergeant. You needn't look so surprised. I was more active then."

"I wasn't looking surprised," Marie said. "Will you have a drink?"

"I haven't had a drink for a long time," Kennan said. "I was with my parents in Indiana, you know. They didn't like to see me drink. I don't think I will, thank you." He got up and walked about the room, looking at the one picture that had been hung, touching the furniture. "Nice place," he said. "You live here alone?"

"No, with Lydia Ferrucci. Everything is hers. Didn't Sheldon tell you?"

"Sheldon? Sheldon Friberg?" Kennan said. "I haven't seen him. I just got in, you know, flew in this afternoon. No, haven't spoken to Sheldon yet. Is he all right?"

"Yes, but how did you know I was here? We just moved."

"There was an address downtown on the card you sent me at the hospital," Kennan said. "I went there and the woman told me you'd moved here. Who did you say you lived with?"

"Lydia Ferrucci, you know, the girl with the bosom, in personnel."

"Yes, yes of course," Kennan said. "Why I wanted to see you, first of all, is to tell you that I forgive you."

"I was sorry about that," Marie said, "I really was."

"I forgive you," Kennan said. "We have to forgive each other or it would be insupportable. You know that as well as I do. Don't you?"

"You don't mind if I make myself a drink?" Marie said. "Or if the smell would bother you?"

"No, that's all right, you go ahead, make yourself a drink if that's what you feel like," Kennan said. "And after telling you I forgive you, I wanted to ask you, why, why did you do it? That's what kept bothering me. There wasn't any reason I could see. You didn't hate me, you didn't know me well enough to hate me."

"Of course not," Marie said, "I liked you, Mr. Kennan, I like you."

"And I never felt you were a wicked person, who would do evil or delight in evil. Are you?"

"Mr. Kennan," Marie said, "when I found out what happened, I felt terrible. When we found you there on the floor. Terrible."

"Then why did you do it?" Kennan said.

"I can't say," Marie said.

"Curious how it kept bothering me," Kennan said. "Right from the first, when I was in the hospital. You know, they'd given me drugs and I was sleepy, but I had to go to the bathroom, you understand my digestion was quite upset. They had told me not to get up, to use those, well, you know what they have in hospitals, but I couldn't bring myself to do that, so I got up. I didn't have a robe then so I wrapped the blanket around me, you know those hospital pajamas they give you that are open in back and don't come down to your knees, and I went in my bare feet in the dark past the other beds and out into the hall. I walked down to the end of the hall, some nurses passed me but it was odd, no one said a word to me. Then I walked all the way to the other end, but no bathroom. Then I started down the hall again, and found it. It was very warm there and when I came out I was covered with perspiration and I began to shiver in the hall, there was quite a draft coming down the hall. I finally got back to my bed and spread the blanket on it as best as I could and got in. My heart was going very hard, you know, BAM bam bam, BAM bam bam, and I was shaking and terribly tense. But then as I lay there I began to relax, and I grew warmer under the covers, and my heart began to go more evenly, and, it's hard to say, in my mind, everything, I mean the city, the city and its buildings, that's what I was thinking of, everything began to take on a more reasonable, that's the word, a more reasonable proportion, I thought that now the buildings are at last assuming a one to one relationship, I thought that, I know, I'm not sure now what it meant but I was sure then, a city with reasonable buildings in a reasonable one to one relationship. And I was almost asleep and then suddenly I came wide awake again and my heart went back to BAM bam bam, because, you see, I had thought of it, why did you do it?"

"Mr. Kennan," Marie said.

"You might as well call me Francis," Kennan said.

"I don't know why," Marie said. "I mean, if I had known what was going to happen I wouldn't have, of course, I wouldn't have. But why I did, I don't know. Oh, maybe it was because you were talking about that priest, and I never liked priests. But no, that wasn't why. Mr. Kennan, there wasn't any why, I just did it, that's all."

"There must be a reason," Kennan said, "and it's important that we find out what it was, find out why a girl like yourself, fundamentally a decent person—you do think of yourself as fundamentally a decent person, don't you?"

"Not just fundamentally," Marie said, "but all over."

"Well, then," Kennan said. "Fundamentally a decent person to do a thing like that. Hold up a man's life to him and make it a nothing, an emptiness. Deny him any value, any at all, as anything."

"Mr. Kennan, there aren't any reasons. Sometimes you just do something, not for any reasons heavy enough to be reasons, you just do it. I just did it, that's all."

"It certainly wouldn't be reasonable for me to expect you to be able to answer right off," Kennan said. "I'll bet you haven't thought about it much, you haven't wanted to think about it, of course. Well, now I've told you that I've forgiven you, you think about it, and we'll talk about it some more tomorrow."

"Tomorrow?" Marie said.

"Not tonight," Kennan said. "I'm quite tired. Amazing how one does get tired traveling. After all, I was just sitting in the plane, letting the wings do all the work, you might say. But one does. I suppose it's the tension, and then the bother of your baggage and all that."

"You're back in your apartment?" Marie said.

"Oh no," Kennan said. "I let the apartment go when I went to Indiana. Didn't know how long I'd be gone, you see."

"A hotel?" Marie said.

"No," Kennan said. "I left my luggage at the East Side Terminal. Amazing how much luggage you can get into one of those lockers. You'd never think it before you tried. You know?"

Marie went to the kitchen and made herself another drink. When she came out Kennan said, "This friend who lives with you, you know her pretty well? I mean, she won't be put out to find me here?"

"I don't think so," Marie said.

"Let's hope not," Kennan said. "Actually, I think I'll turn in now. I know it's early, but as I said I am tired, and I'm used to getting a lot of sleep. The doctor told me I should take a lot of sleep, of course, but also there wasn't much else to do in Indiana. If I can just take my coat and tie off?"

"Certainly," Marie said. "I'll get some sheets."

"No, no," Kennan said. "Don't bother to do that. I'll have to sleep in my clothes anyway, I'm too tired to go fetch my luggage now, so there wouldn't be any point. It won't offend you if I take my shoes off?"

"No," Marie said.

"Don't want to get the upholstery dirty," Kennan said. He took his jacket off, folded it neatly and put it over the back of a chair. He took off his necktie, folded that once, and put it on top of the jacket. He sat down on the couch, took off his shoes and poked them side by side underneath. "Well," he said, smiling at Marie, "good night." He stretched out on the couch, turned to face against its back, put one of the small pillows under his head, put his hands together under the pillow and was still.

By one o'clock Lydia had still not come in, so Marie said the hell with it, wrote out: "*Mr. Kennan, you remember, is here for the night, that's his body on the couch, I guess you better try not to wake him, M.*" Scotch-taped it outside the front door, put a blanket over Kennan and went to bed.

She was awakened an hour later, squinting against the light. Lydia was sitting on her bed, shaking her shoulder. Lydia had no lipstick on, her black eye make-up had smeared and she was quite drunk. "There's a man here out there," she said.

"I know," Marie said. "I wrote you a note."

"I saw it," Lydia said. She got up and pulled her dress off over her head. "I'll wake him up," she said. Her loose hair caught in the zipper of her dress and she squealed. She pulled the dress free, threw it at her bed, sat down next to Marie and moaned. "I feel so terrible." She pressed her thighs together and bent over. "I let Mike do it to me tonight," she said.

"Mike?" Marie said.

"But I didn't come, I almost did but I didn't," Lydia said. "I wanted him to do it again but of course I made like I did come so I didn't know how to tell him and he said he'd better get me home. And outside we started necking again and I got so hot again and then he disappeared. And then when I saw a man inside I thought it was a miracle."

"No," Marie said.

Lydia stood up and stripped off her slip, panties, and brassiere. She wadded them and pushed them against her groin. "Why not?" she said. "I won't hurt him. He'll enjoy it even."

Marie thought for a moment. "No," she said. "He's still very nervous."

"Yes," Lydia said, and made for the door.

Marie slid out of bed, caught up with her and held her by the arms. "Go to bed," she said, "come on, just go to bed and you'll go to sleep."

"Oh please," Lydia said, "someone, someone." She pulled Marie to her and moved against her, hands on Marie's buttocks.

Marie sighed. "All right," she said, "come on." They stumbled to Marie's bed. Marie caressed her. Lydia came to orgasm quickly, pulling, as she did, Marie's head against her great breasts. Then she dropped her arms and lay with eyes closed and mouth open. Marie got up, went to the bathroom and washed her hands and face. When she came back Lydia had turned and pulled the sheet over her. "I'm sorry," Lydia said into the pillow, and was asleep.

Marie threw Lydia's dress off the other bed and was about to get in but saw that the lights were on in the living room. She put on a bathrobe and went out. Kennan lay in the same position, Lydia's stockings were draped across him. Marie dropped them on the floor, put out the lights and went to bed. She said to herself, "Busy, busy, busy," and went to sleep.

When the alarm rang Marie groped in the wrong direction for it and hurt her hand on the wall. She came alive, turned off the alarm, and looked over at her own bed. Lydia was stirring. There was a knock on the door. "Terribly sorry to bother you," Kennan called, "but I do have to go to the bathroom. Are you decent?"

Lydia shot up, holding the sheet to her neck. "Oh my God," she said, "I did that, didn't I? I did. Oh my God." She picked up the pillow, hit herself in the face with it and fell backward.

"Please?" Kennan called.

"Go right ahead," Marie said. Kennan came in, managed to find the bathroom door without looking at the beds, and went inside.

"Oh I'm sorry, I'm sorry, I'm sorry," Lydia said.

"Relax," Marie said. "You do much of that?"

"No," Lydia howled. "I never did, never. Oh my God, I'm sorry, I'm sorry."

"Relax," Marie said. "We going to get our hair cut short and wear neckties?"

"Please, please," Lydia said, sobbing.

"Relax," Marie said. "We get tired of each other, I understand there are a couple of bars in the Village you can always pick up a nice dikey piece for a change."

"Stop it," Lydia screamed.

Kennan came out of the bathroom. "Is anything wrong?" he said, not looking at the beds.

"No," Marie said. "Just unlucky in love. I'm getting up." Kennan scooted out.

Marie got up and said, "We don't do that again, huh?"

"Oh no," Lydia said, "never, never, never. Oh I feel awful. I don't know what to do."

"Relax," Marie said. "It was interesting, once."

"I can't get up," Lydia said from under the sheet, "tell them when you get to the office, I'm sick, I'm dying."

When Marie, dressed, came out into the living room, Kennan had sugar, milk, and three cups of coffee set out.

"That's very nice of you," Marie said.

"Not at all," Kennan said.

Marie explained that Lydia would not be rising now, reassured Kennan that it was nothing serious, drank her coffee, stood up, said, "Well, you'll let us know where you are?"

Kennan chuckled, and said, "Say hello to Sheldon for me. Tell him I'll be getting in touch after I get organized."

At the office, Marie told Friberg of Kennan's arrival and lack of departure. "You mean to say," Friberg said, "he simply folded his hands and passed into slumber? Incredible. How is he?"

"I don't think he's in very good shape," Marie said. "He doesn't seem exactly in touch, or anyway he isn't in touch with what I'm in touch with. I don't know."

"I'll give him a call," Friberg said, and telephoned Marie's apartment, but there was no answer.

When Marie got home she found Lydia and Kennan having a beer. Lydia was in slacks. Kennan had shaved. Two large suitcases, an overnight bag and a briefcase were stacked by the door.

"Well, well," said Kennan, rising with a jovial smile, "the only worker bee among all the drones."

"You finish my beer," Lydia said. "I've got to get dressed, Mike is coming for me." She shuddered and went into the bedroom.

"Very pleasant young lady," Kennan said. "She works at the office, too. Remarkable."

"Yes," Marie said. "How are you feeling?"

"Why, just fine," Kennan said. "I was a little fagged out after getting my gear this morning, but I took a nap before lunch and that fixed me up just right. Then this afternoon I took a nice walk, went up Third Avenue as far as Ninety-sixth Street. I must say, it's a real pleasure to be back in New York again. Oh, I know, it's noisy and tense, but still, there's life there, life, and that's what's important. Isn't it?"

"What's there out in Indiana?" Marie said. "The walking dead?"

"Don't be silly," Kennan said. "Here there's a texture, an inter-weaving of innumerable purposes, a whole universe of struggles and defeats and victories, an unthinkably enormous spectrum of desires and actions, of hunters and hunted. I don't know, perhaps it's merely a function of size and wealth. Although I don't see why I said merely; after all, elementary factors combine to make the great complexities. No, it's different from Indiana."

"You're right," Marie said. "I was silly." The doorbell rang. Marie opened it and recalled that she had been introduced to Mike. He was a stocky man in his early thirties. She introduced him to Kennan. "Call me Francis," Kennan said. Mike sat down.

"We were talking about New York," Kennan said. "You like the city?"

"That parking problem," Mike said, "I swear to God every year I say it can't get any worse and then next year it's worse. They're going to have to do something, I don't know what, but something."

"Not parking, so much," Marie said, "but as a gigantic force-field of exhilarating tensions."

"Exhausting, too," Kennan said, "but I can't see one without the other."

"You're so right, exhausting," Mike said. "You'd think air-conditioning in the car was just a gimmick you don't need, but I tell you, all summer, crawling around looking for a place to park, and then sweating over the wheel to squeeze your way in if you find a place, and then sweating over the wheel to get out because some dumb bastard has pulled right up behind you, I tell you, you need it and next year I'm going to get it."

"You have so much faith," Marie said, "that the city will be here next year? The bomb won't make it one empty parking lot for miles and miles and miles?"

"I thought of that, walking," Kennan said. "I could see sudden light, although of course I wouldn't see it, and hear the thunder to break heaven, and feel myself and the city engulfed. Horrible."

"No, things don't look so good," Mike said. "They're going to have to do something, I don't know what, but something. Hey, how about terrific big bomb shelters all around, they could use them for parking when there wasn't a war? How about that?"

"Great," Marie said. Lydia came out, affixing earrings. Flurry, and Lydia and Mike left.

"Seems something of a clod, that young man," Kennan said.

"Yes," Marie said, "I don't know how it is, but Lydia collects clods. She's not, and with a shape like that you'd think she'd find some better material."

"I was looking through the Morison Navy history," Kennan said. "Sad."

"Well, war," Marie said.

"No, not that so much, but all the lives of naval officers laid out in footnotes, three or four lines. Born, class at the Academy, a handful of posts, retired 1949, died 1951. That's all."

"Tell me," Marie said, "you figure to stay on here?"

"Why, yes, I'd like to," Kennan said. "For a while. Until I get my bearings. But one thing I'd like to tell you right now. Asking why you did that to me, as I was yesterday. I realize now that I was obsessed with it, understandable, I think, off in Indiana, seeing no one but my parents, well, it's easy to get obsessed like that. But today, New York, this apartment with you and Lydia, it's blown the obsession away. Oh, I still want to know, and I want you to think about it and tell me when you decide, but I won't press you for it as I did yesterday, slightly neurotic. I thought I was right that it would be a good idea to come here, and I was."

"I see," Marie said. "Well, I'll put on some dinner."

Kennan insisted that he do the dishes after dinner, and Marie read. When Kennan came out of the kitchen he prowled the bookcase until he found something he wanted. Just before ten the telephone rang. Lydia speaking low and quickly, said to Marie, "Oh, honey, I'm engaged, Mike asked me and I said yes."

"That's wonderful," Marie said.

"Don't kid me," Lydia said, "I don't know if it's wonderful or not, I don't know anything, I don't know about tomorrow, but he asked me and I said yes. But the reason I called, I won't be home tonight. I didn't want you to worry."

"Fine," Marie said.

"I hope so," Lydia said, and hung up.

"That was Lydia," Marie said, "she is in the first place engaged to be married to that clod Mike and she is in the second place not going to be with us tonight." She took up her book.

"To that clod?" Kennan said. "Strange." He put down his book. In a few minutes he stood up and began walking about the room. He looked out of the window into the dark. He came back and passed behind Marie's chair. He touched a picture and walked around the couch.

"What's your trouble?" Marie said.

"I'm nervous," Kennan said. "It was different when there were two of you, even if one of you were not here but only expected, it was different, it was simply a dormitory situation. But the thought that I'm going to spend the night in the apartment alone with you. It makes me nervous."

"Relax," Marie said.

"Don't be silly," Kennan said. "If I could I would. Listen, Marie, you don't feel guilty enough, guilty because of what you did to me, you don't. Oh hell, hell. I can't make myself talk about it, a hand chokes my throat with embarrassment, I can't even stand it when anybody else talks about, you saw how I changed the subject before when you just mentioned Lydia's, her body."

"About sex," Marie said.

"Yes, yes yes," Kennan said. "Of course. Listen, Marie, you don't feel guilty enough about what you did to me to, to comfort me? You don't, do you?"

"I don't think so," Marie said.

"No," Kennan said. "Listen, then would you mind if I went out and picked up a girl and brought her back here? Would you mind that, and going into the other room and leaving us alone?"

"No," Marie said. "I wouldn't mind. But would she?"

"The kind of girl who would let me pick her up wouldn't mind," Kennan said. "Thank you." He put on a raincoat, said that he still had Lydia's key, and went out.

Marie worried for a moment about what would happen when

Kennan came back without a girl, but decided that by that time he would be tired enough to calm down.

In less than an hour the door opened and Kennan, with a courtly half bow, ushered a girl in. She was rather young, mid-twenties, and quite ugly: beefy jaw, twisted nose, sallow skin, heavy figure. Her hair was rather long, black, and matted. She wore a tweed skirt, a sweater, and a suede jerkin, loafers and no stockings. Kennan introduced her as Chris. She flopped down on the couch, stuck her legs out and looked around the room. "What a waste," she said, "what a criminal waste, spending all that money on furnishings, on possessions. Think of all the books and records you could buy, all the wonderful creative experiences, but no, no, people are so mixed up in this crazy society they haven't any real sense of values any more. Are you going to watch us?" she said to Marie.

Kennan asked her, and Marie, if they would like a drink. "All right," Chris said, "but just a light one." Kennan went to the kitchen. "We can get blind afterward," Chris said, speaking so that Kennan could hear, "but I don't believe you should blunt your senses so you aren't receptive to all the wonderful subtleties of the sexual experience, I think it's a very immoral thing to do. And don't you drink too much or you won't be able to give a decent performance." Marie could see, through the kitchen door, the bottom of a tilted bottle as Kennan took a long, long pull. "Are you going to watch us?" Chris said. "I've never had a woman watch me before. Men, certainly, a lot of times, lot of times when I pick up a couple of men one of them wants to watch, but it might be a good idea to have a woman watch, you might be able to tell me something useful about my technique, being a woman. Basically, of course, I'm a very sexual person, but naturally my middle-class upbringing and the lousy system of education we have in this society has left me with some inhibitions, and that's the worst obstacle to developing a satisfactory technique." Kennan came in with three glasses. His hands were shaking. "What's your favorite position?" Chris said to him.

"I don't know," Kennan said, the glasses clattering as he put them down.

"Why don't you know?" Chris said. "It's the kind of thing a man your age should have very firm opinions about, he has enough experience to know exactly how he functions most efficiently. Although it is amazing how often men your age and older, even though they have had a lot of experience, don't know much about all the variations. I will admit, myself, until not too long ago I had enough inhibition left to feel not quite comfortable in anything but the basic position, but I met a simply marvelous man who helped me enormously and got me over that. He was older than you are. I've often found that men slightly older than you are the most satisfactory. Of course, on the other hand, it's horrifying how many men are completely useless, completely unable to give anything like an adequate experience. It's the sad old story of the American male and his mother, of course."

Kennan was pale and shaking quite badly, now. Marie said, "Well, I believe I shall retire."

"Oh, you needn't go yet," Chris said. "I like to talk about it a while before, I find it makes for greater excitement. Some men like to talk about it before, but you'd be surprised how many of them don't, but they can't expect me to ignore what I know about my own functioning, can they? I'll fondle you, if you'd like, some men do, while we're talking." Kennan shook his head quickly.

"Whatever you want," Chris said. "I believe that's the only way to attain satisfactory functioning, to know what you want and do it, without the slightest embarrassment or self-consciousness. That used to be my worst enemy, self-consciousness, in fact I'll admit sometimes it still does bother me a little, especially in the beginning of the experience, in the foreplay, but I tell myself that it's the force of anti-life and I must not give into it. I've been quite successful in freeing myself and I intend to improve even more, until I attain absolute freedom and absolute sexual expression. I think I may be beginning to feel a little excitement now. Caress me outside my clothes and we'll see, but for heaven's sake do it properly, there's nothing worse than a man who expects you to know how to caress him but hasn't bothered to learn the proper techniques to do it to you, the damn selfish pigs." Kennan was shaking very badly, and sweating. He did not move.

Marie stood up. "Out," she said.

"What?" Chris said.

"Out," Marie said. "Out out. Go away."

"Now wait a minute," Chris said. "You didn't ask me here, he did. What's the matter with her?" she said to Kennan. Kennan shook his head.

"Out," Marie said. She took hold of Chris's jerkin and pulled. Chris came to her feet. "Get your hands off me," she said. "Are you going to let her get away with this?" to Kennan. Marie opened the door. "Out," she said. "Go function someplace else."

"Of all the ball-less fairies," Chris said to Kennan, "letting her act like this."

Marie started for Chris, who said, "Don't you lay a hand on me. You're damn right I'm going. God, what a collection of weirdies."

Marie closed the door, went over to Kennan and knelt on the couch beside him. He put his head against the back of the couch. "Thank you," he whispered. "Thanks a lot." He put his hand in front of him. "If I could stop shaking," he said.

Marie pushed his hand down and pulled his head onto her shoulder. "That's all right," she said. "I'll take care of you. You'll stop shaking."

Vernon was nervous about the visit of Mrs. Wheeler and her brother and for the third time charged out of his office, asked Marie an inane question ("Are you sure you have the Stockton file handy?") peered around and popped back inside. Marie erased the error Vernon's voice had caused and continued typing.

Lydia Ferrucci came up. She was wearing one of Mike's shirts, thereby appearing more balloon-like, even, than usual. "I've been calling and calling," she said.

"We have given instructions," Marie said, "that no calls be permitted except from Reception. We are awaiting guests that scare us. A Mrs. Wheeler and a Mr. Forbes, and we cannot leave them dawdling while communication is blocked with trivia either of a business nature or pertaining to real life. You know who they are?"

The phone rang, from Reception. Mrs. Wheeler and Mr. Forbes to see Mr. Vernon. Marie got up. Lydia said, "God, yes, they own the place. That's interesting. I'll go out with you and take a look."

"You still engaged?" Marie said.

"Don't think you're being funny," Lydia said. "I don't know what I'm doing."

In Reception, Mrs. Wheeler was sitting straight on the edge of her chair, hands folded. Alexander was wandering the room, hands behind back. Marie said, "Mrs. Wheeler, Mr. Forbes?" Lydia, following Marie, went around her, headed for the outer doors and the elevator. Alexander turned and stopped, and he and Lydia stood chin to forehead, breast to solar plexus. "Excuse me," Alexander said. Lydia feinted to her left and passed to her right, moving around Alexander, whose small head swiveled after.

"Alexander," Mrs. Wheeler said, marching toward the waiting Marie.

Six minutes after Marie had closed Vernon's door behind them, Alexander came out and closed the door again. He looked at Marie, started away, came back. His face was red. "I hope," he said, "my silly clumsiness, moment ago, didn't embarrass, young woman."

"No," Marie said.

"Acquaintance of yours?" Alexander said.

"Oh yes," Marie said.

"You'll apologize for me?" Alexander said.

"No need," Marie said.

"Please do, please do," Alexander said. He wheeled and strode off.

The next afternoon Mrs. Wheeler received Alexander at her house. Alexander raised his hands. "First, Molly," he said, "before you berate me, let me admit that I deserve everything you are about to say. I don't expect to be let off my proper scolding, but I do want you to know that I am humbly aware of my guilt."

"Really, Alexander," Mrs. Wheeler said, "sometimes I despair of you, honestly I do. For a time you will go along acting in a fashion that is at least adequately reasonable, and then without the slightest warning you do something as shameful as your exhibition yesterday. What can that Mr. Vernon think of you, of us? More important, what would dear Papa think of such a performance? What can we think of it ourselves? How can we expect the Mr. Vernons of this world to feel a proper respect when you act in such a fashion? What on earth could have gotten into you, in the very middle of an important discussion, to make you leap up and mutter some foolish excuse about not feeling well and positively flee away?"

"Molly, you're right, of course you are," Alexander said. "But didn't you see, can it be that you didn't notice, didn't understand? That girl, that girl in the waiting room."

"Girl?" Molly said. "You don't mean Mr. Vernon's typist? A common little thing."

"No, no, Molly," Alexander said, "I mean."

"Oh ho," Mrs. Wheeler said. "You mean that other, that great plump creature. Well, what of her?"

"Not plump, Molly," Alexander said, "if you mean plump all over. A very trim figure, except for those enormous you-know-whats. I tell you, Molly, I've never seen anything like it. And that's what it was, my dear, you see. I don't excuse myself, but that's what it was."

"Alexander," Mrs. Wheeler said.

"But don't you see, Molly," Alexander said. "She, they, were so incredible, so dream-like, that I was unbearably excited, unbearably, Molly. I simply could not sit there talking to Mr. Vernon, why I would have burst, absolutely burst. I threw myself into a cab and positively flew into the little flat. Had to do something, you know, I simply had to do something."

"Well," Mrs. Wheeler said, "I suppose that explains your actions, which I had thought quite mad and inexplicable, but it certainly does not excuse them."

"No, my dear," Alexander said, "I cannot excuse them, as I have said. But will you let me remind you, gently, that it is a very great mistake to believe that human beings act at all times reasonably? Indeed, not simply a mistake, but a sin? That it is the so-called rationalists who are destroying all that is good and decent in society by imposing mere reason on age-old customs and hallowed patterns? Who in the mad pride of their so-called reason ignore and mutilate the deeper wellsprings of man, a creature not only possessed of reason but blessed with sacred and unalterable instincts?"

"I do not think, Alexander," Mrs. Wheeler said, "that under the circumstances I wish to be lectured by you. Whatever your reasons, you behaved badly, very badly. Instincts are all very well, but good manners are good manners. Although I must say, your sudden flight did give me the opportunity to observe Mr. Vernon under the turn of unexpected circumstances, and he showed up very well. Since you have obviously disqualified yourself in this case, I believe I will take it upon myself without further consultation to recommend him for the presidency."

"Molly, you will have to excuse me once more," Alexander said. "I simply cannot put my mind on anything but that unbelievable girl."

"So you flew into the little flat," Mrs. Wheeler said.

"I did," Alexander said. "Went through a lot of foolishness, too, for my pains. Had her dress as near as could be the same way, had her put on those silly foam-rubber things I happened to have around, although I always despise them, pulled and squeezed and pinched away at a great rate trying to pretend it was the other. But of course it was a disappointment. Oh, certainly, I felt better after a bit. But it wasn't the same thing. Molly, I really must have that girl."

"Now Alexander," Mrs. Wheeler said, "I warn you. You've always been sensible so far, or so I've understood, in not playing your nasty tricks on any one of those creatures who could in any way be connected with you. I warn you, Alexander, don't let a moment's foolish infatuation with a pair of big you-know-whats lead you into disaster. Remember, she undoubtedly knows who you are."

"You're right, of course, Molly," Alexander said. "And I will have to be most especially careful and most especially shrewd. Indeed, even in my excitement I took care not to ask her name or indicate any interest, but I did find out that Vernon's little girl knows her, and that will be a start. Trust me, Molly, to come out right, but I must have that girl."

"I hope," Mrs. Wheeler said, "that in your disappointment you didn't treat the poor thing in the flat too harshly. It's not her fault, you know."

"Am I forgiven, Molly my dear?" Alexander said.

"I don't suppose I have any choice, Alexander," Mrs. Wheeler said.

"I must confess," Alexander said, "I was quite uncommonly fierce. Finally couldn't bear to look at her you-know-whats any longer, reminding me of what I was missing, so I turned her over and gave her good and proper what-for on the other side. Then I played a little game I used to a lot, so much I tired of it and hadn't for some time. Let's have a nice martini, my dear, and I'll tell you about it."

"You tell first, Alexander," Mrs. Wheeler said. "I know you and your sly ways. I'll bet you don't have anything at all to tell."

"Do so," Alexander said.

⚹ *13* ⚹

Lydia and Marie got home after work to find Kennan cutting pieces out of the *Times*. "I know," he said, "it is a perfect attestation of my helplessness and futility, but since I am helpless and futile why not attest it? Look, from page three alone I have removed an Air Force General's reflections on creative evolution, a Texas Republican's paraphrase of the Sermon on the Mount and all the advertising except for three girdles and a funeral home. Better, no?"

"Don't be so God damn chipper," Marie said, "we just got out of the subway."

"Partake of my strength," Kennan said. "It takes guts to slice the *Times*."

"Well, negative guts but better than none," Marie said, going behind the sofa to remove her shoes and stockings.

"My positive guts have been borrowed for the national security," Kennan said. "Oh how we are led by fools and dastards."

"Who'd you expect," Marie said, "Pope Joan?"

"What are you two practicing," Lydia said, "Cambodian? I want a drink and then I have to change."

After Lydia's Mike had carried her away, Kennan said, "Is, will Lydia be out all night?"

"She didn't tell me," Marie said.

"Oh," Kennan said.

"Oh what?" Marie said.

"You know," Kennan said.

"Look," Marie said, "I don't want to be hard, but that much managing you've got to do for yourself, find out if she'll be in or out. I know maybe it'll embarrass you, but you've got to be willing to be embarrassed."

"You're right," Kennan said.

"Naturally," Marie said. "Now, listen. I want to ask you something and tell you something. First place, what do you know about Alexander Forbes? Lydia says he and his sister own the place, but what do you know?"

"Forbes? Yes, they do, her name is Wheeler. Inherited just about all the stock, I understand. Don't know anything about him, though, except he's a malefactor of great wealth, not much in the public eye."

"Malefactor?" Marie said.

"I assume," Kennan said. "Why?"

"They both came to see Vernon yesterday, I didn't tell you. Then this morning he came by without calling, told Vernon he wanted to apologize for leaving so soon yesterday, he'd been sick or something. Then this afternoon he called and said he'd lost his wallet, could we look around, and there it was, way under the couch in Vernon's office, how I don't know. Had almost six hundred dollars in it and his initials on it, but no papers at all. Then when I called him and told him we found it he asked could I bring it to his place tomorrow afternoon at three."

"Well?" Kennan said.

"Something wrong," Marie said.

"You think the blood-sucking capitalist bastard has designs on you?" Kennan said. "You want me to go with you?"

"Hah hah," Marie said. "But Lydia, yes. He almost got paralyzed when he saw her. And when he came out of Vernon's office he made some funny noises. A lot of money, you say."

"A lot, but come on," Kennan said. "You're not considering Lydia as a rich man's idle toy?"

"Toy, hell," Marie said. "If she has to marry a clod it might as well be a rich one. Besides, she likes clods. Besides, I give Mike three weeks. Besides, it might be interesting."

The next day Marie brought Alexander his wallet.

Marie said to Kennan, "Man, is that ever a creepy crawly thing. When I was telling him about Lydia he kept on getting red and then white and opening and closing his hands and twitching his eyes and leaning forward and leaning back and not looking at me and then looking at me. When he wasn't looking at me he looked like he was listening to music and when he was looking at me I thought maybe he might make a jump on the chance I'd turn into Lydia by the time he got there."

"You have not, of course," Kennan said, "bothered to tell Lydia anything of this puppetry."

"No," Marie said. "But a rich crawly thing, I guess, if he lives there. Nice place. Big."

"Marie," Kennan said. "I don't want to seem stuffy. Nor do I want more than necessary to accentuate our respective ages, mine the prudent middle years, yours impetuous youth. But I do feel impelled to raise the question, i.e., do you have any slight idea of what the hell you're doing? This cheerful chatter about manipulating our Lydia into a marriage of splendid wealth, fine, I approve of it, it's the kind of loose talk that has shaped our national heritage, it's the sort of thing that warmed the ragged troops sitting at Valley Forge, at Manassas and beyond, its threads are woven into the symbolism of our glorious flag, and so forth. However, if you can seriously believe there is a chance in howling hell that Alexander Forbes, swine of great fortune and distinguished family, is going to marry our Lydia Ferrucci, you are mad, quite mad. Or, if we set reason to the side and imagine the unimaginable, if you think such a marriage would be for Lydia anything but a catastrophe, you are equally if not more appallingly mad. And, finally, if at the most extreme limit of probability, your machinations do succeed to the extent that Forbes and Lydia have any relations whatever, those relations can only be the particularly squalid and disgusting prostitution of Lydia. I don't know whether I am opposed to prostitution as such, but in this case I am opposed."

"Well, you're right," Marie said, "except you're not. It isn't so simple. For the Forbes wanting to marry Lydia part, I don't know.

Not a good chance, sure. But I do know there's no chance at all if I don't do something about it. You never can tell what the dice are going to come out, but you do know that nothing is going to come out unless you shake them and shoot them. I'm doing the only shaking and shooting I can. Now for Lydia, I don't know. She's a funny girl, the poor kid. She's smart, but not very smart. She's got this addiction to creeps, or creeps get an addiction to her. One of these days she'll marry one creep or another. All very dull. Why not make it a creep with a difference? Sure, she probably won't like it, but at least it would be interesting and a change, the money and people and all, and I tell you if she marries just a plain creep she sure isn't going to like that either and it won't even be interesting. And prostitution, what do you think she is, a starving peasant? If she doesn't want to she won't and he doesn't have enough of anything to override her not wanting to. Jesus, if Lydia was prostitution-oriented with that bosom she would be running City Hall."

"I don't get the feeling," Kennan said, "that we are operating in the same universe here."

"Probably not," Marie said.

Lydia came home, to their surprise, quite early in the evening; she had not been expected for the night. "It's all done," she said.

"You drowned Mike," Marie said. Lydia nodded and sighed.

Kennan, guilty with his annoyance at Lydia's appearance, guilty with his relief that there had not been embarrassment, said, "You poor kid. You want to tell us what happened?"

"Oh, talk about it, sure," Lydia said, "talk about it. That's what I do most of, talk about why this man is no good or that man is no good. Christ, what's the matter with me?"

"Nothing," Marie said. "He wasn't any good."

"No," Lydia said. "And it isn't anything that happened, nothing new happened, I just had a couple of drinks with him and then had dinner with him and we talked, I talked and he listened and he talked and I listened and when we finished talking and listening and dinner it came to me that time was just up for talking and listening to Mike. So I said I was tired and came home."

"Ah," Kennan said, "I misunderstood, I'm sorry. I thought it was the end of the affair, not a simple lovers' tiff."

"No," Marie said, "she drowned him."

"That's right," Lydia said. "Goodby Mike, hello some other creep."

"That's the spirit," Marie said. "God, am I a judge of character."

The day after that Alexander hurried to his sister. "My dear Molly," he said, "an incredible bit of luck. Really; I feel just as I did that time at Monte when zero came up twice running."

"You are speaking too loudly, Alexander," Mrs. Wheeler said.

"But listen, Molly, listen," Alexander said. "Just in the forlorn hope, on the odd off chance that she might drop a word to the purpose, I arranged for that typist of Vernon's."

"Unlikable little thing," Mrs. Wheeler said.

"Molly, listen," Alexander said. "To come by the big flat to fetch me something I'd left. And offered her a cup of something for her pains, although I must say she insisted on putting away quite a lot of whiskey instead. I was going to be ever so careful not to mention the girl, so shrewd in maneuvering the conversation so that perhaps her name might be mentioned. And before I could do a blessed shrewd maneuvering thing it all came pouring out, her name, where she lives—they live together, Molly, think of that for a piece of luck—and ever so much about her. She's twenty-five years old and quite unhappy, Molly, she spends a great deal of time at home alone because, the little typist said, prattled away, really, she's quite uncommonly shy and afraid of men. Afraid of men, Molly, isn't that glorious?"

"When you calm yourself, Alexander," Mrs. Wheeler said, "you will remember the terrible dangers involved."

"Yes, Molly, yes, but I tell you I was so excited by this, simply being given the information I wanted on a plate, and that she was shy and afraid of men, had a very strict religious upbringing, Molly, why the little typist was scarcely out the door before I flew once again down to the little flat. The poor creature down there must wonder what demon has gotten into me."

"Well, Alexander," Mrs. Wheeler said, "I will admit that I'm pleased to find you so animated and taking such an interest in life, but at the risk of being a spoil-sport I do insist you listen to me. That girl knows who you are."

"Of course, Molly," Alexander said, "and I have already given the matter thought. After I get her, and I shall, Molly, I shall, I intend to be prudent and careful and make her last the longest time, but when I'm done then there's only one answer, I shall have to kill her."

"Alexander, Alexander," Mrs. Wheeler said.

"I know, Molly," Alexander said, "I know. Dangerous, terribly, I agree. But it is the only way. And please do not think that I intend to blunder forward foolishly without thinking my way through very, very carefully. Indeed not. When the time comes I will have crossed every last T, I promise you, and there won't be a chance to put a foot wrong. But let's not even speak of that yet. There is so much to come before. First to get rid of this one, of course. And then the little web to get Lydia, her name is Lydia, Molly, pretty? And then, my goodness, what glorious times to be had. Shy, afraid of men, properly brought up and, Molly, that glorious, that incredible figure. Think of it."

"To be frank, Alexander," Mrs. Wheeler said, "I would rather not."

⁂ *14* ⁂

When, shortly, the announcement was made of Vernon's impending ascension to the presidency he told Marie that he would of course take her with him.

"You're all right," he said. "You do your job."

"But," Marie said. "Thanks Mr. Vernon, a lot, but. Do you think I can do that? Secretary to the president of the company. Can I?"

"Crap," Vernon said. "Don't get carried away by titles. You'll have a girl to help you out, sure, because there'll be more routine stuff than you can handle, and you'll get a nice raise because my prestige demands it, but you'll just be a secretary like you always were, don't get dreams of glory from the women's magazines how you'll really run the office. It's me that'll be doing the president's work, and it's me it'll be rough on. Rough but good, you understand."

"Yes," Marie said. "You're right, of course you are."

Marie went in to tell Sheldon Friberg of her coming position. He smiled and congratulated her and said, "You'll be glad to learn that I have excused you your perfidy on the grounds that there is a certain nobility in being the first and therefore perspicacious rung in a meteoric career. How soon you figure you can knock off Vernon and take the job?"

"Couple months at the outside," Marie said. "How's Sheila and the kid?"

"Wonderful," Friberg said, "healthy. How's Kennan?"

They both laughed. "That's so funny," Marie said, "but you're right, he is still there. Not so good. No worse, but not much better. I mean, he's cheerful enough usually. But he doesn't do anything, walks a lot and looks at things, reads, that's about it, doesn't seem to be planning anything, I don't know. Maybe a little better."

"Hell," Friberg said, "why shouldn't he be cheerful? Doesn't have to work, living rent, food and duty free with splendid clean-limbed American girls, why if ever a man has consolidated the dream it's old Kennan."

"You know that isn't true," Marie said.

"What part?" Friberg said.

"Well, he's got some money still, from severance, I guess, and he buys more than his share of the food and liquor, and we'd pay the rent anyway."

"And the living?" Friberg said.

"Not with Lydia," Marie said.

"You," Friberg said.

"Once in a while," Marie said. "Sometimes. I feel sorry for him, and he's there and I don't have anybody else in the way right now that I like better."

"Pity," Friberg said, "just pity. God."

"That's it," Marie said. "So not so good."

"Has he asked you?" Friberg said. "Have you told him that?"

"He knows better than to ask," Marie said.

"He still hasn't called me," Friberg said. "I feel a little unhappy about that. I suppose, given Kennan, I can see why. But look, why don't you and he come around to dinner sometime? You can push it. Look, some girl Sheila knew at Ann Arbor a hell of a long time ago, she called her out of the night, she's coming to dinner Friday, why don't you come along?"

"Girl, huh?" Marie said. "Sure, but it seems to me kind of a simpleminded way to try to pull him back into the life stream, I mean under the circumstances. Or is the point to get him off my back?"

"Bitch of my bosom," Friberg said, "get out."

Kennan was most reluctant, saying he didn't feel up to seeing people, saying a domestic interior would be bad for his nerves, saying he felt ashamed to face Friberg and Sheila after his suicide attempt, saying he certainly under the circumstances didn't need any stray imbecile women, good God. By judicious nagging and a free use of her tactical advantage as hostess, Marie forced him to agree. "He'll be there," Marie told Friberg as the two of them left after work Friday.

Kennan was there when Marie and Friberg arrived, drinking ginger ale and talking to a very tall, very groomed blonde girl. "My God, man," Friberg said, "I'm glad to see you. You're looking good, you really are."

"Hello, Sheldon," Kennan said, "I'm all right. You look fine. Sheila looks fine."

Sheila came out of the baby's room and hugged Kennan's arm. "Isn't it wonderful having him around again?" she said. "Really wonderful."

Kennan said, "Oh, yes." Marie and the blonde had a drink, the others ginger ale. Then they had dinner. They talked about children.

The blonde girl said: "I always thought my mother was a pretty shrewd cookie, so when I said I'd decided to go to New York I listened to what she told me. She told me that with my looks and my bounce one of two things would happen. I would right away meet some attractive guy and get married and start having kids, I'm a Catholic, which was all right but the odds were I could do much better right there in Saginaw where I knew everybody. Or I would work into a job in some glamour outfit and meet men who had money and wanted a good time and could take me places and live it up and I'd start screwing around which was all right but wasn't going to get me anywhere in the long run, because why buy a cow and all that bit. I came anyway, but I have to admit I worried about what she said.

"Right away, I was as lucky as I could be. This gal I'd known at Ann Arbor was in New York and I called her and she was making out all right in TV, mostly commercials but some parts too and was living with this nice guy who did public relations and she asked me to a party at his place. There were a lot of big people there but the top banana was Max Harrison the producer who had just opened *Verone*, you remember, smash, smash,

smash, and he and I got along like a firehouse. I told him I was looking for a job and he asked if I could type, he had a girl for shorthand and all that jazz and I said sure and he said come see him tomorrow and that was that, just like that, his executive assistant. I've got this dream of an office, I just got raised to a hundred and forty and Christmas time Max gives me a little piece of whatever show he's working on.

"The first thing Max did was to sit me down by his desk and give me a drink and tell me, 'Honey, one thing I want to make clear. First, a lot of the men you're going to meet through me, here at the office or at parties I got to give and all like that, are going to make passes at you, you're a very good-looking gal and built and you know all about what I'm saying. But first thing is, no. Not with anybody you meet through me or anybody in the theater. You're going to know a lot of my little secrets, and excuse me, a gal in the sack will talk too much. Anybody wants to take you out, show you a time, hit the spots, fine. But that's all. And I'm going to make it easy for you. I won't say so right out, I'll kind of gag it up, but I'll get it across that you're my gal, you and me, we're doing the thing. And if you get asked, you don't say yes or no, but you just leave it up there like it's so but don't want to say it, just throw the line away, you know?'

"I liked Max right away, he looks like a fat little bird, so I stuck out a little and grinned and, just kidding, said, 'And will we be doing the thing, Max?'

"He said, 'Honey, I got married third time last year, she's just about your age. You'll hear a lot of stories about Vivian, and most of them are true, I'm civilized, she's civilized, we're civilized, she goes her way, I go mine. But the bit is, when I want her to be there, she's there, and when Vivian is there, man, she is there. And something else, the stories you hear about the fat slob successful producer and the gals looking for a good part? Well, they're true too, and like this afternoon I've got these German gals, these twins they heard I'm doing *Milkmaid* with the sister bit are coming in, and if I close the door I don't get any calls or see anybody till I open the door.'

" 'Will you close the door?' I asked him.

" 'How I feel,' he said, making a funny face.

" 'Will they get the parts?' I asked him.

" 'They'll get a fair reading,' Max said. 'I'm no fink. No, baby, you and I are going to be buddies, and that's it, I wouldn't feel right otherwise, with a gal working for me in the office here. I want to give you the job because you're a very good-looking gal, that's important, and you're smart and got poise and can talk to people, I saw that last night, and very important, you don't have any ambitions in the theater, Jesus, a gal I once had working for me.'

"Just like Max said, I have thousands, literally thousands of guys making the pitch at me, wanting to take me out and all, and I'm around town as much as anybody, in the columns pretty often you'll see 'Max Harrison's fabulous gal Friday tom-tomming with' and it'll be a name. But it's just a fun thing, oh, they all make a pitch, but not very hard, I give the loving freeze, you know, and they think me and Max and why get into trouble, and so forth. A few times I've been tempted, but Max means what he says, I know it, he wouldn't like it but he'd fire me in about five seconds. So there's that.

"And when I moved into my new apartment, it's not big but it's fabulous, right away I started yakketting with these two guys across the hall, Timmy and Tommy, I'd drop in for a drink before going out or they'd come over for coffee Saturday morning, really nice guys, they're both successful young lawyers, not the annoying squishy-swishy kind of fairy, you wouldn't necessarily know they are except they are. And one day they said they had a thing they wanted to ask me about, the old bit about how they had to go see people socially or have people in sometimes for professional reasons and it was embarrassing and damaging never to have a girl, so would I come with one or the other of them, make like we were going together and all, 'be devilishly hetero-sexual' as Timmy said. They said they knew it wouldn't be very much fun for me, very dull types they had to meet, they said, and I wouldn't be meeting any men, they were all terribly stuffy married types, but they would make it up to me. And they have, they've been darling, they're always buying me things, in wonderful taste, very expensive, I don't remember when I bought myself any lingerie, for example.

"So when I'm not out with some important friend of Max I'm out with Tommy or Timmy. You know, I haven't had the sex bit since I came to New York? And you know something else? I don't care. I'm having a fabulous time, and I just don't care.

"Of course, it can't go on forever, and some day I'll meet my guy. I really would like to have kids, and I'm a Catholic, so when I say kids I mean kids."

Sheila said, "My God, that's terrible, obviously she's never going to have any children at all."

Friberg said, "Wonderful, wonderful. You know, that very rarely happens, oh, sure, you hear a lot of talk about prones, accident-prones, victim-prones and so on, people who maneuver the universe against themselves, but it's mostly nonsense. Yes, certainly, there are enough people engaged in maneuvering the universe to their own harm and frustration, to be sure, to be sure, but the talkers always ignore the fact that the universe does a hell of a lot of malevolent maneuvering on its own, and mostly the situation of the prones is too complex to determine what areas are of the prone's maneuvering and what of the universe's. But here. This splendidly lucid, hilariously uncomplex case. How unerringly she struck for and conquered and exploited the dream of her blonde young heart's dream, love-dream, death-dream: the gorgeous figured outer show of abundant sexuality—abundance the American way, of plenty heaped upon plenty, the cup pressed down and running over, and all, wonderful, wonderful touch, made more real, more palpable than mere translucent life by the beatification of public print. All the splendid show without, and within the equally splendid converse, female caponhood, female eunuchdom, aridity, stasis, emptiness. The whited sepulcher, except that the sepulcher burns and blazes with color and the white is within, white not for cleanliness, white not for purity, but white for absence, white for nothing, white for death."

Marie said, "That stinks. Just because she works for that slob he tells her what she can and can't do and the idiot does it and doesn't do it. Him and his Vivian and his civilization and his German twins. Puke. I'd twin him. Of course, she's stupid to live that way. Not bad-looking, but, man, hard. Poor kid."

Kennan said, "But God, don't you see what an attack on me this is? Before, because I was not in balance, because I was stretched in the unstable—the meta-stable, if you will—attitude of faith, I could have parried this hit. Yes, I would have seen it was pathetic, yes, I would have seen it was self-imposed without awareness, yes, I would have seen it was unfair, but no, no, I could accord myself with her essential no. I had a rule, the rule said no, and whether I lived to the rule or did not there was a rule: sexual intercourse outside the sacrament of marriage and for purpose other than procreation is a sin. Because faith said it. So that whatever the turnings of God's labyrinthine ways, or man's, for that matter, I could, would have said of this girl, odd, perhaps, she should be married, perhaps, the human soul is a great complexity, perhaps, but good, good, whyever and however, she is not pitted with that sin.

"But now I have lost my imbalance and what is there for me to think? Revulsion, but revulsion is not a thought. Why revulsion? Because she refuses the natural instincts of man? Nonsense; civilization is that refusal. Because she does not know she refuses? Nonsense; we are all a web of that ignorance. Because she has chosen the outward manifestation of an inwardness that does not exist? Nonsense; I have no rule to tell me what is outward and what is inward, nor a rule to tell me that such false congruence is bad or good.

"And not revulsion purely, because if I cannot think about my feelings I cannot feel them purely. And I cannot think, I have no rules to think. I cannot think if what I do and want to do with Marie is good or bad. I cannot think if what I should do should be good or bad. I do not know, I do not know."

Marie and Kennan took the subway home late in the evening. Kennan sat folded into the seat between Marie and a fat colored man. The signs in the car told him what to gargle and what to drink, what to chew and what to swallow, Miss Subways told him what to love and the sign for shelters told him to die, but he could not take their advice as serious or disinterested. "I shouldn't have gone," he said.

"They were glad to see you," Marie said.

"I know it," Kennan said, "and I them, but I shouldn't have gone. That terrible woman."

"Oh, that," Marie said. "I see. Shook you up. And her a Catholic, too."

"My God, was she?" Kennan said. "I don't remember her saying that."

"At the end," Marie said, "when you were looking kind of bleared with it all. That worse?"

"Of course it's worse," Kennan said. "Don't you see? On top of everything else it's a miserable travesty of what I believed when I could believe, of what I thought when I could think. And now that I can't think I have no tool, no lens, no tweezer, to peer and pick at what I thought when I could."

"You can't think?" Marie said.

"No," Kennan said, "I don't know how to think any more."

"Well," Marie said, "that's too bad. But we can get you through it. I'll think and tell you what to. All right?"

"It would be better than nothing," Kennan said. "Tell me."

"Right," Marie said. "Now, thinking, I was thinking. We want to know more about this Alexander. Especially, does he have a girl, there wasn't one on show at his place, but I'll bet a type like that has her stashed away in some expensive little apartment, with gold pants and a poodle, you know, ha ha. So what I want you to think about and do is, simple, follow him around a couple of days, see where he goes in to, who he goes out with. Okay?"

Kennan began to laugh very loudly. The fat colored man against him turned his head and frowned, and after a few moments said, "If you don't mind, mister, to make less noise? It's been a trying day."

Kennan stopped laughing and said, "I'm sorry. Something funny."

"I guessed that," the fat colored man said.

Marie and Kennan got off at Seventy-seventh Street. They walked upstairs, past the store, now closed, that sold fake African fertility symbols, and walked home. Lydia was asleep and they had, at Kennan's request, sexual intercourse.

❈ 15 ❈

"Quite simple," Kennan said. "He came out of his place around eleven, walked over to Park and got a cab downtown. I got a cab right behind him, had told the driver to go on down until I told him to stop. Alexander turned off east on Thirty-first, I got out and walked over, in that traffic it was easy to keep up with him, he got out just past the corner of Second and went into a house down the block a little. Let himself in. Didn't come out. I waited three hours in a bar on the corner with a view."

"Too bad," Marie said. "I'd have liked you to have a look at her. What kind of a house?"

"A little house," Kennan said. "Four stories. Garage on the ground floor. Ugly. Top floor looks unused, windows shut up. What do I do now?"

"Pick him up from his place the same time tomorrow. If he goes down there again, do whatever you want to do and come back after a couple hours. I want to get a look at the competition."

"All right," Kennan said.

The next day Kennan said, "Didn't show at all." The next day he said the same.

"I know," Marie said. "I called his place, he's away for some days. Probably tomcatting around some resort with that popsy of his. Maybe. Saturday we'll go down and ring her bell, though, maybe he's tomcatting around without her."

Saturday they went down and rang the bell, but there was no answer. "Oh well," Marie said, "I expect they'll be back and we'll see."

All the next week Kennan went once a day, in the afternoon, and rang the bell of the house on Thirty-first, but nobody ever answered.

When Alexander got back he went to see his sister. "You're looking tired," she said.

"Perhaps a touch," Alexander said. "Fairly strenuous business, you know, getting rid of them. Nothing a good night's sleep can't fix. And then, to work. Plans all laid, Molly my dear. My, I can't tell you how I am looking forward to this. Lydia. Lydia. Oh my."

"Perhaps it might be wise," Mrs. Wheeler said, "if you delay a day or two and take some rest. Foolish to overtire yourself needlessly."

"Couldn't possibly wait, my dear," Alexander said, "not possibly. Would go mad. I tell you, Molly, you don't seem to realize how excited I am, the anticipation I feel. Haven't felt like this for years, donkey's years. But don't you fret yourself. Once it's done, once I've got the lovely creature safe and sound, I'm going to go very easy, I promise you that. I want Lydia to last the longest time, the longest time ever. You know, Molly, it's a funny thing, the human mind, have you ever thought that? Here I am, never spoken a word to the girl, never touched her hand, and already I feel a little melancholy at the thought of the time when she'll be all used up and have to go. Even though I know perfectly well by that time I may be tired of her. Odd."

"Tell me, Alexander," Mrs. Wheeler said, "what is the longest time you've ever kept one of your poor wretches? They come and go so I've never been able to keep track. But I don't suppose you really know, with your dreadful memory."

Alexander chuckled and pulled a notebook out of his jacket. "Right you are, Molly," he said, "worst memory in the world, that's why I write it down. Tell you in a jiffy."

"Goodness," Mrs. Wheeler said, "you don't mean to tell me, Alexander, you have everything written down, their names and what they look like and the dreadful things you did to them and the horrible things you made them do? You must be very careful, Alexander, what if that should fall into improper hands?"

"Yes, I thought so," Alexander said. "The longest was two years ago, January 14 all the way through to April 25. Let me see, was that the little dark girl with the long hair or was, what? Oh, Lord no, Molly, of course I don't write down what they look like or what we did, where would be the sense in it? And as for their names, why, after the first day or so I usually couldn't tell you their names for the life of me, after all, there's no one else there, and if I feel the need of a name I just use any that pops into my head, they learn who I'm talking to quick enough. No, all I put down is the date they come and the date we leave. Don't know why, exactly, just a sense that it's right to have some sort of a record. After all, that's what history is based on, some sort of a record, and there's nothing more important to human civilization than history, is there?"

"Any name that comes into your head," Mrs. Wheeler said. "Alexander, tell me, do you ever call them Molly?"

"I think that question is in damned bad taste, Molly," Alexander said.

"Oh nonsense," Mrs. Wheeler said. "After all, any name that pops into your head, it's the name you say most frequently, isn't it?"

"Of course it is, but," Alexander said. "All right, Molly, since you asked. I have noticed that I do use Molly sometimes. When they've done badly or haven't followed instructions or something and need to be severely punished, I've noticed that sometimes just before I start, got them all safely rigged up but haven't started to punish them yet, I call them Molly, say something like, well, Molly my dear, you've done badly and you're going to get punished for it, it's too bad, but I'm really going to have to hurt you this time."

"Oh," Mrs. Wheeler said. For some moments, Mrs. Wheeler and Alexander sat in silence in the sun-bright room, in embarrassment, mingled with a little pleasure.

"Where's Lydia?" Kennan said, and Marie said Lydia was working a few minutes late but she, Marie, had come on home to buy food before the stores closed, Lydia had suggested she call

Kennan and tell him what to get but Marie didn't trust his judgment even with a potato, come on, he could carry.

"Where's Lydia?" Kennan said, after they had gone and come
and were having a drink, Marie a martini and Kennan a weak
Scotch and water. Marie said she'd be along.

"You won't guess," Kennan said, "but I thought about looking
for a job today. I actually gave it cool and rational consideration."

"Hey," Marie said. "You're feeling pretty good?"

"Don't come clinical at me," Kennan said. "I just thought about
it. On the one hand, it did strike me as the normal thing to do,
although, now that I mention it, I do see the damnedest number
of able-bodied men around in the late morning, say, or the early
afternoon, going to the dry cleaner or walking a dog or whatever,
who certainly aren't working normal work, but then I suppose
they aren't normal or they would be, the world knows that. On
the other hand, although I'm not repelled by the idea, neither do
I positively look forward, anticipate with joy, resuming the old
office shuffle. Now, if I had a reason to get back to work. Can you
give me a reason?"

"Money," Marie said.

"Disappointing," Kennan said. "I have been given to understand that here in America we have, uniquely and affluently,
transcended that smothering materialism which curses the darker
world to eat its bread only if moistened by the sweat of its brow.
We must have a higher reason. Yes, of course, when I run out
of money, which won't be all that far off, I will have to go back
to work, but I am striving to lift myself to a higher plane. Can
you give me a higher reason?"

"No," Marie said.

"Well, what's keeping Lydia?" Kennan said.

By nine Marie had telephoned the night line in Personnel, but
nobody had answered. By ten they had eaten dinner and almost
exhausted hypothesis, all of which broke on the rock of Lydia's
certainty to telephone or have someone telephone, "Unless, of
course," Kennan said, "it's something truly apocalyptic like being
run down or pushed under a subway."

"That doesn't happen," Marie said.

"People tell me so," Kennan said, "but it does."

"No," Marie said.

"Nothing makes life feel so thin as empty waiting, waiting when you don't know why," Kennan said. "Like fabric too long used about to wear through, not tear, it's too worn for that, just wear away to no fabric. Like the sound, or lack of sound, not even a silence, just a lack, in your bedroom in the morning when you were a boy home sick from school. Like waiting in the war."

"By God," Marie said.

"I'm sorry," Kennan said. "No time for doubtful rhetoric."

"By God," Marie said. "That Alexander. I'll bet it's him."

"But we agreed, she would have called," Kennan said.

"Maybe, maybe not," Marie said. "I'll call him." When she hung up she said, "A maid or something. Said he was back from his trip but out for the evening, he might be in briefly tomorrow, did I want to leave a message." She stood up. "All right, come on," she said. "We'll go down poke around the love nest. By God, if it's going to be that rich crud Alexander he's not going to get her so cheap and easy."

"Wait, wait, wait," Kennan said. "In the first place, what makes you so sure this has anything to do with Forbes?"

"I'm not sure," Marie said, "I want to find out."

"In the second place, if it is Forbes she's with, what business is it of ours? A free adult, and so forth. What do you fancy, bursting between them as their lips touch, crying Hold, stop, this merger is unsanctioned by the SEC?"

"Come on, come on," Marie said, "let's get our thumbs out."

"But good Lord," Kennan said, "even if she is down there, what fools we're going to look, like what, like irate parents fetching a late child from a five-year-old birthday party."

"So," Marie said, "if she's not down there she's not. If she is down there and everything is gracious like a Scotch ad, we'll look foolish, but I don't like her not calling. And if she is down there and something's wrong, we better get there, and I don't trust that Alexander and she didn't call and it smells bad. So let's move."

The telephone rang. "Quick," Lydia said, "come down and get me out of here."

"Where?" Marie said. "Alexander?"

"Jesus, yes," Lydia said, "I don't know where, someplace on Thirty-first."

"The love nest," Marie said.

"Jesus," Lydia said, "come on and get me out."

"Where's Alexander?" Marie said.

"I locked him up where he put me," Lydia said. "The bastard had a heart attack."

"Coming," Marie said.

When Lydia opened the door to them, she was wearing a man's wrapper, holding a hand over her middle, stooping slightly and limping. "Come upstairs," Lydia said. "I want to see if the bastard is dead."

"Are you all right?" Kennan said.

"Jesus," Lydia said.

Upstairs was a neat, pleasant room hung with tapestries. "He's gone," Marie said.

"No he isn't," Lydia said. She pulled a tapestry aside, took a key ring from the pocket of the wrapper and opened the door. "Only two keys," she said, "the big one for the door and the cabinets and the little one for the handcuffs."

"Jesus," Kennan said.

The other room was smaller and had no windows. It had a bed, metal wall cabinets, two of which were open, and two armless chairs. Alexander, wrapped in a sheet, sat slumped in one of the chairs. He was quite gray. He blinked at them and whispered, "Help."

Lydia stood over him, said, "I'll help you, you bastard," and raised her hand. She said, "I can't touch the bastard any more. You hit him." Marie hit him in the face with the back of her hand.

"Don't," Alexander said. "I'm not a well man."

Lydia limped out into the other room. "Bring him out," she said. "I don't want to stay in there."

"Should we get you to a doctor?" Kennan said.

"I don't know," Lydia said. "I want to sit a minute. Those stairs were rough."

Marie and Kennan dragged Alexander into the other room and dropped him in a chair. "A doctor," Alexander said, "take me to a doctor."

"What happened?" Marie said.

"This terrible burning sensation in my chest and down my left arm," Alexander said, "and I believe my vision was affected, yes."

"Shut up," Marie said. "What happened?"

"God," Lydia said. "Well, when I came out of the subway and started to walk east I think he came out behind me, anyways he said my name and started to walk along. I knew who he was of course and he said he'd seen me at the office and remembered me and knew what a good job I did and blah blah blah. Then he asked me, started insisting, I must have a drink with him, if I would be so courteous as to spare a few minutes for a middle-aged man, blah blah blah. So I said okay, I would, I just wanted to call you first and say I'd be late, as a matter of fact I was, you know, a little flattered, he seemed so glad to see me, God, what a world. And he said I could call from his house. And we walked a little and we came to his car he had parked there, and we drove down here, I thought it was a funny place for him to live. And we drove the car in the garage and came up the stairs, up here, and the door to the other room was open and he motioned me to go through and I did and the door locked behind me and there I was. First I thought it was some kind of nut joke, then I started to yell and bang on the door, then I looked for a window but there wasn't any, then I just sat and worried. Must have been an hour and a half. I couldn't imagine what was going on. I got scareder and scareder."

Alexander sat up straighter, holding the sheet around him. That's it, just it," he said. "First effects of anger and what you call it, adrenalin, fade away. Worry, anxiety, fear, realization of loss of control of situation. Always the way."

"Shut up," Marie said. "We'll fix you later."

"There wasn't any sound I could hear from outside or anywhere. Then he came into the room real quick, came bursting in. I started to stand up but I was only halfway when he hit me in the middle. I went down again and was coughing and breathing and couldn't do anything while he was swarming over me, when I could sit up and notice he had my hands behind me in those damn cuffs he has and my ankles to the legs of the chair."

"Boy," Marie said. "Are we going to fix him."

"What's the matter with you?" Kennan said to Alexander. "What is it?" Alexander shrugged.

"Then he started talking to me, pulled the other chair over close and started talking. Telling me, oh God, every kind of crazy thing, that I was helpless, I couldn't do anything about my situation, he kept calling it my situation, that all I could do was make life easier for myself by obeying him and trying to please him and if I didn't all it would mean was punishment, situation, obedience, punishment, obedience, punishment. And games we were going to play, he kept on talking about games. God. Then the bastard took my clothes off. He went and got a scissors and cut them where he had to, kept on telling me he would get me other stuff if we wanted to play games where I wore clothes. He wasn't even excited yet, seemed pretty calm, except when he finished getting them off he grabbed my damn breasts and squeezed hard and closed his eyes and made a noise like a horse. That's when I tried to jerk away and ram my shoulder into his balls but he stopped me easy and said something like that was the only time he wouldn't really punish me for disobedience, then he kicked me a couple, no three times in the leg up here, look at it." Lydia spread the robe to show the great dark bruise on her thigh. "Then he took his clothes off, God, so ugly, and I just about gave up and figured the only thing was to get it over with and get out of that damn quiet room, except he said something about we were going to go slow, very slow, he wanted me to last weeks and weeks and weeks, and I didn't see what I could do. But he didn't come at me yet, he opened the cabinets and showed me, Christ, whips and belts and metal things, kept on saying I'd get to know them, then he got out some boxes full of pictures and started showing them to me, Christ, you go in and look at them, all pictures of girls he did things to, you ought to see some of them, the looks on their faces, and he got hotter and hotter and was squeezing me and rubbing me and then he started saying, all right, all right, we'll just get this out of the way before we have some real fun, and he unlocked one of my legs and threw me on the floor, twisting my ear, God that hurt, and was coming at me, when he stopped and bent over and stayed that way holding his side, then he dropped. It didn't take me long to drag over and get the keys out of his pocket but I was so scared he'd come to and I didn't know what to do, before I got the thing off he started to move and I didn't know what to do so I dropped on him, put my belly over his face and he stopped moving. When I got the leg thing off I came out here and shut him in, but I was shaking and shaking and it took me a long time to figure out how to get my hands where I could see what I was doing. When I got the wrist things off I still couldn't call for a while, I just sat. God, you go look at those pictures."

"All right," Kennan said, standing, "the police and then we'll get you to a doctor."

"Wait," Marie said.

"What for?" Kennan said.

"Just wait," Marie said. "How do you feel now, kid? Think you need to see a doctor right away?"

Lydia shook her head. "No, I'm okay, the bastard."

"Really, please," Alexander said, "there'll be plenty of time for making amends after, but I've had a terrible scare, I must see my doctor, his name is Carson and he lives and practices on Seventy-third Street, could one of you call him, perhaps, or perhaps we'd better not disturb the poor man but go to his office, if one of you could drive me or obtain a taxi, perhaps?"

Marie got up and went to the other room. Lydia closed her eyes and rested her head on the sofa back. Kennan looked at Lydia, then at Alexander. Alexander looked ahead.

Marie came back after a while and said, "Boy, those pictures. All those poor kids. I guess you killed them when you were done."

"No, no," Alexander said, "never killed a soul in my life."

"One way or another, missing or complaining, the cops must be interested in what happened to them. Give the cops you and the story and the pictures, be lots of fun."

"Can't we discuss this after I've seen my medical adviser?" Alexander said.

"Don't be silly," Marie said.

"But I may have another attack and die at any moment," Alexander said, "you have no right to imperil a human life like this."

"Do," Marie said.

"All right," Alexander said, "if that's the kind you are, all right. What form of blackmail were you considering, then?"

"What form would you suggest?" Marie said.

"Stop this nonsense," Kennan said. "Blackmail, for God's sake. We call the police, of course."

"I'm not so sure," Marie said. "I figure we give him to the police, oh, well, yes, there'll be a terrible mess and scandal and family shame and his sister, that mean-looking cow, will have five kinds of fits and everything, but they won't hang him and they won't hurt him, much, and probably he'll just get stuffed away for life in a psychiatric hospital. I mean, after the cops finish working him over and all, even cops have sisters and human feelings. So if we can find a way where on the one hand we can get some good out of the mess ourselves and on the other arrange a worse punishment than the cops, why we ought to think about it."

"Hear, hear," Alexander said.

"No," Kennan said.

"Why not?" Marie said.

"Justice," Kennan said.

"Law isn't necessarily justice," Marie said. "Everybody knows that."

"This isn't an occasion for piddling sophisms," Kennan said. "Look at Lydia." Lydia opened her eyes, then closed them and shrugged.

"All right, look at Lydia," Marie said. "What good will the cops do Lydia? Bad publicity and bad bother, that's all, and no compensation for a miserable time. Certainty he won't be able to start up again? No certainty. Revenge? If she wants revenge it's not enough."

"The police," Kennan said. "It's the right way."

"All right, look at Lydia," Marie said. "She's the one went through it, not you or me. Ask her. Kid, you want necessarily to call the cops or do you want to talk about another way?"

Lydia remained silent, her eyes closed, for a moment, then she said, "What did you have in mind?"

"Fine," Marie said.

"Wonderful," Alexander said. "Now, apart from my most solemn promise not to indulge in any of this sort of foolishness again, and believe me, the fright I've taken this evening would be enough to prevent me quite without my solemn promise, how much money for each of you would you take as an adequate testimony to my, ah, good-will?"

"Shut up, you bastard," Marie said. "Lydia, you want to marry this crud?"

Lydia opened her eyes. "God, no," she said.

"Okay," Marie said, "I'll marry him."

"Don't be ridiculous," Kennan said.

"Oh no," Alexander said. "I couldn't possibly, thank you. My sister, and so forth."

"She'd like the cops and the newspapers better?" Marie said.

"Well," Alexander said. "Well, perhaps not."

"You see," Marie said, "if I marry this crud, in the first place I can make damn sure he doesn't start up his cruddishness again, and in the second place I can be a nice built-in revenge for his past cruddishness and in the third place I can control enough money to compensate Lydia. Works out fine."

"Complete nonsense," Kennan said. "Insane nonsense."

"Now," Marie said, "you're thinking he can agree and then afterward refuse or skip out. But he can't, we'll have the pictures and this place and the story, he can't unless he doesn't want ever to come back and he's a sick man. Or he could yell blackmail and get us in trouble, but he can't, aside from everything coming out it was his idea, trying to keep us from telling the cops, I momentarily wavered, an unsophisticated young girl dazzled by his promises. Or that mean cow sister of his will scrape up the lawyers to stop it. She can try, but if she tries the mess goes up anyway, and he's a sick man and he'd be smart not to tell his mean cow sister till after. Oh, hell, there'll be problems when we're married, sure, but everybody tells me it's not realistic to go into marriage all cloudy-headed, thinking there won't be any problems."

"Insane," Kennan said.

"Really," Alexander said, "don't you think we can work out some other simpler way?"

Marie got up and stood over Alexander. "Look, you cruddy little bastard," she said, "I'm fed up with you acting coy. You think being married to you is such an undiluted pleasure, all right, I'm willing to blast out to the cops and wait until you start getting your next heart attack in a cell or in a State loony bin. Besides, what kind of a gentleman talks like that about marrying?"

Alexander looked at Marie for a moment, and said, "Yes, there's that. Perhaps a bit of a rest might do me some good."

"Right," Marie said. "Then that's that. Let's go."

Lydia insisted that she needed no doctor's examination, just wanted to go to bed. They dropped her off at the apartment, then went on to Alexander's doctor. After the examination in a small room, Marie insisted on being present when the doctor delivered his opinion. "After all," she said, "I want to know the state of his health, fiancée and all."

The doctor, who had a thin mustache, looked puzzled, but Alexander said nothing. "Well," the doctor said, "I'm happy to say that it's not nearly so serious as it might have been. Of course, it's not trivial, never is, and a man your age, well, although it could have been more serious it might soon be unless we take it seriously. Ha ha?"

"What?" Alexander said.

"Definitely a coronary, of course," the doctor said. "Not a major one, and very possibly not to be repeated for twenty years. But we must take care, avoid excitement and strain, physical, mental, and emotional. For example, we must be very moderate in our use of alcohol."

"I drink very little," Alexander said.

"And as little tobacco as possible," the doctor said.

"I don't smoke," Alexander said.

"And for the immediate future we should refrain from, we should abstain from," he looked at Marie.

"Sexual intercourse," Marie said. "That's all right, one of the reasons we're marrying is to take care of him."

"Of course," the doctor said, "but a nurse, after all, and might it not be a good idea to wait a few months?"

"No idea at all," Marie said. "And while we're here, you can take blood for the test."

When Marie and Alexander came out into the anteroom, Kennan was gone. "Your friend's gone," Alexander said.

"It doesn't do you any good," Marie said.

"No," Alexander said.

Marie and Alexander were married two days later at City Hall. Lydia was one witness, an elderly man loitering in the hall the other.

It was her second step up.

✳ 16 ✳

"Gone, eh?" Friberg said. "Poor Kennan drifting into the dark, a thin figure carrying a small bag, merging with the night, a wanderer, his frail tentative root unrooted, drifting again over the illimitable nameless face of the American land, arriving, perhaps, at some future morning in some filthy Midwestern town, the anonymous rooming house, the anonymous job, the pale smile for the girl next door he doesn't talk to, the quiet drinking alone at the end of the bar, the rapid random tumble on the unwashed Polish prostitute, nights alone to sleep, mornings alone to wake, and then one random time, gone again, drifting into the dark, nothing behind to remember, nothing ahead to expect. Eh?"

"Stop worrying," Marie said. "I don't know. He just went off, was gone when I got back. Most of his stuff is still in the place. I don't know."

"What do you propose to do to replace worry?" Friberg said.

"Nothing," Marie said. "Nothing to do."

"Then permit me to fill my own vacuums," Friberg said. He laughed. "And you wouldn't care to tell me how you engineered Mrs. Alexander Forbes?"

"Engineered?" Marie said. "Don't be insulting. A bride gets selected, a bride gets plucked."

"Yes," Friberg said, "speaking of which."

"No," Marie said, "we aren't. Speaking of it, that is. But I wanted to talk to you, to see if you could give me any ideas on what to do. I mean, I'm quitting here, of course, and I'll have enough money, I guess, but what am I going to do?"

"Why, the activities proper to your new station, I assume," Friberg said. "Serving on charity committees to raise funds for obscure nervous disorders, attempting to elicit rational discourse from your partners at dinner parties, observing the mating habits of the servants, what did you have in mind?"

"Shit," Marie said. "I'm serious."

"Well first," Friberg said, "you'd better tell me something of the life-style you intend to adopt. I presume you'll start off with a long honeymoon voyage to Brindisi, or beyond."

"No," Marie said. "Alexander has to rest and he says he can rest best out in his Long Island place for a few months, but I don't want to stick myself out in the hills there so I'll stay in his apartment and Lydia will come in with me, she's thinking of quitting too, did you know? I wouldn't mind going someplace, but Alexander says even if you go someplace and stop there it's not as restful as your own house, and I don't care all that much to make him go. But what will I do?"

"Alexander says, is it?" Friberg said.

"Oh, well," Marie said, "sure, he's a pig, but after all."

"I see," Friberg said, "meaning, of course, that I don't, but anyway. What would you like to do?"

"I had one idea, I wanted to ask you," Marie said. "It's yours, really. You always used to go on how trade magazines are all a big tub of lies, never tell the truth about products, never tell the truth about companies, never tell the truth about people, just a snow job to try to make everything and everybody look good, bring in the advertising. Well, I thought about making Alexander let me start a real trade magazine, start with shoes, say, so you could do it, tell what's really going on in the industry, what company is screwing what, who's pulling this sleazy deal, really tell about the trade. What do you think?"

"I sometimes forget," Friberg said, "that you are a very young and, if not technically innocent, inexperienced girl."

"Scared," Marie said. "All that talk was talk."

"I'm sorry," Friberg said. "It's a touch unnerving to have one's previous righteousness, uttered in the safety of inaction, subjected to the killing light of the real world. But, no, it won't work. Whatever you can get Alexander to do, and I have full faith in your omnipotence, it would have to be done through an organization, and organizations are semi-independent entities. There are some things they can't be made to do. This organization, for example, simply cannot be made to scream to a stop, turn in its own length and start emitting truth. To build an organization for that purpose? No, it would ridiculously over-demand a fortune one hundred times larger than Alexander's doubtless considerable one, and of course not for an instant or a penny would the family and lawyers permit it. And, to get back to the personal element, I would not dare, I would, as you say, be scared, to have anything to do with such a monstrous perversion of our order. I would never get a job again in my field, and I'd need a job immediately. See?"

"I see," Marie said. "Too bad."

"Yes," Friberg said. "But I begin to see what you are driving at when you ask what you will do. You mean, I gather, to do good?"

"Certainly," Marie said.

"Difficult," Friberg said. "Difficult to know what to counsel you. If, of course, it were the dear old dead depression days we read so fondly of, why you could, for example, start your own Communist Party and be away running in no time. But it's more complicated now. I'll think about it, though, and let you know if anything comes to me."

"All right," Marie said.

"Sorry," Friberg said. "But speaking of family, how did they react to the marriage? Seemly exultation that the thin Forbes strain is to be bolstered by a healthy inoculation of Slovak blood, a little fertile soil on their blue genes? Or perhaps a certain coldness, a perceptible distance, toward one whom they have not, after all, known very long?"

"I don't think he's passed the word yet," Marie said. "He was saying something about going to see his sister today, but I wasn't listening."

As Alexander advanced across the room toward Mrs. Wheeler, she leaned forward to peer at him. "Alexander," she said, "you are looking drawn. I've been worried these last days when you didn't come around that you were overtaxing yourself with your new little friend, and I believe I was right to worry. I thought you were going to be ever so prudent and easygoing, I thought you wanted the poor thing to last. I'll bet she's simply in shreds. You always were a terribly greedy little boy, always snatching at the pleasures of the moment and cramming them down, so to speak, without the least thought for the pleasures that tomorrow may bring."

"Molly," Alexander said, "do be quiet an instant and listen to me."

"You're not in trouble, Alexander," Mrs. Wheeler said. "I warned you about this girl, remember I did."

Alexander sat down. "Molly," he said, "please be quiet. I am not in trouble about that girl. I'm. Well, Molly, the facts are that I've had a bit of a heart attack. And I've been married."

"Oh, Alexander," Mrs. Wheeler said.

A half an hour later, Mrs. Wheeler sighed and said, "What puzzles me, Alexander, is why you really wanted to marry that little, that girl. Otherwise you would have let the lawyers handle everything."

"No," Alexander said, "I didn't want to let the lawyers handle everything. And I didn't want to marry her, you know. I wanted to be told what to do, and it just happened that she was telling and that's what she was telling."

"And you are fully aware that it's only your money and your name she's after?"

"The money, certainly, why else?" Alexander said. "The name, no, I rather think not, doubt if it means anything to her."

"Of course it does, Alexander," Mrs. Wheeler said. "It means a great deal."

"Certainly it does, Molly, if you know about such things," Alexander said. "But don't be provincial. Have you never been to the Bronx?"

"And you have no plans?" Mrs. Wheeler said.

"Rest, Molly, rest, that's apparently the only thing I can do. Rest and have a bit of a think."

"I was always afraid one of those girls of yours would get

around you some way and pull you into an unsuitable marriage."

"It wasn't like that, Molly," Alexander said. "And please, not now."

"Not now, not now," Mrs. Wheeler said, "but if you don't let me patch things up now it will be too late when you're ready. All I can say is God be thanked you had children by poor Alice before she died. At least the family will go on, however bad a father you've been to them."

"That's right, Molly," Alexander said. "That's all right. I just need to get away and rest."

✳ 17 ✳

Some weeks after Marie had moved into Alexander's apartment she telephoned Friberg. "You and Sheila," she said, "tomorrow night. A housewarming party, you might say, except when Lydia and I started figuring who we wanted we kept crossing everybody off except you and Sheila."

"Very flattering," Friberg said, "but a little restricted, a little lacking scope, surely. No nice young man with a clean smile for you, for Lydia?"

"Oh well, sure," Marie said. "There's this nice young man of Lydia's and this other nice young man that's mine. After all."

"Yes," Friberg said. "I'll approve of them?"

"God, I wouldn't think so," Marie said.

When Sheila and Friberg arrived Marie took them on a tour of the apartment. She pointed to the door of Lydia's room and bath, then they walked a bit and she showed them the door of her room and bath, then they walked a bit past rooms that Marie said had, at the moment, no specific function, then, coming around the long way, they passed through the dining room and she pointed out the door to the kitchen and Mrs. Ferguson's room. "Who?" Friberg said. "The loyal family retainer?"

"Yes," Marie said. "She'll be out with some food later. She's all right. A little servile. I figured I might have some trouble with her, but no, she was just worried I'd fire her. If I could, which I don't know for sure. But she's all right. Grovels a little."

"Boy," Friberg said, "tradition is shot to hell."

"It's a lovely apartment," Sheila said. "I mean stuffy and ugly and all, but so much room."

"I wish I knew something good to do with it all," Marie said.

"Harbor the homeless, the dispossessed," Friberg said.

"I thought of it," Marie said, "but I don't know any. Except Kennan."

"A lot of work to keep it up," Sheila said.

"Yes," Marie said, "this woman comes in every day. She won't talk to me much."

"Fine," Friberg said, "doubtless black, doubtless oppressed, doubtless of a family that lives in foetid squalor. Have them move in."

"I thought of it," Marie said, "but I doubt if she would. She doesn't seem to like me much."

When they returned to the living room Houston and Piselli were sitting as they had been left, each a drink untasted in his right hand. They were both burly men in, Friberg judged, their middle forties. Houston, however, was the balder. They had surprised Friberg. Under cover of the record Lydia had just put on the phonograph, he indicated discreet curiosity to Marie. "Detectives," she said in a firm, carrying voice, "private fuzz. Alexander put them on to watch me and we started talking. One or the other was always hanging around or following, so we got to talking."

"That's right," Piselli said, saluting with his glass, "and I'll admit I'm not easy in my mind about the operation, and that's a fact. After all, we hired out to this guy to let him know what his lady and her friend was up to, if anything, understand, if anything, and I'm not at all easy in my mind now that it's us they're up to. No, nothing illegal there, we put in reports like we're paid to do, but once in a while it strikes me as kind of a failure of moral obligation."

Houston, lighting a cigar, said, "Nonsense." He puffed, coating his blue suit with ash. "Soft-headed nonsense. I'm surprised at you, Piselli, I thought you were sounder than that. We contracted with the client to report on visits from, visits to, and any other

activities involving men. It's implicit in such a contract that those
men are other than ourselves and it's explicit in the Constitution
of the United States that no man can be forced to be a witness
against himself, yes, that's right, the Fifth Amendment you're
always talking about, and I'd say it was time somebody else beside Commies and crooks got the protection of the Constitution.
What's the matter, Piselli, you going fuzzy-headed? Next thing
you'll be talking like a do-gooding one-worlder." Houston put
down his cigar, and rose to dance with Lydia. He did a firm,
competent two-step, despite the music.

"Now wait one minute," Piselli said, but was ignored.

Later, while dancing with Lydia, Friberg expressed his surprise about Piselli and Houston. "I know," she said, "I know. But
it happens. We were lonely. There wasn't anybody else around.
They were around. Nobody else was. We were lonely. It happens."

"I don't think I approve," Friberg said. "It's aesthetically displeasing."

"Oh nonsense," Marie said, "you're just ashamed to say you
think it's wrong. I agree, it is, I disapprove."

"Well?" Friberg said.

"I don't know," Marie said. "Suddenly getting married, engi-
neering like that, and not having to work and not knowing what
to do, how to do what I want to do. And not being sure, it's the
first time I can remember in a long long time, not being sure what
I was doing was the right thing, I don't mean little right or little
wrong but not being sure what I was doing was moving in a direction I want. Having nobody around but Lydia was too much on
top of that."

"They much better than nothing?" Friberg said.

"Not much," Marie said.

Later Sheila went to call the baby sitter. When she came back
Piselli asked her about her child. "I got five myself," he said,
drawing his wallet, "oldest eleven, youngest fourteen months."
He handed over the pictures. Sheila said, "Nice, nice." "I guess
you think," Piselli said, "a man with a wife and five children
ought to be either on the job or home with his family?"

"I thought this was your job," Sheila said.

"I'm off-duty now," Piselli said, "it's Houston's tour. But the girls wanted me to come to the party. But I can tell you, I don't feel right about it. We got a nice little house in Woodside."

"Can it, Piselli, can it," Houston said, dancing past with Marie. "Man wasn't designed to be monogamous, you know as well as I do, I thought, that's the role nature gave women, protect the blood lines and the family, stands to reason. God, man, next thing you'll be spouting United Nations talk."

"Now damn it, Houston," Piselli said, but Houston and Marie had danced away.

Sheila and Friberg left early.

The next time Friberg saw Marie, some weeks on, she came and visited him at his office. "You look terrible," he said.

"I'm tired," she said. "Never get to bed any more."

"Oh? Your Bobbsey twins lost their ardor?"

"They're gone," Marie said. "I mean they're there watching, but we don't mess around with them any more."

"Well that's a small blessing," Friberg said.

"Yes," Marie said, "and I put the fear of God in them, they report anything I'll squeal and get them fired. So that's all right."

"What's all right?" Friberg said.

"Oh, some guy Lydia knew and his friends, actually his friends, lots of them, without the guy. Man, queers crawling up the walls and falling off the ceiling, day and night, especially night. Last night Luke and John, two of them, they'll tell you they've got a very sound relationship, is what they tell, they insisted on giving a reading of *Vogue*, well, Luke kind of chanting and John on drums. Noisy. I think they're still there, someplace. Mrs. Ferguson quit. Somebody kept goosing her."

"What are you going to do about it?" Friberg said.

"I hired another one," Marie said. "But it's a grind."

"No, no," Friberg said, "the inversion invasion. Or have you decided to be the queen bee?"

"Not as a career," Marie said, "but it passes the idle hour. Actually, there's not much I can do about it. Lydia's decided she's going to save one of them from himself, Tom Harrison, a miserable piece of foppery and snottery, but that's what she's decided."

"Oh God," Friberg said.

"Yes," Marie said. "And where Tom Harrison goes there goes the horde and there we are. You might drop by some evening and take in the sights. If the spirit moves us we put on quite a show."

"I disapprove," Friberg said.

"So do I," Marie said, "it's, how you say, aesthetically displeasing."

When Friberg went, after working to early evening, to drop in at Marie's, he rang the bell, waited, rang the bell again. Calling himself an idiot for not having telephoned (although she had implied it was always open house and fair frolic), he turned to the elevator when Marie's voice said, "Who's there?"

"Me," he said.

"Oh," she said.

A long pause, and the door opened. He went in and followed her back down the hall to the living room. She was limping slightly.

The living room had no one else in it and was dim. Friberg sat, looked around, said, "The revels are all ended?"

"You bet," Marie said. She swung her feet up on the couch.

"Where's Lydia?" Friberg said.

"In her bedroom, crying," Marie said.

"What for?" Friberg said.

"She feels like crying," Marie said. "Honest to God, what a silly question."

"And what's your trouble?" Friberg said.

"It's funny," Marie said.

After an acceptable period Friberg said, "What's funny?"

More pause. Then Marie swung her feet out and jumped up. "Ah, the hell with it," she said. She turned on several lamps. "I'll go scrape up Lydia. You have a drink, I know you don't, but have one anyway. The hell with it."

"Why are you limping?" Friberg said.

"I kicked a wall," Marie said, "or a fairy bit me or something. You hang on."

First Marie came back and made drinks, then Lydia came in, newly made-up and no less stacked than ever she was, then the telephone went off and Marie answered it and said, "Come on, come on," and soon five or seven people arrived and there was the music of glass and vocal music and instrumental music and a young man said to Friberg, "My mother's joined the Peace Corps and I'm free at last," and a young woman said to Friberg, "My fiancée's an optician and I'm proud, do you hear me, proud," and Friberg was very bored.

Going, he looked for Marie but could not see her. Lydia was in a corner with several. As he left the room, however, Marie came up and walked him to the door. "Smart of you to leave," she said, "things'll start getting rough just about now."

"Rough?" Friberg said, halting. "Looks to me a seemly young middle-class crowd."

"That's it," Marie said. "Brrhh." She opened the door for him. "But it's all right, I can take anything for a while. I'll find out."

✻ 18 ✻

Alexander, sitting back in the big chair, loosening and tightening his wrist-watch band, looked about the room and said, "Well now, gentlemen." The five other men in the room suspended their drinks attentively. "I have given, I assure you, given every waking moment of the past week to the question you have presented me. There has been, on the one hand, the very real consideration," and stopped as he saw five pairs of eyes swivel from him to his right. He turned and saw Marie coming in, close the door behind her and, smiling slightly, seat herself. Alexander frowned and said, "My dear, these are some men with whom I have important business. Gentlemen, my wife." Pause for surprise, then bustle as the five, led by Mr. Walter Downey, rose to their feet, followed quickly by Alexander. Marie nodded. "Go right ahead," she said. "Nothing to be afraid of."

"Delighted to meet you, Mrs. Forbes," Mr. Downey said. "I will admit I had no idea of Mr. Forbes' good fortune in so youthful and attractive a helpmeet."

"It is a surprise," Marie said. "Sit on down."

Led by Mr. Downey, they did. Alexander looked at Marie again, then decided best to get on with it. "I was saying, gentlemen. The very real consideration that for a man of my age and experience, lack of experience might be more accurate, such a first step is one to be examined with the greatest care, the greatest prudence, the greatest caution. On the other hand, of course," and Mr. Downey did not move his large, well-cared-for body nor shift his gaze from Alexander, but his nostrils did dilate. "There is the fact, overwhelming in its insistency to every honest and far-sighted man, that never in its history has our beloved country stood in straits more dangerous, more fearful, never has there been greater need of men in the councils of government who possess sound principles, deep vision, profound awareness of the decencies of human existence. That being so, I have the honor to accept your most flattering proposal, and place at your disposal all my energies and all my assets in the contest for the seat of Member of Congress."

Mr. Downey said, "You may get pretty tired in the race, Alexander, but I doubt if we'll have to call on quite all your assets. However, I know we all think you've made an excellent decision, and we all have the utmost confidence of your victory in the primary and the election." He leaned forward to rise.

Alexander raised a hand. "Please," he said. "Hear me out. There's not a great deal more. You may believe me or believe me not—and I know perfectly well how pride and ambition cloak themselves in self-deprecation and reluctance—but I honestly do not think I would have accepted your proposal if it had been simply a matter of the election fight against Aldo Bompelli, whom of course I know quite well. Aldo is a Democrat, true, but when you have said that you have said all you can against him. As far as I know, Aldo's record in the House is as good as you could expect. True, on occasion he's been forced to go along with his party, but on the basic issues, the gut issues, Aldo has voted the right way and I see no reason to believe he wouldn't continue to do so. No, if it were just running against Aldo, I'm not sure I'd have the incentive to take this great step. It's the primary that's important to me. This Link, whom I intend to fight and destroy in the primary, is another matter. He would be a disgrace to his country whatever he called himself, and calling himself a Republican makes the disgrace a veritable stink in the nostrils of the godly. Peace, co-existence, disarmament, relaxation of tensions, more civil prying from Washington, more centralism, more economic strangleholds, more damned interference in a man's right

149

to live his own life—well, gentlemen, you can accept my word that I feel very strongly about the possibility that Mr. Link might throw his poisons down the well of the Congress, and I'll stop at nothing honorable to make sure that after the primary Mr. Link is, is a missing Link."

Several of the men chuckled. Mr. Downey said, "That's very true, of course, Alexander, and I'm sure we're all at one with you. But let's remember that this is a double fight, first the primary, then the election, and we're not going into this thing to win the primary and then lose gracefully to Aldo Bompelli. We're in it to win all the way."

"Of course, Walter," Alexander said. "All the way."

Going down in the elevator, Mr. Downey turned to young Krantz and said, "I thought the fact sheet on Forbes said he'd never remarried?"

"Yes sir," Krantz said. "That's what it said. Nice-looking little piece. I guess I better check into it."

"I guess you better," Mr. Downey said.

On the street, under the canopy, Mr. Downey and Krantz said goodbye to the other three men and watched them march away. "Someday," Krantz said, "you or me or somebody is going to forget to wind them up. It'll be too bad."

"You talk about them to me," Mr. Downey said, "how do I know you don't talk about me to them?"

"Good God, Mr. Downey," Krantz said, "that's no comparison and you know it, sir."

Mr. Downey chuckled. "Prudence, boy, prudence, just as the old fart upstairs said."

"What are the chances, Mr. Downey?" Krantz said.

"To beat Bompelli? Not bad, not good. It's marginally a Republican district, and Bompelli is a good campaigner, a good organizer, but he's been in a long time, he's maybe a little tired, a little cocksure. We might take him."

"And the primary he's got such a hard on about?" Krantz said.

"That," Mr. Downey said. "Nothing. God almighty, boy, do you think good, honest, home-owning Republicans are going to vote for a boy who wants to talk to Russians? Not only talk but listen, like they were people on this earth too? No, the election maybe, maybe not, it's a rough fight, but for the primary we won't have to draw a hard breath."

"Yes sir," Krantz said.

"You know," Mr. Downey said, "come to think of it, the one thing that gave me any pause at all for the primary was the relative ages. Our misguided countrymen, or maybe it's the God damn women, have an incurable predilection for young fools like you or Link over mature, responsible types like Forbes. That young new wife of his will be a help. Proves there's youthful virility together with the seasoning. We'll have to think about ways of using her."

"Proves it?" Krantz said.

"Within the meaning of the act," Mr. Downey said. "My God, boy, what are you suggesting? A prime-time TV display of candidates' virility?"

"Well," Krantz said.

"No," Mr. Downey said. "Take the word of a mature, responsible, seasoned veteran of the American political scene. I haven't the time to explain it to you fully, but it simply is not practical."

"Yes, sir," Krantz said.

Marie obtained an appointment with John Henry Link, representing herself as the president of the Political Committee, New York State Council of Young Homemakers. Link, as she entered his office, stood up. He was a tall, large, youngish man with curly brown hair. He shook her hand.

"Mrs. Polichek," he said.

"Call me Marie," Marie said.

"I will admit," Link said a little later, "that I am delighted to find an organization such as yours taking an interest in politics, and politics at the grass roots, at that."

"Grass roots?" Marie said. "Here?"

"Yes, perhaps, ah, sewer or Con Edison level would be more applicable to urban life," Link said, "for it is undoubtedly true that the old image of a rural Jeffersonian America is sadly in."

"Yes yes yes yes," Marie said. "Now, what we want to know is what we can do to help you beat Forbes in the primary."

"Why," Link said, "that's very kind, very flattering. I suppose you'd like a general survey of my position on those many areas, that quite wide spectrum, where I differ from Mr. Forbes. Or, let me say, believe I differ; Mr. Forbes has not yet, as far as I know, taken specific positions on many points of vital interest to the informed electorate. Now first, in all fairness to you and your organization, I want to make it clear that I am on some matters what some people call a radical, and I don't think I'm ashamed of that label. For example, I believe that."

"Yes, yes, yes," Marie said. "Of course, naturally, who doesn't."

"Why, I'm afraid that you'll find an uncomfortable number of people who don't. Perhaps you haven't followed me completely. On the question of, oh, for example, Communist China's admission to the United Nations, I take the firm stand that the matter should be openly debated. Or on nuclear disarmament, I believe we must face the fact that it is a, perhaps the, most important task facing us and must look beyond the stale reiteration of frozen positions to some sort of breakthrough in ideas and attitudes."

Marie closed her eyes. "I hold," she said, "that oxygen-breathing organisms must give high priority to obtaining and maintaining a supply of air at least adequate to their minimum needs." She opened her eyes. "Come on. Now, like I said. What kind of help do you need to beat Forbes?"

"I hope," Link said, scratching on his blotter with his thumbnail, "you won't misunderstand my question, but you realize my position. You and your group, you are not in any way affiliated with the Communist conspiracy?"

"Homemakers, for Christ's sake?" Marie said. "No."

"Well, there are innocuous-sounding fronts, and all that," Link said.

"Uh-huh," Marie said.

"All right," Link said. "You want to help and you ask what you can do?"

"Right," Marie said.

"Time and money," Link said. "Volunteers to canvass and re-canvass, to talk to the voters weeks before the primary and to get them interested in voting the primary in the first place and get them interested in voting for me and make lists of those who sound as if they will and get them out on primary day and check them off and make lists of voters who've moved out of the district and make sure the opposition doesn't vote them and hand out campaign material and, well, there's plenty of work for the willing. And, of course, money."

"Well," Marie said. "Homemakers, after all. What with, you know, knocking the kids around and the morning martini and comparing husband's sex lives with other homemakers and maybe a quick couple of shags behind the friendly neighborhood tavern, there's not so much time left in a day. I mean, we all don't organize like I do. How much money?"

"Why, that would depend entirely on what you felt you could give," Link said.

"Naturally," Marie said, "but how much?"

"You embarrass me," Link said.

"Say five thousand?" Marie said.

"Good God," Link said.

"Now I'm not sure I can get it," Marie said. "But I'll try. What else?"

"Why, why I'd want to think about it," Link said, "I am, I must say, somewhat overwhelmed with this unexpected generosity." He looked at his watch. "I suppose you have a husband and kids to get back to."

"Not especially," Marie said.

"How many children do you have?" Link said. "I, to boast a little, have three."

"Me too," Marie said, "there's little Alexander, and little Lydia and little Francis Xavier. What did you have in mind?"

"Why, it's almost five," Link said, "and if you are free I thought you might like to come home and have dinner with us, meet my wife and the kids. If you'd like?"

"Oh," Marie said, "sure."

"You'll excuse me while I telephone," Link said.

Link parked in the driveway of the small new house and they went in. Mrs. Link was at the door, a thin woman in printed cotton slacks and shirt. Behind her was the roar of many childish voices. Link introduced them, then excused himself to go "say hello to the kids." Mrs. Link led Marie into the small glassy living room and said, "Martini?" Marie nodded.

"Well," Mrs. Link said, sitting with her glass. "Young Homemakers getting behind John's campaign, hey?" Marie nodded. "That's a laugh," Mrs. Link said. "You know, the first thing that crossed my mind when he called me was he was trying to scrounge a meal for some poppsy of his, not that I know about any, but what else does he do in there all day, and besides, it's the best explanation for what I will delicately call a decline in vigor, I'm sure you follow me, but you're not?"

"No," Marie said.

"I'm sorry," Mrs. Link said, "but I didn't get your name either of the times, it's been the usual murderous day and I'm a teeny buzzed."

"Marie," Marie said. "You catch a couple of quick boffs behind the friendly neighborhood tavern today?"

"Goodness, no," Mrs. Link said, "those loafers it's too much like work. There's this guy three houses down, he's a writer and you know how they are, home all day, fell by as per usual."

Mr. Link came in from the children's room, frowning. "Mandy," he said, "that's a nasty bruise Kiki has."

Mrs. Link finished her drink. "It's all very well for you to ride that old-hat permissive hobby-horse," she said, "but I have to live with them. You put them to bed while we girls have another."

At dinner, Marie pushed the sludge on her plate around a bit, and put her fork down. "Yes," she said to Link, "I understand about you needing money and people, but I was hoping there might be some other thing or things to be done. More specific. More explicit. More immediately effective."

Link swallowed a large mouthful of sludge, smiled a compliment at Mrs. Link, and said, "I don't think I understand exactly what sort of thing you have in mind."

"Well, exactly I don't know either," Marie said, pushing her plate a little to one side to evade the odor, "I was hoping you would have some ideas. Something like, oh, framing Forbes on a narcotics charge, say, or threatening to break his legs if he doesn't quit. Something like, I don't suppose they're very good."

"Oh well, now," Link said, spooning a little more sludge into his plate, "that sort of thing. But surely if we start thinking along those lines we have to ask ourselves the age-old question of means and ends. Assuredly I believe with all my heart that the interests of the United States would be better served by my nomination and election than that of Forbes, yes indeed. But am I justified in working to that goal by means which are surely, in spirit if nothing else, a denial of the democratic process?"

"Who's talking about your ends?" Marie said. "I'm talking about mine. Knocking off Forbes."

"I know, dear," Mrs. Link said. "He's always like that. But me, I was always more interested in the reverse problem, good means and bad ends, it always seemed more pertinent. I remember. I remember when I was in Berlin after the war, working for the Army. What a time, you remember?"

"No," Marie said. "That would be about when I was five."

"I was twenty," Mrs. Link said. "What a time. I'd never been away from home before. I didn't know anything. Oh, sure, I'd had a couple boys in high school and a couple after, but I didn't know anything. I remember the first time I went to one of those clubs, tiny little places in the cellar with rubble for a roof, tiny little places with little tables and a bar and not much light, and girls, my God the girls. I remember the first time I went, I went with a lieutenant from back home, his wife was in my class, he was in the Adjutant General's office, he said he'd show me around. We sat down and I looked at the girls, they were at the bar, some of them, and some of them sitting at empty tables and some standing against the wall and some walking from table to table where there were men and some were dancing in the tiny space, dancing with each other, and I didn't understand at first, I thought, sure, they were there to be picked up, maybe, if the man played it right and bought them enough drinks and offered them enough or just was nice, my God I thought I was back at the junior prom at high school. Until the man I was with asked if it would be all right if he danced with one of them, he'd heard something about this place and I said sure it was all right with me and he got up and went over to one of the girls, and they started to dance and in a minute they stopped, he stopped, and made a funny twist and came walking back to the table, a funny look on his face, a grin but funny, and sat down and said, 'It's true what I heard about this place, the minute we start to dance she opens my fly and says, please, very cheap, very good, anything you want, please, actually opens it.'

"Then I looked at the girls harder. You know, it was funny, the way they were dressed. Some of them tried to be smart, elegant, but there wasn't one thing they wore that looked like they didn't pick it out of a trash barrel. And some of them said the hell with it and just wore to show as much as they could. That was funny, the two ways.

"Then the man I was with said he hoped I wasn't shocked, it was like that, and I said no, I wasn't shocked, I was maybe a little surprised. And he said, Surprised? A few months around here I wouldn't be surprised at anything. Why, you know, no, you don't, but there's a place around here where they specialize in mothers and daughters, both of them, I mean, at least they say they're mother and daughter and they show you papers to prove but of course you can get papers for anything. And a place around here where they have a guy who was, who says he was a light-heavyweight champion before the war and for a pack of cigarettes you pick out any girl in the place and she takes her clothes off and they put on gloves and he belts her around, he really belts her around, and then for another pack of cigarettes some guy comes out and does you know what to her on the floor. And they've got a place around here where every girl she carries a picture of a guy, a soldier who she says is her fiancé or husband and a prisoner of war and she says wouldn't you like to do to me what my fiancé or husband would want to do except you're healthy and free and he's rotting in some prisoner of war compound, they even promise to write him a letter about it, but of course you can't believe that any more than you can believe they really have fiancés or husbands although of course a lot of them do.

"But that isn't what I started to say.

"What I started to say, was about the major, the Luftwaffe major. I was walking after work with a man I knew, an English officer, and we passed a group of Germans working on a rubble pile, sorting out the bricks that could still be used, you know, and this English officer pointed at the man who seemed to be the foreman and he said, 'See that chap, the stocky built one? Luftwaffe, major. A first-rate officer, absolutely first rate. I was on the Intelligence side and we knew about him, we did indeed. Few months ago I found myself looking at him, doing that job of his, and recognized him. Went over and introduced myself, got to nattering. Seen a good deal of him since. Fought the whole war right over again. Must have been a really first-rate officer. Keen, assiduous, tireless with detail, firm but fair, absolutely cold-blooded in action, brave, resourceful. Career officer, of course, the air force his whole life. Said to me once, "I do not like, I do not like at all, the idea of killing other men, even in war. It is strange, then, is it not, that at the same time I cannot imagine a life that brings out the best in men as does the Service. It is too bad that the Service must sometimes be used." No politics at all. Detested Hitler, he says, and I believe the man, but detested all politicians. Asked him what he thought about the concentration camps and exterminations and that sort of thing at the time, he said, "I knew about them, of course, although I did not then realize how far those madmen had gone. But there was nothing I could do, so I simply did my best not to think of it." Then one day, evening, actually, we were drinking beer, and I put it to him, I said, "You are, I believe it thoroughly, a man who has selflessly loved your country and tried to serve it, a man who loved his Service and tried with enormous success to carry out its finest traditions. Yet is it not a fact that because of you and others like you, less worthy, most of them, I believe, but like you, that we are today sitting in the rubble of your capital city with the stink of millions of murdered men, women and children in our noses?" And if you will believe me, when I said that, tears came into the man's eyes and he said, "I know, I know. It cannot be, life cannot be so cruel. But it is true."'

"I always remembered that," Mrs. Link said.

"Bastard Germans," Marie said. "Now, what are we going to do about Forbes?"

"Why," Link said, "I suppose, in the last analysis all that we can do is put our case before the people who, in their collective wisdom, by that miracle of democratic synthesis in which a multitude of individuals, not all well-informed, not all well-intentioned, combine to give that decision we can but hope is the best decision, which, indeed, has so often proved to be the best."

Marie narrowed her eyes and said nothing.

Later, talking of the problem with Friberg, he said, "Well, yes, I admire your sturdy attitude, very much in the American tradition, not to say that of the West, in its largest sense. Not to submit meekly to events but to dominate them; not to be molded by the universe but to mold. I do not, however, I must confess, see any easy practical answer to your problem."

"Thanks," Marie said.

"Well, what the hell," Friberg said, "you want me to arrange for the massed photographers of the urban press to burst in on the shabby hotel room as Alexander, grinning playfully, disembowels his mother?"

"That's the idea," Marie said, "only his mother is long disemboweled."

"I'll think about it," Friberg said.

When Marie got home Lydia was sitting alone in the living room. She was wearing an old skirt and a tortured white shirt.

"Alexander?" Marie said.

"Out someplace," Lydia said. "I noticed he doesn't much like to stay around if I'm here alone. Don't like it much myself. Listen, Marie, I think I'll get out of here. It's fine, not having to work, and having a nice place to live and all that, but I think I'll get out, get a job, go back to where I was before."

"What for?" Marie said. "Nothing to do with the time?"

"That's it," Lydia said. "That, and Alexander, who doesn't give me happy memories, and the creeps I've been playing around with. I don't know, maybe living here, not working, has nothing to do with it, God knows there were always creeps, but I have the feeling they're getting worse and I can't do anything about it, I'm not in control. So maybe if I go back and start over. Brush my teeth a lot. Get to bed early. Work hard. Buy clothes that de-emphasize the bosom."

"No," Marie said, "it won't help, but if you want to try. Except listen, first you've got to help me. Frame Alexander so he loses the damn primary. Or better, has to drop out. Or something. Now think. Frame him with you?"

"No," Lydia said.

"No," Marie said. "All right, how?"

Lydia shrugged. "Frame how? Really or really in pictures or fake pictures?"

"What a nice methodically dirty mind you have," Marie said. "Let's see, I guess fake pictures is as far as we can get from reality, so that's best. We need a photographer, then. Hey, that creep photographer of yours, what was his name?"

"Norman," Lydia said. "Oh no, then leave me out. He'll want to take more pictures, and I've gone so far beyond those sweet innocent days that I'd cry."

"Don't be silly," Marie said. "A man has a habit like his, he gets his fix or he kicks it. If he hasn't kicked it he's found some other way of getting his fix. Okay, you got his address? Then look him up in the phone book and we'll take off."

"Hadn't we better call first?" Lydia said.

"No," Marie said, "what I remember from the time he saw us last, he'd go underground."

Norman lived one flight up in a well-kept house in the West Village. Marie pressed the bell and, eventually, Norman opened the door. He did not immediately recognize them, but started a defensive speech, "Ladies, ladies, you don't have to say anything, I'll sign your petition, I ought to give out rubber stamps with my signature," then recognized them. He froze for a moment, tried to slam the door, but Marie was leaning against it.

"My God," he said, "it's the killers."

"Now, now," she said, "be calm, be cool. We are not here in a destructive or educational capacity. We come in honest search of an honest craftsman, and will repay his honest efforts with honest money."

"It's Norman the lens not Norman the creep we want," Lydia said. "Hello, Norman."

Norman backed one step and said, "You're level? You promise?"

Marie and Lydia promised and went into the apartment. Standing in the middle of the living room was a very, very thin girl with dark brown ringlets, weakly pretty. She was barefoot, wearing dungarees and a T-shirt enormously too big for her, like hippo skin. Norman hesitated, then interposed himself between the girl and Marie and Lydia, putting a protective arm around her. "I'd like you to meet my wife," he said. "We just got married a couple of months ago. Her name's Betty Ann. That one's named Lydia and I'm blocking the name of the other one, the terrible one."

"I'm very glad to meet you," Marie said.

"Wait," Norman said. "Honey, go get dressed." The girl murmured something.

"Hell," Marie said, "not for folks like us."

"No, baby," Norman said, "you get dressed. I've got my reasons." The girl slipped off to another room.

"You'll see," Norman said. "You can sit down over there." He indicated one side of a large round table. He sat down opposite. He glanced at Lydia and looked away, smiling slightly, drumming fingers on the table.

"How you been, Lydia," he said, "anything much new?"

"Not much," Lydia said.

Norman's wife came out of the back room and stood near the table, self-consciously posing, but also smiling slightly. She was still barefoot, still wearing dungarees and a T-shirt, but the T-shirt was not now too big, it was barely big enough to encompass the tremendous humps jutting forward, two feet forward, it seemed, at least, from her chest. "Now how about that?" Norman said. "How about it?" He jumped up and, tenderly holding her arm, guided her to a seat at the table. She sat down. The humps hovered far over the wood.

"Best foam rubber," Norman said, "light, fireproof, washable. Guy I know in the East Village did them for me. How about that? Hey, Lydia, I don't know if you remember, but I used to be kind of an unhappy guy, one way or another, you remember? And you know why? You just said it yourself, before. I was two people, I was, I was Norman the lens, Norman Win, a God damn good photographer, you ask anybody in the business, who made himself a God damn good enough living. But I was also Norman the creep, Norman the schmendrik, Norman Winogradow, who at the age of thirty-four still had pimples. Well, by God, I'm still two people, I'm still Norman the lens and I'm still Norman the creep, with pimples, but I'll bet you I'm the only Norman or anybody else with a wife who tapes in at 63-18-27. Now what do you think about that?"

"I think," Marie said, and Lydia kicked her hard on the calf. Marie moved her legs and said, "I think she's absolutely wonderful."

"Oh yes," Lydia said, "I think she is."

Norman leaned back, smiling broadly now, and put his hand on his wife's. She looked up quickly at Marie and Lydia and then down again, still smiling her weak sweet smile. "So okay," Norman said, "what's the business?"

"Well," Marie said. "It's mostly a technical problem, but there are certain aspects of policy we've got to thrash out with your guidance. Thing is, we've got to fake a picture to knock some guy out of a political race. Now, there's no reason the picture would ever have to get itself published, but it's got to be good enough to convince the guy, and a couple of other men, he's got to drop. I can get you some snapshots of the guy, I suppose, and all you have to do is work him into whatever we decide. Women? Fags? Heroin? I haven't made up my mind. What do you think?"

"No, no, no, no," Norman said. "Let's wait a minute. First thing, how much you willing to pay? Remember, that kind of montage shot, it's going to be any good at all, takes time and talent. Five hundred bucks?"

"Sure," Marie said.

"Christ," Norman said. "Now, second thing, old snapshots are no good. I'll want a negative to work with, preferably one I shoot myself. That stop you?"

"Let's see," Marie said. "No, I don't see why. You can be, what? Oh, a free-lance photographer taking pictures of all the candidates and their families, hoping to sell a story to *Life*, say. Okay?"

"Wait a minute," Norman said, "you said a guy, nothing about families, kids and women."

"Oh no," Marie said, "the only family is me, it's my husband. But you'll take pictures of him alone, too, of course, the rest is just packaging."

"Your husband?" Norman said. "It figures. Well, that's okay. Now, what kind of a fake you want?"

"How about with a couple of women, all naked and tangled up," Marie said. "Can you do that?"

"Sure, I can do it," Norman said, "but is it worth doing? I don't know how hard a push this guy needs, but it seems to me you're going to push, you might as well push. So he's tangled up with a couple naked women. So? So maybe he thinks that's bad but maybe he figures the American public will think if he's smart enough to promote a couple naked women he's smart enough to vote for. Hey, I've got an idea. We take a shot of Lydia, you know, and,"

"No," Lydia said.

"All right," Marie said. "How about fags? Maybe him in drag

with a couple of the boys. Lydia can supply the boys." Marie rubbed her aching calf.

"Can she now?" Norman said. "That's interesting. But I don't know. We got to ask ourselves, is American politics ready for fag shots? First of all, there's the fag vote, I don't know what district he's running in, but you remember what Kinsey said. Then there's the little old lady vote, they'll just think it's cute, he likes to dress up funny. Then there's the sophisticate vote, they'll be scared to vote against in case anybody thinks they're square about fags. I don't know if it's such a good idea. You know American politics, you got to balance, balance, balance."

"Norman is so brilliant," his wife said. "I sometimes cry for sheer happiness."

"Honey," Norman said, "I'm embarrassed."

"What does that leave us?" Marie said. "What is the American voter prepared to abhor en bloc?"

"What're his politics, liberal?" Norman said. "We could show him shaking hands with, oh, a Russian soldier."

"Not liberal," Marie said. "He'd claim he was stealing the soldier's Mickey Mouse watch. Hey, how about giving himself a fix, big needle in his arm."

"So the voter thinks he's a diabetic, no," Norman said. "It's a problem, it is a problem."

"May I say something?" Norman's wife said. "If it wouldn't be interrupting too much?"

"Honey," Norman said, "you go right ahead and say whatever you want. She's not loud," he said to Marie and Lydia, "but she's deep."

"It seems to me," Betty Ann said, "that it's no good doing something simple like just having him embracing nude women or just being homosexual or just being a Communist spy or anything straightforward. If I understand what Norman has been saying, we want to appeal to the widest spectrum of the American voter. Then why not show him, let me see now, kissing Paul Robeson while they're both standing on Old Glory?"

"She's got it," Norman said, slapping the table with one hand and squeezing his wife's shoulder with the other. "By God, my honey's got it. It's all there in black and white and red, everything you could want."

"You really think so?" Lydia asked.

"You could get somebody who looks like Paul Robeson, I guess," Marie said, "but would anybody know?"

"Easy," Norman said, "we'll fake it like it was out of a say West German newspaper with a translation of the caption, perverted American politician attempts seduction of notorious Negro Communist. Who is going to not believe a West German newspaper?"

"You know," Marie said, "I think she's right."

They made arrangements for Norman to call Alexander and get an appointment for a sitting. Marie and Lydia said goodbye and left. On the street, limping a little, Marie said, "You double-uddered bitch, why did you kick me?"

"I thought you were going to say something nasty," Lydia said. "I'm sorry."

"Bitch," Marie said, "bloat-titted bitch. Why would I say something nasty?"

"I know, I know," Lydia said. "I'm sorry, I apologize. It's me, I guess, the rotten shape I'm in. I think the worst of everybody, even you. You can kick me back if you want."

"Good," Marie said. "Ah, the hell with it. I'm too glad things are moving. Let's go home and get a drink. Maybe Alexander will be there, we can study his profile."

"Marie," Lydia said, "don't you wish Kennan were back?"

"God, yes," Marie said. "I'm frustrated."

Alexander's sitting for Norman went off, Marie considered, with pleasant smoothness. Alexander was, of course, pleased at the attention, hopeful that the pictures and story—Betty Ann, flat again, came as the writing segment of the team—would gain attention to him. He had many suggestions for photographs; informal shots of the Forbeses at home, Alexander expostulating some point of interest with, perhaps, pedagogic finger raised, the severity of the gesture belied, perhaps, by the warm expression about the eyes, Marie gazing at Alexander over the rim of her teacup, the tenderness of the posture belied, perhaps, by the contempt about the eyes. "But are you certain my expression was quite warm enough?" Alexander said. Marie said it was.

A few days later, Marie and Lydia went downtown to Norman's place to inspect the work and to pay the commission. They were very impressed. "It looks good," Marie said.

"Sure it looks good," Norman said. "I'm good."

"He is," Betty Ann said, big again.

"I like the touch of not having them quite naked," Marie said. "It lends weight."

"That was Betty Ann's idea," Norman said. "Just what she said."

Taking the pictures, Marie and Lydia went to Friberg's office and borrowed a typewriter and desk. "Crafty," Lydia said. "No trouble-making flat-feet can trace the letter to you."

"I hadn't actually thought of that," Marie said. "Just Alexander might come home in the middle."

Marie considered for a moment, then wrote:

Dear Mr. Downey,

They tell you are all mixed up in the political rackets with this no-good scum A. Forbes I know all politics is rackets but Mr. Downey how can a man like yourself even if mixed up in politics who calls himself a decent Christian gentleman how can you mix up with this scum Forbes. I'd like to know that. Maybe it is that you have been duped by this scum Forbes you do not know the kind of scum he is. Well here you are Mr. Downey here is the kind of scum he is. Not just a fairy scum, not just a Commie scum but even a Red nigger-lover scum. How about that Mr. Downey. They say no word of honest people is good any more in the dirty game of politics but maybe this once they are wrong. I hope so.

Sincerely,
An American

P.S. If they are not wrong and you stay mixed up with this scum I will see that honest people find it out.

A.A.

"Right," Marie said. "That ought to forward the cause. Okay, here's the address, you type out an envelope and I'll say a word to Friberg."

"Leading a busier and more fruitful life?" Friberg said.

"I hope so," Marie said, "I really do. But it's hard, very hard. One weak woman pitted alone against all the forces of the dark, candor and sweetness her only weapons."

"Who dat, angel-child?" Friberg said.

Two days later Alexander received a telephone call from Mr. Downey. He was not at the moment home, Marie said, but was expected in an hour or so. Mr. Downey asked if he might come over and wait. Marie said he could.

Marie introduced Lydia as a friend and Mr. Downey and Krantz settled themselves. Krantz immediately commenced light conversation aimed at Lydia, mentioning with brittle facility the latest nuclear tests, the latest Soviet triumph in space, the latest African massacre, the latest Mississippi atrocity. Mr. Downey, speaking softly, interrupted him in the middle of atrocity. "Mrs. Forbes, I hope you won't think I'm being impertinent or prying, but the relation of a candidate to his backers is, after all, a peculiarly intimate one. I wonder, now, have you known Mr. Forbes a long time before you married him?"

"No," Marie said. "Practically no time at all."

"Might I ask how you happened to meet him?" Mr. Downey said.

"Through Lydia," Marie said.

"Is that so?" Mr. Downey said. "And you've known Mr. Forbes for quite some time, Miss Ferrucci?"

"No," Lydia said.

"Well," Mr. Downey said to Marie, "I've always been led to believe that long courtships are the best, I courted my wife for two years before we married, so I guess we can say you're a very lucky young woman to have married both in haste and happily."

Marie had no reply.

After the pause, Mr. Downey said, "Now, I wonder, I suppose you've met a lot of Mr. Forbes' friends and acquaintances, I'm sure he's proud of his new young wife and likes to show her off, I'd imagine he has a wide circle, wider than you might expect from many a man of Mr. Forbes' background, a great variety, all manner of interesting folk. Wouldn't you say that?"

"I don't know," Marie said, "you two are the only friends of his I've ever met. You are interesting, though."

Krantz laughed, shortly, and Mr. Downey said, "Is that a fact? Well, I suppose newlyweds like yourself are happiest spending time alone with each other, is that it?"

Marie shrugged. After the pause, Krantz leaned toward Mr.

Downey and said, "Look, sir, we decided already it's all but hopeless, whatever the case is. Let me stop being polite and come out with it." Mr. Downey thought a moment and nodded. "Mrs. Forbes," Krantz said, "the fact of the matter is that we've heard some pretty rough accusations against your husband, about his politics, and worse, about his, his, well I don't want to shock you, but about his private life, his manhood, if you understand me, and, worst of all, about his choice of, ah, friends in that private life. Now, have you anything you can tell us in regard to all that?"

"I don't understand," Marie said. "Private life? Manhood? Friends?"

Krantz grimaced. Lydia, on cue, said, "I think, dear, the man is implying that Alexander is a homosexual with unusual taste in partners, is that right, Mr. Krantz?"

Krantz said, "Yes, yes, now don't you be offended Mrs. Forbes, we've just had this accusation, some kind of nut, probably, but we've got to find out about it, you see that?"

"Oh, certainly," Marie said, "I can see that."

After the pause, Krantz said, "And what do you say about it?"

"Oh, mercy," Marie said, "is that what Alexander does? How awful." She giggled. "I wonder if sometime he'd let me watch."

The pause lasted a long time, until Alexander came in. Surprised, he took Mr. Downey and Krantz into the study. They were there not more than half an hour; Mr. Downey and Krantz came out alone, said quick goodbyes to Marie and Lydia and left.

In the elevator, Krantz said, "I claim we're lucky. Even if it is too late to get another candidate, this could have come further along when we'd really be tagged associates of his."

"Yes, yes, no doubt," Mr. Downey said. "Tell me. You really believe there's something in it? Oh, sure, we both know it's probably a good fake, although for the life of me I can't see Link having the guts or gall to pull anything like this, and who else would we don't know, but even so, you really believe there's something in it?"

"Sure," Krantz said. "Smoke and fire."

"It never comes to you that perhaps the man is completely innocent? That the man was as surprised and astounded as he seemed to be?"

"Sure it's probably a fake," Krantz said, "but no man is com-

pletely innocent, and certainly not a man somebody hates enough
to pull a fake like that on."

"Christ, I wish I were young again," Mr. Downey said.

"What do you think of the wife now?" Krantz said.

"I don't know a thing," Mr. Downey said. "It's out of my depth."

"A kook," Krantz said. "And that other one, with the boobs,
huh?"

"Very pleasant young ladies, both of them," Mr. Downey said.
"But I can't say as I'd find it peaceable to spend much of my time
in their company, one or the other, unless I had the word of the
Holy Father that they really had my best interests at heart."

"Boobs," Krantz said, "but I think I know what you mean."

✳ 19 ✳

"It has become quite clear to me," Alexander said, "that these are extraordinary times demanding extraordinary measures."

Marie, reading, nodded her head and continued reading. Alexander was at a window, hands behind his back.

"I will spare you the unpleasant details," Alexander said, "but the fact of the matter is that some days ago I was forced to retire from the primary election, and forced in an indescribably, in a lewdly unprincipled manner. I don't know whether that ignorant lout Link is directly responsible or not, and it doesn't matter. It was obviously the work of someone of his convictions willing to go to any lengths to destroy a man of my convictions politically. Very well, within narrow limits, they have succeeded. But, as history shows us often happens, it is the kind of success which will prove in the long run a disaster, I can promise you that. If any man or conspiracy of men think that they can make me the figure of a fool and, even more important, prevent me from exposing their unholy plans for the betrayal of this country, they are wrong, dead wrong. Do you hear me?"

Marie nodded and continued reading. Alexander turned, walked over to her and said, softly, "My dear?" Marie looked up. "My dear," Alexander said, "I visited my doctor this morning. He pronounced me fit, quite fit. I asked him, subtly, of course, by indirection, if it would be prudent to resume a normal life, in moderation, to be sure, in moderation. He assured me there was no medical reason against. Fine news, eh?"

"Swell," Marie said.

"Well, then, my dear," Alexander said. "I must admit I am more than eager. After all, here we are living as man and wife, and our marriage has not even been, as they say, consummated. Farcical, eh?"

"Screamingly so," Marie said.

Alexander touched his finger tips to Marie's shoulder. "My dear," he said, "perhaps it is an admission I should not make, but I really don't think I can wait until this evening. Do you think it would be utterly improper if we retired now?"

"Go bugger yourself with a stereopticon," Marie said.

Alexander sat down facing her. "I was afraid," he said, "that was the point of view you would adopt. You wish to punish me for what you consider my past misdeeds, is that it?"

"That, yes," Marie said, "plus the fact I find you physically loathsome."

"I see," Alexander said, "I see. In that case, my dear, I have no recourse but to turn elsewhere for solace. You can understand that?"

"No," Marie said. "No more little house, no more beatings, no more pictures. No."

"I see," Alexander said. "Then what would you have me do?"

"That's interesting," Marie said. "I don't suppose it really would be kindly to cut you off completely. Let me see. All right, we'll permit you a certain amount of professional help. Only the best kind of call-girl, of course, I don't want to be afraid to go to the john. And I'll have a chat with them beforehand, here."

"A chat?" Alexander said. "Whatever for?"

"Why, to make sure they are proper for you, Alexander," Marie said, "and to make sure they understand what you are permitted and what you are not."

"A chat," Alexander said. "Why, do you know, that's rather exciting."

"Hell," Marie said. "Well, I'll try to make it as little exciting as I can."

The girl, who arrived at the apartment at five the next afternoon, was tall and slim, attractive, well-dressed, dark-haired, little older, it appeared, than Marie. Her name, she said, was Sybil Shore. She seemed very mildly surprised at the absence of Mr. Forbes—on orders in the study—and Marie's invitation to sit down for a moment.

"May I take you into my confidence?" Marie said.

"Certainly," Sybil said.

"Because I will need your advice," Marie said.

"If I can," Sybil said.

"To be frank, then," Marie said, "a primary reason why my husband has called upon your services is that, as a result of his callous and wanton brutality, I am temporarily unable to fulfill the usual domestic offices."

"You poor kid," Sybil said. "Men can so often be monsters, can't they? I hope you have a good g y n. Here, let me give you the name of mine, he's really first rate, I've been going to him for years." She reached into the enormous black bag she carried, scribbled into a notebook, tore out the page and handed it to Marie.

"Thank you," Marie said. "You're very kind. So incapacitated, I have agreed to let my husband have, at decent intervals, other outlets, under supervision."

"I think that's very wise," Sybil said. "The alternative would mean him running about who knows where with who knows what, which could end unhappily."

"Exactly," Marie said. "However, under the circumstances I prefer his enjoyment to be as minimal as possible. I do not know whether you normally permit men to cause you any serious discomfort or, indeed, pain, if they are so inclined."

"Never," Sybil said emphatically. "I am far too attractive, too competent and therefore too much in demand to have to suffer that indignity."

"Excellent," Marie said. "Then I hope you will make it perfectly clear to him that should he attempt any such activity you will, you will what? Scream like a siren, knee him in the short hairs?"

"I don't think there is any need for details on that score," Sybil said. "I assure you he will not indulge in any of that sort of nonsense."

"Fine," Marie said. "But further than that, I wish, as I say, his pleasure to be as moderate as possible. Can you so arrange?"

"Certainly," Sybil said, reaching into her bag again for notebook and pencil, "give me just a moment to arrange my thoughts. I assume you mean," she said before writing, "such moderation not to go as far as complete fiasco?"

"Fiasco?" Marie said. "Why not?"

"No," Sybil said, "I really would not advise it. It might act to send him in a desperate, therefore less controllable, quest to prove himself again. Extreme moderation short of complete failure, I would think."

"As you say," Marie said. She watched Sybil, forehead wrinkled, jot notes and mutter to herself. Soon Sybil finished, gazed at the page, nodded in satisfaction and dropped book and pencil back in bag.

"Now," Marie said, "there is one final point at which I very sincerely hope you will not take offense. It might seem perfectly rational to you, upon further reflection, that your own enlightened self-interest would dictate you ignore our conversation and concentrate on giving maximal satisfaction to my husband, in the reasonable expectation that you will thereby create future demand. However, I will quite easily know it if you do, and shall in turn do all I can to prevent my husband seeking your services again. If, on the other hand, you do comply with my wishes, I will also know it, and will insist that he remain your client."

"That seems fair," Sybil said.

"Hey," Marie said, "you make out pretty good in this racket, huh? You sure sound like it."

"Oh, sure," Sybil said; "I do very well. But I earn it. And I don't live in a place like this."

"I was lucky," Marie said.

"Of course, I haven't met your husband," Sybil said.

"Not that lucky," Marie said. She got up, walked out and to the study, opened the door and said, "All right, Alexander, you may come out now."

Sybil and Alexander gone to his room, Marie fidgeted, made herself a drink, wandered the room, looked out the window, wandered more. "I wish," she said, "I wish." For a moment nothing happened, then the doorbell rang. Marie hurried to throw it open, stared, and said, "Mister Kennan, you've come home."

"Oh no," Kennan said, "I'm staying at the Waldorf." He came into the apartment. "Hello, Marie, you're looking very well," Kennan said. They embraced and kissed.

"My God I'm glad to see you," Marie said.

With a drink, Kennan said, "Yes, I spent a few weeks in pretty bad shape, well, rotten shape. Drinking and mooning, mooning and drinking. But the damn puritan training took over and I stopped. And I spoke to a few people and got this job. Damnedest job in the world. Well what it is is just doing public relations, release writing, newspaper contacts, house organ, that kind of thing, for this big long-haul trucking company. The thing is, all of them, all of the top men and most of the middle men at the office, the office is in Trenton, they're crooks. I don't mean ordinary business crooks like everybody else, I mean real hoods. They've all got records, they've all served time, I wouldn't be surprised if personnel doesn't screen them for at least one notch on their forty-fives. Fascinating."

"That's wonderful," Marie said. "It really is. Are they all dark and Italian and speak badly?"

"Every last one of them," Kennan said. "How are you? Is that pig, God, Marie, I know I didn't have any rights, but when you married him." Kennan put his glass down, turned to Marie next to him in the couch, embraced and kissed her.

"Sure, sure," Marie said when they had stopped kissing, "it was just necessary. Come on, we'll go to my room before he comes out and you have to make conversation with him."

After they had intercourse, and talked a little, Kennan said, "That's wonderful, Marie, that makes everything better or at least not so terrible. You're not really married to him."

"Of course I am," Marie said.

"But you said you're not, it wasn't consummated. It could be annulled."

"But it isn't," Marie said. "Look, marriage is a technicality, a piece of paper. Anything else it is hasn't got anything to do with the technicality. So we're married."

"God," Kennan said.

"If we weren't," Marie said, "what I'm going to do to him wouldn't be so much fun."

20

The advertisement, written by Alexander, typed by Marie, was sent to the *National Review* and, in time, appeared. It read: *WANTED, bright young hard-driving self-starter to exec action program.*

There was one answer, and it seemed the right one.

Norton Ford, as he sat in Alexander's study, was a stocky man in his early thirties, brown-haired, brown-eyed, full-faced, vital. He had ten years of experience in the personnel department of two large industrial corporations; superb experience, as he explained to Alexander, really getting to know what makes people turn over, but now, as he explained to Alexander, he wanted to move into something that gave deeper rewards than money alone, "Although, frankly, sir," he explained in his deep voice, "I can't afford to overlook money as a consideration. But I agree with you right down the line, this country is being nibbled, no, strike that, gobbled to death by the mush-heads and the bleeding hearts, the idealogues and the social engineers. Quite frankly, I'm not one of those who see the Kremlin behind every baa-bleating do-gooder in this country. Oh, sure, the Kremlin has its people in it up to their shoulders, both shoulders, and lots of them, more than I dreamed before I started to study this thing. But that's just part of the cancer, and not the biggest part, and I'm convinced that if it ever gets to be the biggest part we've still got a few men wise and principled enough to cut off that threat at its source. We have them now, but will we have them in a few years time, have them in positions of authority? Not if the present momentum of events keeps up, we won't. God almighty, sir, you read that filth in *The New York Times*, you know what I'm talking about."

"Quite," Alexander said. "Perhaps I've had certain experiences in these matters that have instructed me even more than the filth, as you call it, and very properly, very properly, in that newspaper."

"Of course you have, sir," Norton said.

Norton was equally full of good ideas on the subject of specific action. "Troops," he said, "we've got to enlist the troops. Get them to join us, get their names and addresses so we can communicate, so we can warn them and rally them. Now that's a problem. But how about this? We take advertisements in the *News*, lay it right on the line, are you with us or are you with them. I think you'll find, sir, that there are more people in this country who haven't sold out than you might hope for. Oh, these won't be the best educated people in the world, but as you know, most of the so-called education the liberal dome-skulls pass out these days does more harm than good. Destroys principles. Saps foundations. These will be real Americans."

"Advertisement," Alexander said. "Yes. Full pages. Get an organization. Yes."

"And maybe the *Journal-American*. For a start. When the ball starts rolling here we can move on to the other cities. Los Angeles. San Francisco. They're hotbeds."

"Yes," Alexander said.

An office, Norton explained, would be necessary. Nothing elaborate, but it would be necessary. Alexander suggested that at the beginning, at least, it might be a good idea to save expenses by establishing an office in the apartment. "Heaps of rooms," he said, "I'll have one of them fitted out for you. And we'll hire a girl for the typing and so forth."

"Fine," Norton said.

"No," Marie said, leaning against the door.

Norton started, Alexander jumped. "My dear, please," he said.

"No need to hire anyone," Marie said. "I'll do it. Lydia and I will both throw our shoulders in."

"Why, that's awfully good of you," Alexander said, and introduced Norton to her.

Before he left that evening, the details had been settled. Norton would come in every weekday evening after work. "Hard on my family, sir," he said, "my lovely wife and lovely girl. But it's something I believe in and I know they do too." Alexander would pay him one hundred and fifty dollars a week. "That's generous, sir, more than generous," Norton said. "I'll try to live up to your faith in me." Starting Monday.

Norton went home to New Rochelle and told his wife Aileen. She, lustrous, dark-haired, cool slim-bodied, possessed, firm-chinned, was pleased because he was pleased. "Not just all that extra money," he said, "but if things work right, if I make things work right, I'll be able to leave the office and do this full-time. Think of it, a chance to do something really worth while, really useful, really creative. My gosh, not many men get a chance like that."

"But you won't leave your job until you're sure," Aileen said.

"Of course not," Norton said, but he was sure already.

Norton thought and worked over the weekend and Monday evening he had the draft of an advertisement to show Alexander. They went over it together, made a few changes, Marie typed it up. It appeared in the two newspapers that Wednesday. It read:

ARE YOU A RED?
ARE YOU A BLEEDING HEART?
ARE YOU A "LIBERAL" DOME-HEAD?

(These lines in 36 point extra bold. Then:)

Maybe not. But there sure are a lot of them around, aren't there? Most everywhere you look, that's the kind of cowardly rat you see these days, isn't it? In the government, in the so-called universities, on the TV, in the newspapers. All around, lots of them, every last ugly one of them working and scheming against YOU, against the kind of America YOU want for YOURSELF and YOUR kids. True? Sure it's true. Don't you know it?

Well, what are you going to do about it?

Dollars to doughnuts, the answer is NOTHING!

And if YOU, a decent patriotic guy like YOU is doing nothing, is it any wonder THEY are winning? Any wonder that day-by-day they're selling America down the river? No!

All right, you say, what can you do? YOU CAN JOIN THE AMERICAN FORCE!

The AMERICAN FORCE is a new, fast-growing organization of decent patriotic Americans dedicated to protecting themselves and their kids from the Reds and the "liberals" and the do-gooders that are working night and day to destroy us. JOIN THE AMERICAN FORCE and you will get up-to-the-minute inside scoop on what's being done to you behind your back, JOIN THE AMERICAN FORCE and you will receive down to earth instructions on WHEN, WHAT, HOW you can act to save America.

What does it cost you to JOIN THE AMERICAN FORCE? It costs you NOTHING.

Simply put your name and address on a postcard or in a letter and send it to . . .

And at the bottom the advertisement said:

The American Force. President, Alexander Forbes. Secretary, Norton Ford.

The result was more than gratifying. By the following Monday over three thousand cards and letters had come in. Twenty-three of them included money, in sums ranging from a quarter to five dollars, totaling eighteen dollars and fifty cents. One envelope was empty. Two envelopes held obscene imprecation, both neatly typed. There were over three thousand names and addresses.

Late Tuesday evening, Marie, Lydia, and Norton finished opening all the letters, Alexander watching. "Gosh," Norton said, "this is exciting, it really is. I wasn't too confident in my own mind that we could get that many people out of their apathy. But just with one ad."

"Your credit," Alexander said, "your idea, you wrote the thing. Damn fine piece of work."

Lydia sighed. "Is that all?" she said. "I'll go to bed." Marie said yes, and Lydia edged by the piles of cards and paper on the desk, on chairs and on the floor, and went out.

"It's a beginning," Norton said, slapping his hands together, "it's just a beginning but it's a beginning. Oh my gosh, I've got all kinds of ideas. Pamphlets. Meetings. A party. Yes, by gosh, sir, you know what we have, right in this room? We've got the beginnings of a party, a party that can really come to mean something, first in this city and then in the whole country."

"Possible," Alexander said. "Long road to go before then, though."

"You're right, sir," Norton said, "of course you're right. There's an awful lot of work to be done just to start. My thinking was that we should answer every one of these, perhaps with a letter over your signature, welcoming them into the Force, perhaps include a membership card and a statement of principles. Oh, certainly, there's a lot of work to be done."

"Well," Alexander said, standing up, "not tonight, it's getting on. You can make a good start tomorrow."

"I'll certainly do that, sir," Norton said, and went home and told his wife the good news. She was happy because he was happy.

Before going to her room Marie went to see Lydia who was lying in bed, watching television, as, recently, usual. Marie turned off the television set.

"Feeling any better?" she said.

"No," Lydia said. "Feeling depressed is what I'm feeling. Like yesterday. Like tomorrow."

"You want a drink?" Marie said.

"No," Lydia said, watching the dark rectangle.

"You don't want to have or do much of anything, right?" Marie said.

"That's right," Lydia said. "I don't want to do anything. I don't want to make an effort and talk to anybody, I don't want to make an effort and think about what to do. I just want to lie here and look out my little window you just turned off."

"That's all right," Marie said, "you don't have to make the effort. I'll tell you what to do."

When Marie had finished telling her, Lydia giggled, a little, and said, "What if I don't want to?"

"You do," Marie said, "even if you don't know it yet. It's a thing every girl wants to do, just once, anyway, for the experience, wade in and rape a man. I might do it myself, but it wouldn't look right. Besides, it has to be done."

"Well, if it has to," Lydia said. "He looks clean. All right, turn the box on."

"Tally-ho," Marie said, and turned the box on.

When Norton came, early, since he had so much to do, he went into the office room and stood happily, looking at the cards and letters on most of the room's surfaces. Lydia came in and he said, "Good, let's get going. I've got hold of an outfit to do the mailing but we'll have to make a master list first," and found himself standing face to face with Lydia, who was smiling. "Gee," he said. Lydia began to unbutton her dress.

At midnight, five days later, Alexander entered the office room without knocking. Lydia, quite naked, was asleep face down on a pallet made of over three thousand letters and cards, many of them worn and soiled. Norton, bleary, was buttoning his shirt, barefoot. He stopped buttoning his shirt. "Sir," he said sadly.

"I see," Alexander said. "Yes, I quite see."

"Sir," Norton said. "I goofed. I admit it, I did. It's been a horrible week. Every day I'd tell myself, no, no more, tonight I'll get down to work. And then she'd be here and I wouldn't. And my wife, she suspects something. It's the first time anything like this has happened. Sir, can't you consider my guilt and my regret as punishment enough and let me go ahead with the work? Sir, please?"

Alexander, gazing down at Lydia's round respiring form, said, "No."

When Norton had left, not quite crying, Marie consoled Alexander. Only a week's time, she pointed out, was lost. "It's not simply that," Alexander said. "I had a good opinion of that young man. I did. Hard-working, assiduous, right-minded. A man prides himself on his ability to judge people's form. I was wrong. He was as weak, as loose-principled, as prone to easy unearned gratification as all the so-called liberals he talked about. And now who's going to do the work?"

"I will," Marie said.

Discussing the matter with Kennan the next day, Marie said she wasn't quite sure in what direction to proceed. "I mean, there is this list of self-certified imbeciles and I'm sure it would be desirable and I suppose with a little thought it would be practical to knock them all off, but I don't know. It's not a really creative answer."

"I wouldn't think so," Kennan said.

"Well then," Marie said, "I suppose you're suggesting a campaign of terror. Telephone calls at midnight threatening hideous bushwhacks by the Black Muslims and all that usual line. Keep them preoccupied and nervous. But again, I don't know. It seems there ought to be an answer less humdrum and routine."

"I would certainly think so," Kennan said.

"How about massive re-education?" Marie said. "Send them worthy tracts containing the best thoughts of noble minds as applied to the searing questions of our day. Do you think that would elevate them from the hog wallow? I suspect the weight would just press them deeper."

"Probably," Kennan said.

"Then maybe straight, down-to-earth man-to-man talk about come on now fellers I know those other idiots with the voices are always telling you idiots this kind of crap but come on now, fellers, you just know it just ain't so and a red's a black's a man for all o' that, I mean look at Schlesinger Junior and Max Lerner for Christ's sake they ain't pretty but they ain't mean. Or do you think that would be both ineffective and nauseating?"

"Both," Kennan said.

"Look," Marie said, "when I invite criticism I expect it to be constructive criticism."

"It's obvious," Kennan said. "So obvious that I'm not surprised you overlooked it. What we do is go on the way they were going, but more so. Really give the imbeciles something to worry about. Give their masters something to worry about too, if we're lucky; worry whether things haven't been pushed a touch too hard and are going a touch too far."

"Of course," Marie said. They embraced. They stopped embracing when Lydia wandered into the room.

"Stop embracing," Lydia said. "I find myself sexually saturated and even the stray and idle dirty thought will give me a headache."

"Sex isn't dirty," Marie said, "it is a triumphant fulfillment making one one with the tides of the universe."

"Hell," Kennan said.

"Still," Marie said, "I have to thank you. You carried out your assignment with craft and assiduity. You should have seen her," Marie said to Kennan, "she'd sleep until one, have an enormous breakfast, go back to bed, doze, hardly televise at all, dreamily sketch out new and startling variations for the evening's enterprise, doze, get up at six and eat an enormous dinner in the kitchen and whammo at seven, bright-eyed and bushy-tailed for the world's work."

"A creep he may have been," Lydia said, "but an active and vigorous creep. His wife must be a very withdrawn-type girl. He knew that ours was an arrangement bearing the seeds of its own destruction and figured to get it while it was there. By the way, he asked me to marry him."

"You could do worse," Marie said.

"Who couldn't?" Lydia said. "No, you were right, it was an interesting thing to do once, without even pretending emotional attachment, but I guess I'm a child of my times. Oh well, back to fallowness and waiting for my prince. Speaking of which, where's Alexander?"

"In his room with his woman of convenience," Marie said. "I think the sight of your rosy red ass last night really wound him up. He was up stuttering for me to get her over about dawn this morning. Very cool, that girl."

"I'd like to meet her," Lydia said.

Sybil Shore came out of Alexander's room shortly after. She was very trimly and tautly dressed in white linen. Marie introduced her to Lydia and Kennan and gave her a drink. "Is he away for the night?" Marie asked.

"Yes indeed," Sybil said. "He's not a young man, you know. Well," she said, sipping her drink, "this is very pleasant."

"I'm not sure, but I think so," Kennan said.

21

In consultation with Kennan, Marie drafted, redrafted, and wrote the first issue of Last Stand, the bulletin of The American Force. Once she had worked herself into the proper tone she found the stuff came without much difficulty. It was the achievement of the proper notes of querulousness, peevishness, crankiness, that took the effort. Factual matter on which to rest the tones was easily at hand; a few minutes glancing at the *Times* was sufficient.

Kennan had suggested that brief paragraphs, rather than longer exercises in dialectic, would suit. So that Marie had several pages of:

Don't believe the guff you hear about the Reds' favorite Supreme Court Judge stepping down. It's all a fake. Besides, if he retired he'd live in Moscow, and the Great American Public isn't quite ready for that. Or is it?

Report from one of the forcibly des-integrated schools in Maryland: Rapes, up fifty-five percent; robberies, up sixty-two percent; muggings, up one hundred and four percent. Guess who's having Congo-style fun? You're right.

Word that one of the last hard-line pro-American anti-Red generals in the Air Force is going to be framed and fired soon. Stage management courtesy of the pinky-lifting no-winners in the State Department.

And so forth. "Well," Kennan said, "it's all right as it stands. But they can get that sort of thing from a lot of places. The common discourse of our era. Try to go a little further."

So Marie wrote:

Latest Kremlintrap—they've started training Africans (mostly right off the trees from the Congo) to teach in New York schools. You hear any complaint from city officials? You bet you didn't— they're all for it. They're sure there won't be prayers in the classroom then.

Tomorrow morning on the subway, take a good look around. How many faces you see look American? What's your guesstimate of how many have redparty cards on their hips? Latest expert figure: 36.7 percent.

Senator Barry (Baruch) Goldwasser's screams of support for more atom testing are a fake. He'll swing into line for American suicide with all the rest.

"Not too bad," Kennan said, "especially for the first time. It takes a while to get away from reality, I guess."

Alexander looked over Marie's typescript. "Yes," he said, "I think you're being wise. It's vulgar of course, quite vulgar, but we must do our best to speak in the tones of our audience or we will simply not be heard. Now, I've been working on some little thing myself. Give it a glance, my dear, tell me your reaction."

Marie glanced through the two pages, single-spaced, he handed her. It began, "The betrayal of national conscience," and went on, in Alexander's familiar style, "inner softness . . . the tyranny of cowards . . . spiritual dereliction . . . Western civilization as we have known it . . . self-reliance . . . bulwarks against chaos . . . little time left."

"That's fine, Alexander, just fine," Marie said.

"Actually," Alexander said, "our separate efforts blend very well. Yours for the less lettered reader, mine for the more thoughtful."

"Except," Marie said, "if we put yours in too it's going to make it more expensive to do, quite a bit more."

Alexander waved. "Damn the expense," he said. "We're in a war for a cause. Besides, I've spoken to the lawyers. They're quite certain The American Force can be listed as a tax-free political organization."

"As you say, Alexander," Marie said.

Kennan, looking with Marie at the first copy of Last Stand, said, "At least it's a start. I don't imagine there'll be much reaction, but then there is so much shouting into the void. I remember, just after the war, at the University of Michigan, some of us got out a few issues of a paper trying to work up some enthusiasm for putting all nuclear weapons under international control before they started spreading. Got absolutely nowhere, of course, talking into a dead microphone, no reaction at all."

"Of course," Marie said, "that was sensible. It might make a difference."

"Maybe, but I doubt it," Kennan said.

Kennan was wrong. The reaction was astonishing, both in numbers and enthusiasm. Over three thousand copies of Last Stand had been sent out. In two days the letters started coming back in, letters of acclaim ("Haven't seen so much sense and guts in years"), offers of help ("Send me fifty extra copies if you can I will give them where they will do the most good I am with you against the reds and the niggers"), letters of warning ("You are doing great work but it is no use, it is too late, they will get you for this"). Ten a day, twenty a day, thirty a day.

"Fantastic," Kennan said. "You know, in promotional mailings, a response of three percent is considered good. We've got over a twelve percent response already, and still they flow. Fantastic."

"Of course, we're not asking them to pay anything," Marie said.

"Not yet," Kennan said.

"I must say," Alexander said, "I am pleased. Who would have thought there was such a residue of sense in the American people after all these years?"

For the second issue (which would have a doubled circulation, so many were the new members of The American Force; one man enrolled twenty-seven in his Yorkville neighborhood) Kennan counseled Marie to urge her fancy higher. "I'm not saying that you should sever all connection with reality, but I am saying the connection should be as tenuous as possible, as close as possible to not being at all."

"Reality?" Marie said. "Come on."

"No, no, of course not," Kennan said, "I don't for God's sake mean real reality, the world that's actually out there. That's got nothing to do with the people you're writing for. I'm talking about their reality, the absurdity they live in."

"Yes," Marie said, "but it's harder to do than to say. Their reality is so absurd, they're so cradled, nurtured, weaned, trained, and molded in absurdity, that it's hard to lift one foot off it, let alone make the connection tenuous. I mean, in a world that has a Strategic Air Command, how can you connect tenuously to the absurd? You've got it up to your ass."

"Well, try," Kennan said.

Marie tried. She wrote, among other paragraphs:

We always knew those so-called "culture exchanges," fancy doubletalk for a lot of spies and agitators being shipped in from Russia by your government, were a screaming fake. But now word is beginning to leak out that you're being sold out at the other end too. Those American actresses and actors and singers who get sent over there in a try to make the deal look good are told they better play ball with the red bosses, or else! There's a special apartment near the Kremlin (we'd give the address if it meant anything to you, or if any responsible official cared) where the American girls *and* boys are made to show themselves like so much meat—so the red bosses can take their pick. Does your daughter want to be a singer?

Farmers say they smell some mighty suspicious goings-on. Swarms of high-paid government bureaucrats asking prying questions, poking their noses where they don't belong. One guess: the long-expected plan to nationalize, which means socialize, *which means communize,* the American farmer is getting started. And *that* means some day real soon you could be a government slave on some Minnesota potato farm. Like the idea?

Friend of ours has a son whose lifelong ambition has been to go to West Point. When the boy got his application papers he answered all the questions until he came to a bunch of fancy doubletalk about motivation and ambitions. The boy didn't take the easy way and double-talk back, he just wrote "I want to kill commies." They played it pretty cagy, all right—took him into West Point and then six months later threw him out on some phony charge about academic—yes, academic—standing.

Did you know that the so-called American government employs almost *half* as many professors as it has generals? Think about that when you try to sleep tonight.

"It's hard, hard," Marie said. "Every time I think I've got a good one I stop and look at it and it starts to get familiar and I realize it's just like something I read in the newspapers or heard on television. It's not fair."

Alexander's essay was, Marie gathered from the glance she gave it, not very different from his first. The second issue of Last Stand went out.

The answer was an explosion. Twice a day sweating men in gray dropped mailsacks on the floor of the office room. A mud of letters and cards slithered everywhere, treacherous underfoot. Kennan took two steps and hurled backward, landing on his rump with an impact that toppled another bundle over his head. "Quit the slapstick," Marie said, "this is getting serious. You okay?"

Kennan pushed himself up. "The malevolent slime," he said. "It's unbelievable." He plucked a handful of letters. "Look, at random, not previously examined, I swear to you any three will have you groping for the vomitorium, listen. 'Just a note to tell you I thought your second issue even better than your first. Of course as an informed citizen who takes care to keep her eyes open I am aware of what is going on in this country but so many I am afraid are blind and your efforts may help to open their eyes. God bless you.' All right, reasonable diction and orthography, at least not uneducated, the tone not blatantly corrosive or palpably mad. What in the hell is happening in this poor country? Another, hmm, business envelope, letterhead, Swanson and Pine, public relations, 'Gentlemen, your out-spoken fact-sheet, Last Stand, has been drawn to my attention. I hope you'll allow me to say that I think you are doing a first-rate public service in alerting the American people to definite tendencies at large today. Congratulations. In pursuance of your goal, has it occurred to you that the services of a professional public relations team might prove eminently useful? I would be very grateful for the opportunity to come in and kick this ball around with you. Signed Arthur A. Swanson.' Well, hardly typical, a businessman crawling down the spoor of the prey. But still, what in the hell is happening in this poor country? Again, 'Dear Sirs, I am an eighteen year old high school senior and very interested in public affairs. I have read both issues of your magazine which you send to my parents. I showed them to my civics teacher who said they were irresponsible.'"

"My God," Lydia said, "where did he come from?"

"'Could you please send me more information and proof so I can prove to my civics teacher that you are not irresponsible?'"

"Hell, the minds of youth," Marie said. "Quick, Lydia, send him a letter saying we're irresponsible as shit."

"I was wrong," Kennan said. "I thought we could be ridiculous and people would laugh and begin to see how ridiculous they've been and how ridiculous the things they read and hear and breathe are. But it's gone too far. The corruption is encysted."

"What are we going to do?" Lydia said.

"We've got to stop," Kennan said.

"Then Alexander will get somebody else like my active creep to do the work and I can't do it again," Lydia said. "These letters, too uncomfortable."

"You're damn right they are, that's why we've got to stop it, not just us doing it," Kennan said.

"No," Marie said, "not just like that, wasting all the work we've done and leaving the harm. We've got to stop it but we've got to find a way to make at least some good come out of it, something, even one sane word said somewhere. Otherwise it's too much waste and harm."

Alexander came into the room with his tweeds. "Aha," he said, "gloating over your latest success. You've earned the right, I'd be the last man in the world to deny you've earned the right." He took from Kennan's hand the letters he had been reading and shuffled through them. "Public relations firm," he said. "Now that's a thought to chew on. Not, of course, you must not misunderstand me, that anyone could have done a better job than you people, oh no, I don't mean that at all. Still, you can only do so much, not fair to expect you to do more than you can, and some chap like this might take some of the load off your shoulders." He reached out for another batch, opened one of them and chuckled. "Not a completely satisfied member. 'How come you say Goldwater is dirty Jew. He is no such God damn thing. Who told you this? You must be some kind nut to say a filthy like this. I

wish you would write more about the black man. They are everywhere more and more, worse and worse, all of them hating. My
daughter has a black teacher he shows no respect. Write about
about that not lies.' Signed something Mayewski. Amusing. Nice
to have a flow of constructive criticism from the readership. You
might think about it, actually, there might be a lot of, what was
that word that disappointing young man used, a lot of mileage
for us on the black business." He scowled. "Remember what that
filthy picture did to me."

"Alexander," Marie said tightly, "go call Sybil. Go ahead, call
her."

"My dear," Alexander said, "you embarrass me."

"Go ahead or I'll embarrass you more."

"My dear," Alexander said, "please. Very well, if you insist, I
can't imagine why."

"And tell her to see me on her way out," Marie said. When
Alexander was gone Marie sighed and said, "I could kill the
bastard."

"That would solve part of the problem," Lydia said.

"Oh no," Kennan said. "We shouldn't do that. Not even him."

They were still worrying when Sybil Shore appeared. Marie
gave her a drink, closed the door and said, "He's away?" Sybil
nodded. "There were some things I wanted to ask, if it's all right."

"Might I use your telephone first?" Sybil said. "My answering
service." When she came back from the phone she said, "That's
all right, I've got an hour."

"Before your next appointment?" Kennan said. Sybil nodded.
"Tell me," Kennan said.

"No," Sybil said. "I'd be delighted to talk to you, but I won't
talk about how I got into this life and I won't talk about clients."
Kennan looked ashamed. "That's all right," Sybil said, "I always
get asked. I just don't answer."

"Now," Marie said, "you don't have any medical training, of
course."

"I do, in a way," Sybil said. "Two years of nurses' training. Not
that I haven't forgotten a lot. You see, what happened was that a
doctor I knew had as a patient what the doctor called ideal nurse
fodder. He was sick, old and rich, of course, but not so sick and
old that he couldn't be titillated and grateful for it and not so

rich that there were dynastic considerations to prevent a massive bestowal. And, my doctor said, he couldn't possibly last more than eight months. Ideal. So I quit school and the doctor recommended me as perfectly competent and my God for eighteen months what I didn't have to do for that old bastard. Eighteen months it took him to go and every day of those eighteen months he had me jumping and hopping and twisting and hanging from the chandelier by my big toe, why there were weeks, complete weeks when I never got a garment of clothes on, not that at his age it often came to much but he wanted to make sure it came to as much as was humanly possible. So of course he kept promising me a handsome bequest, a handsome bequest, Dolly, he would say, now let's try it that way again. And when the old bastard went he left me the handsome bequest of fifty, that's right, fifty dollars. But I met a lot of his relatives and friends at the funeral. That's how I got into this life."

"You know," Kennan said, "it really serves you right."

"What is that supposed to mean?" Sybil said. "Are you some kind of silly snob who looks down on prostitutes?"

"No, no," Kennan said, embarrassed again.

"I'm not complaining," Sybil said. "I never complain."

"Good," Marie said, "then you not only have a lot of practical experience, and I suppose a lot of information from your friends, but some theoretical background. Now, given the hypothetical case of a man who's had a mild heart attack under sexual stimulation, been told by his doctor to knock off stimulation for a while, then told he can resume. What are the chances of him dying under serious and prolonged sexual stimulation?"

"No," Sybil said, "your chances aren't good. It's possible, but very unlikely. The body protects itself to a degree, you know. No, it's not the body the body has to fear, it's the mind. He's much more likely to go because of strong emotion, rage, say, especially when he's not permitted to act on his rage. If you want my opinion."

"Now that's interesting," Marie said.

When Sybil had gone, Kennan said, "That's wrong. Of course I don't look down on prostitutes. How can I look down on them? But I do think it's an unfortunate, unhappy life. That's what I meant by it serving her right, after trying to extort money from the old bastard."

"Not extort," Marie said, "value for services performed, except he cheated her out of the value. I don't know how unhappy she is."

"Not extort," Kennan said, "but it's ugly." Marie and Lydia began leafing through the letters and cards. "Damn it, it is ugly," Kennan said. "Isn't it?"

"Yes," Marie said, "it's ugly. But it doesn't serve her right. Especially if prostituting is what you think it is, not what she seems to think it is. Ugly, but she harmed no one."

"Well, yes," Kennan said.

In a few days Swanson of Swanson and Pine, public relations, showed up to Alexander's summons. He was a natty stout man with a very shiny skin on his head. He and Alexander were closeted in the study for some hours. Alexander was most enthusiastic about the meeting. "Scope," he said, "that man has scope. And organizational know-how, as he puts it himself. Why, do you believe it, he outlined an entire campaign, just sitting there, thinking fast after I'd told him what we have here, an entire campaign. Getting members who live in the same neighborhood together, organizing study groups, voting them in primaries and elections, rallies for all the members, I can't begin to tell you what that man thought of. I'm optimistic about that man, I really am."

"Great," Marie said.

22

"Really, Molly," Alexander said, "you've no idea how busy I've been these months. And not silly make-work, either, but honest productive toil. So do forgive me."

"All right, Alexander," Mrs. Wheeler said. "If you cross your heart and swear you've not been avoiding me, influenced by that child bride of yours, why then I suppose I must forgive you, as ever."

"You are good, Molly," Alexander said. "Molly, do you realize that there are now over five hundred Troops of The American Force in Metropolitan New York? Five hundred, Molly, only think, and ten to twenty adults in each? And uncounted children influenced. Molly, isn't it exciting?"

"And how is your child bride, Alexander? I must say you seem in excellent spirits. Is it because of her or is it this educational work, which I must admit I find largely incomprehensible."

"She's splendid, Molly, just splendid, a happy marriage, you know, there's nothing to say about them, an excellent wife. But you mustn't be like that, Molly, incomprehensible indeed. Any infant could understand. What I am doing is to create an organization by which I can force, absolutely force, Molly, the politicians to pay attention to me, consider me, and, yes, fear me. You have no idea, Molly, what cowards they are, our politicians. At the slightest, most inconsequential, emptiest threat they quiver and bolt. And the organization I am building, with, I must say, the very loyal aid of a number of people, my good wife not last among them, is neither slight nor inconsequential. Oh, Molly, I really am going to obtain the opportunity to do good work."

"I'm very glad for you, Alexander," Mrs. Wheeler said. "And speaking of your good wife, might I pry a little?"

"Not prying, Molly," Alexander said. "Sisterly concern."

"Yes," Mrs. Wheeler said. "But I suppose my question really has been answered, when you tell me that both of you are very happy. I must say I'd been concerned to think how she would react to, to your little tricks and treats, you know. But I gather she must endure them, or even enjoy them, I suppose."

"Yes, well, yes," Alexander said.

"Tell me," Mrs. Wheeler said, "is there anything especially terrible, I mean, after all this time I imagine you must have progressed to a frightful stage, knowing you? Especially if it's the sort of thing she enjoys and encourages, as it must be. Although if she does I'm not sure it's all that much fun for you, poor dear."

"Molly," Alexander said. "Well, Molly, I'll tell you the truth. I don't do any of that sort of thing any more. Not at all."

"Oh, Alexander," Mrs. Wheeler said. "You mean she made you stop?"

"Not exactly, Molly," Alexander said. "It would be too difficult to explain."

"I expect you miss it terribly," Mrs. Wheeler said. "You always were so vivacious telling me about it, so full of joie de vivre."

"Not at all, Molly," Alexander said. "I won't hear a word against my good wife. Oh, I admit the thoughts have crossed my mind from time to time, I'll admit that. But, no, it's been arranged otherwise. And I will say also that recently, throwing myself into the work I've been doing, I can't tell you how enthusiastic I am, there haven't been any thoughts. At least, very many fewer. Sublimation, I suppose. But Molly, to talk about you. You won't mind if I say it, I hope, but I'm not at all happy about the way you are looking. Peaked, I think, definitely peaked."

"I know," Mrs. Wheeler said. "Alexander, do you remember that last summer on the farm with Poppa and Momma before Momma passed on?"

"Oh, perfectly," Alexander said.

"Yes. I sickened and grew weak and the doctors simply could not find out my trouble. I've been thinking and thinking about that summer, Alexander, not because I feel the same now, nothing a little girl feels, I suppose, is the same as a woman of my age feels, but because I think it is the same kind of feeling. A weakness and, now don't you dare laugh, a thought of impending loss. And then Momma died."

"Molly," Alexander said, standing up suddenly, "you stop that this instant, do you hear me?"

"Sit down, Alexander," Mrs. Wheeler said. Alexander sat down. "I'm sure it is nothing serious and will pass away. But since you asked I told you. I've been to the doctor and he finds nothing. I suspect it's simply growing older. Alexander, do you find that things, everything, becomes less and less interesting?"

"Oh no, Molly," Alexander said. "Why, you know how tremendously interested and excited I am about the work I'm doing. Molly, do you realize how things are, how paltry and pale and identical our political parties are? Do you realize the tremendous leverage, I get that from my man Swanson, what tremendous leverage even a small organization with definite, realistic views can wield? As Swanson says, in a vacuum even a little, well, bad smell, you know, makes a mighty bad smell."

"Yes, yes, but Alexander. For example. Just a few months ago you were so enormously excited by that girl you'd glimpsed only once, that girl with the big bosom. And now I understand she lives in the same house with you and you've not even mentioned her. You see? Or is it perhaps that you have been enjoying her and, a married man, have felt that delicacy prevented you from mentioning it? Really, you needn't be delicate with me, Alexander."

"No, Molly," Alexander said, "I haven't, I haven't at all. Yes, I find her exciting still, but, but things have been arranged differently. That's simply the way it is."

"It strikes me, Alexander, that for a grown man, you speak a great deal about things being arranged."

"Well, Molly, perhaps so, but then after all I've had enough experience of things being arranged for me by you."

"Are you comparing me with that little snip?" Mrs. Wheeler said.

"My wife, Molly, remember, my wife. No, not at all, you're quite different, you two, quite different. But, after all, I'm the same."

"Let's speak," Mrs. Wheeler said, "of something else. You are quite interested, then, in this political work you are doing?"

Alexander laughed. "Oh Molly," he said, "what have I been saying? Don't you see? If I bring it off why then I'll be managing too."

"Tell me frankly, Alexander," Mrs. Wheeler said. "I can see that you have thrown yourself quite thoroughly into this business and I won't pretend to you that I understand it or find it very interesting, but I can see that you do. But, quite frankly, weren't you happier before, in the days when you had that snug little house downtown and those poor little girls you would tell me about with such a sparkle in your eye?"

"Happier?" Alexander said. He got up, sat by his sister on the couch and took her hand. "You are a devil, Molly. You know everything, you always have. Yes, I was happier then, Molly, much happier, much. But it can't be helped, Molly, I've been pointed in another direction and given a push, and it can't be helped."

"I was, too," Mrs. Wheeler said. "I enjoyed your stories so much. I did. Alexander, you don't suppose you could think back, rack your brain, and tell me some stories you never told me? For example, I distinctly remember you started to tell me about a tiny, tiny little blonde girl, but we were interrupted and you never did. Do you remember?"

"I remember," Alexander said. He paused. "No, Molly, I don't think I'd better do that. I don't think I'd better."

Mrs. Wheeler put her hand on her brother's hand, and they sat in silence.

✳ 23 ✳

Marie, Lydia and Kennan (with, Kennan said, "the kind of sickened terrified fascination with which one contemplates one's own castration") had decided to investigate meetings of Troops of The American Force, each to a different meeting, in capacity as officials of The Force. All arranged by letter, they went, and returned.

Marie got back first and was drinking when Lydia came. They drank until Kennan came. When Kennan came he drank.

"More horrible, more horrible," Kennan said. "I'd expected, what? At least half comic. Little old ladies in tennis shoes, as the lieutenant governor said. But oh no, not comic in any regard, beneath the thin surface of raw raging hilarity.

"You will perhaps understand that for me the horror was heightened, or more accurately, perhaps, one dimension of the horror was that they were all Catholics, Irish, German, Polish, Slovak, but all Catholics. No, nobody said so, there was no Pope play or Bishop banter or parish prattle but I knew, I knew, my nose is excellently tuned to my own.

"Clean but shabby apartment. Hot. Taste still hungover from American Gothic; much furniture, much decoration, much gewgaw. Lower middle class. Middle middle age. Nine women, five men. Troop chief Mrs. Zonia Gorman. Irish. Catholic. Tall. Dry.

Her husband Thomas present; tall, squeezed, a telephone company employee for thirty years. Rates and schedules department.

"Chatter. I chatter much, all impressed with emissary from Headquarters. I chatter much and well, drinking coffee.

"Mrs. Gorman summons order. Rapping spoon on coffee tray. And she said, 'Hail Mary full of Grace have you all read your Last Stand,' their Last Stand, our Last Stand, my Last Stand. They murmured yes.

"Mrs. Gorman barked, 'Hail Mary full of Grace report of the letter writing committee.' Then plump Mrs. Octracki filling tight and hard the disciplined glitter of her uniform strode to the great map wall in the air-conditioned underground steel air and with her pointer touched a city and said, 'Hail Mary full of Grace overkill,' the city blackened on the map, she touched a city and said, 'Hail Mary full of Grace counterforce,' the city blackened on the map. When she had blackened six of our cities she turned, lifted chin, tightened lips, looked eagles in her eyes, nodded, strode to her seat.

"Chief Gorman barked, 'Hail Mary full of Grace report of the books committee.' Then gray Mr. Kaufmann in his great black robe leaned forward and said to the little girl looking up at him, 'Now, Selma, you were heard to tell your friend Jeannine that you knew where babies come from.' 'Yes, sir,' said the little girl, 'I found out.' 'But you've been told where babies come from,' Mr. Kaufmann said, 'they come from God.' 'Oh, yes, sir,' the little girl said, 'but I didn't mean that I meant what men and women do to make.' 'Enough,' roared Mr. Kaufmann. 'It is the order of this court that the body of Selma Richter be carried to stone cell underground and that she be flung upon the stone of that cell to lie in slime and muck, to lie in that slime while the legs of insects and the teeth of mice torment her body, hungry and thirsty and blind in the dark to lie on the slimed stone until the torment of her body has driven from her mind the gutter filth that babies come elsewhere than from God, Hail Mary full of Grace.' Then Mr. Kaufmann turned to the pudgy, balding young man looking up at him and said, 'And you, sir, were heard to be crying at night?' 'Yes, sir,' the young man said, 'I couldn't help it, I felt simply terrible. Anton, this boy I've been living with, or really he's been living with me, it's my apartment after all, though I've never, never made a thing of it, Anton, this boy, really a wonderful boy, in his way, good looks and beautiful manners and so lively and cheerful when he wanted to be, but recently he's been, oh, restless, I could feel it, restless, and then three days ago he called and said he probably wouldn't be home that night and he wasn't and the next day when I came home he'd come and taken all his things and there wasn't even a note or anything and when I call him at his job he won't speak to me and he hasn't called me and I've heard he's living with that Michael on Riverside Drive. And before I used to look forward so much to coming home and getting there just after Anton or just before and we'd change our clothes and mix up some really good martinis and talk about what had happened during the day and laugh at things and in a while we'd make dinner, both of us helping, and we'd eat and the evening and, oh, wonderful. But now I dread coming home, I've tried going with other boys but I don't want to, so I go home and the place is empty and I'm empty and there is no end to it. So I cried.' Mr. Kaufmann's lips were pulled back from his teeth and he said, 'Men do not cry. This disgusting perversion of God's and nature's law is a cancer that must be ripped from a healthy community, it is a rot that must be ruthlessly destroyed in a healthy society. The order of this court is that you be carried below ground and the proper officer be deputed to tear from you your genitals. Hail Mary full of Grace.' And Mr. Kaufmann swept from the bench as the court rose.

"And then we had more coffee and more chatter, I had to chatter a lot, and we all went away," Kennan said. "I feel sick."

"No," Lydia said, "mine wasn't like that at all, not at all. Mine was in a very nice apartment, new. There were quite a lot of people, as many as thirty, maybe, half men and half women, everyone but me was in couples, married. All quite young, late twenties, early thirties. Very nice appearance they all made. Men in dark suits. Women in cocktail dresses.

"I got a drink, Scotch and water, and a couple came up and introduced themselves. They asked me what I did at Headquarters and when I told them I had to do with Last Stand they said what a marvelous thing it was, 'really,' the man said, 'in the tradition of the early part of the century muckrakers, Tarbell and Steffens and so forth, but this time revealing the scabs of the

Liberal establishment. Of course,' the man went on, 'aside from the eye-opening revelations, no, not perhaps revelations, we all know the kind of thing that's going on in this country, the documentary evidence, let's say, which is so important and necessary, in addition to that I must say I think your paper has another splendid quality. I mean the style, that delicious parody of those hordes of lice who feed the American people what the establishment wants them to know.'

" 'Simply marvelous,' the woman said.

" 'Frankly, between ourselves,' the man said, 'I've noticed that too often our fellow conservatives, however worthy and right-thinking, tend to adopt the establishment tone of heavy-handed humorlessness, officialese, bureaucratese, a sort of distillation of the dusty soullessness of the establishment man, you know, the kind of scum who works for a quote respectable unquote foundation and drinks beer from a can because he thinks it's earthy and hates God. Well, your paper certainly is a refreshing breeze.'

" 'Simply divoon,' the woman said. 'I always read it to our Ricky, he's four, at bedtime, he's hysterical for it.' The man frowned and they drifted away, chatting heatedly.

"Another couple drifted up and introduced themselves and the man said, 'You know, a friend of mine told me something you might want to put into that excellent paper of yours, kind of a tip to turn the tables on the barbarians. Whenever anybody in his shop, he's VP in one of the big fund-raising outfits, starts talking about integration and voting registration for the poor down-trodden Negro and all that soft-headed jazz, why he pretends to get really mad and says didn't they know his family was from the south and his sister was almost raped by a nigger, he comes right out and says nigger, and they ought to know better than to talk like that in front of him. And when they say, kind of stunned, no, really, how awful, I didn't know, why he goes on to say yes, and they certainly took care of that nigger's ass for him, they certainly did. And as far as I know he's never been south of Jersey City. Of course, I wouldn't dare try to get away with that kind of thing in my shop, it would be suicide for me, but a lot of your readers might.'

" 'Wait till you get your promotion, dear,' the woman said.

" 'For God's sake, Alice,' the man said, 'stop pushing me.'

"I got myself a drink and the host called order by clapping his hands together. It took a time, but when they were quiet he said, 'All right, boys and girls, calm it a little, we won't be long and you can go back to your gossip.' (There was a titter.) 'Now, the one thing I wanted to talk to you about today, and I know from speaking to a number of you this evening that I'm not alone in my concern, is.' And a man standing close to the speaker called out, 'World peace.' (There was a laugh, a loud long laugh.) 'No,' the speaker said, smiling, 'not world peace,' (There was a laugh.) 'nor, for that matter, the danger of fallout,' (There was a great loud laugh.) 'nor hunger in the poor, pardon me, backward, pardon me, emergent nations,' (The great loud laugh was an artillery salvo; the woman standing next to me had her hand over her eyes, was shrieking between hiccups, leaned her forehead helplessly against my shoulder.) 'nor any of that jazz. But seriously, but seriously, now,' (He had to say it several more times before the laughter gargled away.) 'there is something to which we should turn our urgent concern. As several of you know, a bill is being prepared in the Congress of the United States establishing stand-by internment camps for political unreliables in case of emergency. This is quite plainly another in an endless series of attempts to hoodwink the American people by fake measures not seriously designed to do what they are supposed to do. Now don't laugh, but how many internment camps does this pseudo-bill envisage? Now don't laugh, but a great big whopping FOUR.' (Intakes of outrage, a sea of hisses, two women together cried, 'Traitors.') 'Exactly. So I urge each and every one of you, without delay, to write your Congressman and your Senator demanding—not asking, not urging, but demanding—an adequate internment program. I think we can agree that at least one hundred high-security camps is the minimum number consonant with the national safety.' (Cries of 'More, more.') 'Thank you.' There was applause.

"A woman next to me started talking about her children. I felt sick."

"No," Marie said, "mine wasn't like that, but I won't talk about it. I feel sick."

"We've got to do something," Kennan said.

"We do," Marie said.

24

"Well," Friberg said in his office, "you seem to have arranged, with cool calculation, a nice stinking mess."

"Don't tell me," Marie said.

"My, my," Friberg said. "Periodicals, clubs, organizations and now even a monster city-wide rally. My, my."

"There is nothing so powerful as an idea whose time has come," Marie said.

"I thought it wasn't funny," Friberg said.

"It isn't," Marie said. "I'm laughing to stanch the blood. Oh, hell. I'll think of something, I guess. You got any ideas?"

"None whatsoever," Friberg said. "Except that your known genius for improvisation get off its ass."

"Yes," Marie said.

"Speaking of which," Friberg said, "what of your demon lover?"

"He's all right," Marie said, "worried about this, but all right. Why the ungenerous tone?"

"Hell," Friberg said. "The bastard never called me, never wrote, nothing. We were never the grandest of chums, but still, it is as if I had ceased to exist. Annoying."

"These things happen," Marie said. "You scared him, I guess, not you but your domesticity, and he decided he didn't want that scare any more. Maybe. Who knows?"

"The human soul and its writhings is, you suggest, unfathomable?"

"If it's human enough," Marie said. "Okay, I got to go meet this Swanson example of complex humanity and decide about the hall. My best at home."

"The hall?" Friberg said. "The hall where Alexander Forbes is going to rally his legions to the Free Christian West? You are a busy one."

"I know, I know," Marie said. "I've got to keep some kind of control. Or at least be where I can control if I can think of what to signal the engine room."

"How about Full Reverse?" Friberg said.

"You sound like me a while back," Marie said, "when you were trying to tell me it was a complicated universe and I wasn't being convinced."

"I'll say one thing for you," Friberg said. "It's a complicated universe, and you do a damned good job of making it more complicated."

"Can't let the damn thing run down," Marie said. "That was Kennan's trouble. He tried to simplify."

"I do not," Friberg said, "want to hear about it."

When Marie arrived at the West Side Assembly Swanson was waiting on the sidewalk. "Wonderful timing," he cried, firmly helping her out of the taxi, "just got here this minute myself."

Marie looked at the building's anonymous façade. "You wouldn't think," she said, "that behind this anonymous façade will be lit a torch to act beacon for all America."

"Ah, no," Swanson said. "I've been checking into their arrangements, seating and public address and so forth. I think you'll find them suitable."

"Swanson," Marie said. "I want a word with you."

"Mrs. Forbes," Swanson said.

Marie drew Swanson under the marquee, against the wall by the entrance. "Look Swanson," she said, "I've been watching you, my old eye's been boring right on in. You think you're so damn opaque, you with your executive gray hair and businessman's stride, your glib PR vocabulary and easy enthusiasms. But boy, I see through you as if you were a mere paltry book. You got that?"

"Ah so?" Swanson said.

"So," Marie said. "I know. Despite all that greasy old oil you give to Alexander, I know you hate this mess, the stinking newsletter and the stinking clubs and the whole stinking vicious fart of it. But you play along, you help, you suggest. And boy, do you hate yourself for it. You got to, you keep on saying, you're in business, the money's there, you've got a wife, a family, a house, a car, you've got no choice but to mine the shit-pile, but boy do you hate it."

"No, ma'am," Swanson said, "I don't hate myself, I love myself, in a purely non-technical sense. It's you damn white people I hate. That's right, I don't look it, I pass, but I happen to be a colored man myself. You see a couple of my sisters, you'd be in no doubt. And I don't hate what I'm doing, I enjoy it. Why, girl, why wouldn't I enjoy setting up something to help the white-faced bastards cut each other's God damn lily-white throats, help destroy this flatulent white society in blood and violence? Oh, sure, all the talk about non-violent resistance is all right for talk, and maybe it'll do some good, too, but I figure with Reverend Martin Luther King pulling at one end and me pushing at the other, why, girl, we'll have us here a black republic yet."

"I'll be darned," Marie said.

"You'll be discreet, too," Swanson said, "I've got affidavits to prove I'm a liar."

"Not a word," Marie said. "Let's go check the place."

Marie and Swanson sat through the fat manager's exhaustive exposition of the services supplied with the hiring of the hall. Marie fidgeted with her pearls, stretched her legs out before her, shifted from right ankle on left to left ankle on right, smoked; Swanson sat squarely, feet flat on floor, without expression or movement except for, from time to time, lifting one hand and gently running its finger tips in a half circle from the center of his forehead to the end of his chin. When the manager had finished, Marie said, "Fine, that sounds fine, wonderful what you do for the money, don't see how you make a profit, don't you think so, Mr. Swanson, we'll take it, of course."

Swanson opened his mouth to agree, but the fat manager insisted that first they must make personal inspection of the facilities. Marie and Swanson tramped behind as he pointed out the

202

rows of empty seats, the dais, the lights, the electrical equipment. Finally done, they returned to the office and signed the rental agreement. "At last," Marie said. "You like the hard sell, hey?"

"I don't like to think of myself as just a manager," the manager said. "I like to think of myself as a salesman. There's the art, there's the challenge. Get your customer in one hand and your goods or services, as the case may be, in the other and ram, ram, ram, he need it or not, he even like it or not, ram, ram and make it stick. Kind of like an art, I think of it."

"Good-day," Marie said.

Outside, Swanson grinned and said, "See what I mean? I didn't notice you voiced any, but surely you can't have any objections, on the high principled plane, at least, if not the low personal one, to busting up that culture complex, whatever comes after, demons dusky or devils dark."

"Swanson," Marie said, "white, black or with a liver in the Mac-Bright tartan, don't be an ass. It is not my intention to destroy, it is my intention to purify." Swanson laughed. "Laugh," Marie said.

25

The evening before The American Force Rally, Alexander, previously all cheer and optimism, began to worry. "But I mean," he said, "if absolutely no one turns up, we'll look pretty silly. Make us a laughingstock. Harm the cause."

"Now, now," Swanson said.

"But how can you know?" Alexander said. "Or that smooth young man you hired for master of ceremonies. Didn't like his looks. How do you know he won't forget what he's supposed to say? At best. For that matter, have you any reason to suppose he's with us, he's not one of them, he won't suddenly turn on us, try to undo our good work?"

"One of whom?" Marie said.

"Please," Alexander said. "I'm even worried about my own speech. Oh, I've got it all by heart now, I believe, I've worked at it diligently enough. But it's not a thing I've done before, in front of all those people. What if I lose control?"

"Now, now," Swanson said.

"Or you do, or even Marie," Alexander said. "My dear, are you quite sure you want to insist on making a speech? Aren't you afraid you'll, somehow, stumble?"

"No," Marie said.

"Well, perhaps you're right," Alexander said, "the voice of

women, solidarity with husband, all that sort of thing. But still. Don't you think we should have gotten at least one well-known figure? A general. A senator. A somebody?"

"Now, now," Swanson said. "We went over and over that. We don't want any outsider to use us as a forum for his own publicity. And we want to stay in charge of the movement ourselves, you at the top, of course, me for public and press relations, Mrs. Forbes for staff work."

"That's a damn poor ordering of hierarchy," Marie said.

"Apologies," Swanson said. "Just the three of us running things, a tight, principled, dedicated, mutually loyal little band. Right? Right."

"I know," Alexander said, "but still, I'm nervous."

"Alexander," Marie said. "Go to bed. Prepare for your emergence on the world stage by a sound sleep. And don't dream."

"Perhaps you're right, my dear," Alexander said, made his goodnights and left.

Swanson looked at Marie. "Why do you regard me so, treacherous hireling?" Marie said.

"Wondering," Swanson said. "I am just a simple black man, but I was wondering if you were planning to pull some show of your own tomorrow."

"Like what?" Marie said.

"Like if I knew I wouldn't wonder," Swanson said.

"What would you do if I did?" Marie said.

"Watch," Swanson said.

"Swanson," Marie said, "go prepare for your emergence on the world et cetera."

"Sleep well," Swanson said.

The next afternoon Marie and Lydia went to the hairdresser. Lydia had her long black hair put into an enormous stiff bell. Marie had tippings of silver added to her brown curls. They went home, had a light early supper, began to bathe and dress. At seven Alexander called in to Marie that he was leaving to meet Swanson at the hall. By eight Marie and Lydia were ready in their new long dresses from Bergdorf, Lydia's black, Marie's scarlet brocade, inspected each other, nodded, and went down to get a taxi.

It was a warm pleasant night in spring, in the middle of May. When they got out in front of the hall, Alexander and Kennan were standing together, watching the hordes shuffle through the entrance. "Lord, Lord," Alexander said, "it actually worked, it actually did. Look at them, they came."

"Wonderful," Kennan said to Marie, "you look really wonderful. And so do you," to Lydia. "Both of you look absolutely superb."

"Thousands," Alexander said, "Swanson says there'll be thousands, he says we won't have room for them all, some will have to stand and will be turned away. I'm so excited I, I, I don't know when I've been so excited."

"Remember the ticker," Marie said. "That sick old pump." She motioned with her head at Kennan and he and Lydia moved some paces aside with her. "The muscle all fixed?" Marie asked.

"Fixed," Kennan said. "I've got them sitting on the dais where you said. Alexander's so star-eyed he didn't notice, but Swanson asked. I said it was your orders and he let it go, looking thoughtful."

"And you gave them simple, easy to follow instructions?" Marie said.

"As ordered," Kennan said. "After a certain amount of detail work they seemed to get what was wanted. God, what a wonderful company to work for. Ask for muscle, muscle is supplied. No questions. Speaking of same, are you ready to answer any?"

"No," Marie said. "I'd feel too silly if it doesn't work. Let's go." They rejoined Alexander and the four of them slipped through the people stream and down the building to the other entrance. As they got to it, Swanson came out. "Thousands of them," he said, "I'll be damned. Come on, we'd better get on the dais. It looks dumb with all those people staring at nothing. Give them a stare at what they came to hear from."

Standing at the entrance to the dais was the big plump afternoon television personality, Jock Gallagher, their master of ceremonies. He had never seen Lydia before, and stared. Marie and Alexander greeted him. Then the six of them moved into the glare of the dais.

Two big men were sitting there already. Alexander, moving toward his rehearsed place just in front of them, frowned and turned to Marie. "All right," she whispered. "From the Troops.

Help keep order. I'll introduce them afterward." Alexander nodded and sat down, Marie next to him.

Alexander whispered in Marie's ear. "Good idea. They look like gorillas."

"Don't breathe in my God damn ear," Marie whispered. "They are."

Marie looked out at the audience. There were some lights shining in her eyes, but not very brightly. It was, however, curiously difficult to distinguish faces in the audience; the fact of composing an audience seemed to blend them.

Swanson nodded, and Jock Gallagher stood up to the microphone. Quickly the drone of the audience, remarkably quiet anyway for so many, dimmed. "Dear hearts," Jock began, the words written for him by Swanson. He congratulated them on their interest in public service as evidenced by their presence here tonight, he told a small joke about two pickaninnies in Alabam' who were afraid to go *anywhere*, which received a gratifying laugh, and introduced Swanson as one of the founders of The American Force, a man high in its councils, a strong right arm of its president himself, Mr. Alexander Forbes, from whom they would be hearing before long. There was gratifying applause as Jock sat down and Swanson approached the microphone.

It had been decided that the more elevated philosophical data and historical precepts which guided The American Force would be most suitably presented by Alexander, that Marie's speech, while touching briefly on wider matters would deal with Alexander himself and what it meant to be the wife of a man so dedicated, so consecrated, while for Swanson was reserved the acid polemic that constituted so much of their journal, Last Stand. Swanson had relied heavily on Marie's contributions to Last Stand, but he delivered himself with a rousing vigor that Marie, through her worry about her own speech, admired. Waving his arms and his voice, Swanson produced the deadly machine-gun bursts that had so quickly captured so avid a readership of Last Stand, and that now found equal response as attested by the gasps, the moans, the cries of the audience. Retiring into thought, Marie heard only random key phrases: "rape of the Christian West . . . mongrelization of America . . . conspiracy of the slavemasters from Harvard . . . cowards who value life over death . . .

fluoridation of water . . . scum in the Warren Court . . . red-hearted, yellow-bellied black-skinned slime befouling . . . hit first, hit hard and trust in God . . . it's just because you people are decent that they hate you."

When he had done the audience rose and screamed wordless ovation, pounding their palms. Swanson stood before them, bowing slightly from time to time. When, after a time, the storm showed no signs of slackening, he turned and went to his seat. As he sat down he glanced across at Marie, smiling slightly.

Jock stood at the microphone while the noise died. His sure show-business instinct, honed fine by years of trouping in afternoon television, told him that this audience was with them, so he omitted the small prepared joke and swung right into the next introduction, saying that they could now look forward to hearing from the young lady who had the great privilege of sharing the life and work of Mr. Alexander Forbes, a young lady who, despite or perhaps because of her youth, had demonstrated an incredibly sure grasp of The American Force, and who had contributed enormously to its success, almost as much indeed as Mr. Alexander Forbes himself. He presented Mrs. Alexander Forbes. There was much applause.

Marie came to the microphone and said, "Well, look," and paused. Then she went on. "You know, I'm glad Mr. Swanson over there told you all the things he did. I'm glad because that means I don't have to say them. I'm tired of them. After all, they come from that no-good sheet Last Stand, and I write most of that. I mean, I make up all that crap out of my head, and I'm tired of it. (Animation in the hall.)

"But there was something I wanted to tell you people, and something I wanted to ask you. What I wanted to tell you is that you people are absolute idiots to believe all those stupid lies. And I wanted to ask you, why do you people believe all those stupid lies?"

There was animation on the dais as Alexander struggled to get up. But the two big men behind him held him easily down. Alexander shouted, "Stop her," but of course Marie had the microphone.

"I don't want to blame you too much," she said. "I mean, I understand it's not easy for you people. You get lied at so much, all the time, your newspapers lie at you and your television and your radio. Your government lies at you for the government and a lot of people lie to you against the government and your companies lie to you and your unions lie to you. Sure, I understand that. But what do you have to be so dumb for and believe them?

"And it should be so obvious, even to ones as dumb as you, that they're lying to get themselves something. Take my husband Forbes, over there, for example. Even if you can't tell he's the kind of son of a bitch who likes to tie girls up and kick them in the belly, can't you tell he's lying to get you to follow him and put him in some lousy office so he can do more lying? Can't you tell?"

There was a crash on the dais as Alexander in his writhing knocked over his chair and escaped the heavy hands. On his hands and knees he shrieked at Marie, "Whore, whore," started to rise, and collapsed. Swanson stepped to the microphone and said, "Is there a doctor in the house?" There were many doctors in the house and they all agreed Alexander was dead.

"How tragic, how unspeakably tragic," Mrs. Wheeler said, "that we should first meet under these circumstances."

"It is, really," Marie said.

"I am sure I do not understand why," Mrs. Wheeler said. "I cannot tell you how many times I urged, I pleaded with Alexander to effect an introduction. After all, his only sister, his wife. But no. In that curiously stubborn manner he sometimes showed, he would not. Can you explain at all why?"

"No," Marie said, "I can't. I hadn't thought about it. I'm not close to my family, so I suppose I just took it as natural. But maybe, now that I do think about it, he was ashamed. Ashamed to introduce me to you. Or, of course, to introduce you to me."

"But why on earth?" Mrs. Wheeler said.

"I couldn't tell you, really," Marie said. "I would if I could but I can't."

There was a considerable silence while both the ladies sipped their tea.

"I hope you don't think me heartless," Mrs. Wheeler said, "if I don't ask you to go over the circumstantial details of Alexander's passing. The lawyer man told me, of course, what happened, but, to be perfectly frank, I'd rather not hear the details."

"I agree with you," Marie said. "Whatever purpose it serves, it's not pretty."

"Purpose," Mrs. Wheeler said, "oh yes. To believe that there is a purpose. It is a great thing. Tell me, my dear, do you believe that?"

"Yes," Marie said.

"I won't ask you about your beliefs," Mrs. Wheeler said. "It is not really a fit subject for discussion. Besides, I'm sure they're all true, in their way."

Marie said nothing. There was more silence and the ladies finished their tea.

"I do hope," Mrs. Wheeler said, "that in your grief you find nothing to mar the sorrowful memory of Alexander. I am aware, as elder sisters are always aware, I suppose, that Alexander had his little faults. As of course we all do. But I know that Alexander, oh, years ago, perhaps, was sometimes harsh, even hard, in his, in certain areas of his life. If that was the case with you, I want you to feel perfectly free to confide in me, if that confidence will wash away the tiny imperfections of your memory of Alexander."

"No," Marie said. "Not with me."

"Oh," Mrs. Wheeler said. Then she said, "I understand that you have yet to speak with the lawyers?"

"Not yet," Marie said.

"I am not, of course," Mrs. Wheeler said, "acquainted with the details of Alexander's affairs. But there will be dreadful taxes, of course. And, as you know, Alexander had children by his first wife, poor Alice."

"No kidding?" Marie said. "I didn't."

"Oh yes," Mrs. Wheeler said, "poor Alice. She died. And then, of course, Alexander and I were very close, very close indeed. But I am sure you will find that Alexander has been just as generous as it is possible to be. Under the circumstances."

"Whatever, I'll not complain," Marie said.

"That's a dear," Mrs. Wheeler said. "And now, my child, you will excuse me?"

"Of course," Marie said, going.

✻ 27 ✻

"Do you want," Friberg said in his office, "to tell me exactly what happened?"

"I don't think so," Marie said. "Not exactly. Besides, that part is mere unenlightening history. We must look forward."

"To what?" Friberg said.

"That is the question," Marie said. "Anyway, to continue. So this morning I see the lawyers. Jesus."

"Jesus?" Friberg said.

"Well, first they go on about how I must realize the almost confiscatory nature of inheritance taxes at a certain level and they go on about I am aware that Mr. Forbes had commitments due to his prior marriage. Sure, sure, I say, how much, I mean I didn't, but that was my position. Then they go on about how Mr. Forbes had made certain arrangements to ameliorate the loss to taxes but that these arrangements were not quite as complete as might have been desired. Sure, sure, sure. Then they start on Alexander's share in this joint."

"Oh?" Friberg said.

"Well, you know how it is with lawyers when they're working. Not thoroughly human so it's hard to tell what's going through their cunning little minds. But I gathered, and I gathered I was meant to gather, that a little while ago old Alexander decided to screw his sister, so he left his share in the joint to me. I further gathered that this made everybody uncomfortable, especially his sister, and the lawyers went on how it was in violation of previous agreements perhaps not strictly binding if put to the legal test but which certainly needed to be considered and about how such division of ultimate responsibility might tend to depress the value of the property and about how some accommodation might very properly be made on both sides. And then a very gentle hint that the sister might make trouble if I didn't play along. So what I finally gathered was I sell her Alexander's share pretty cheap and she doesn't make trouble."

"You need a lawyer," Friberg said. "Those are hers."

"Just what I was thinking," Marie said, "especially after all that poor-mouth in the beginning. Bad tactics. Then, pretty casually, they mention how much I get if I play."

"Yes?" Friberg said. "Come, come, the point, the point."

"Well, what with this thing and that, what with my part of the loot and selling the share of this place and some kinds of trusts and so on, annual present income sixty-five thousand dollars, give or take a dollar."

"Great God," Friberg said.

"Right," Marie said. "So I figured, hell, why be greedy. I'm sure the sister is screwing me, certainly, but after all there are more important things in life than money and to descend into the arena with her would be sordid and besides."

"Besides?" Friberg said.

"A couple of besides," Marie said. "So I said yes."

"Yes," Friberg said. "Well. Are you to be congratulated? A husband lost, a fortune won?"

"You are damn right I am," Marie said. "Wow."

"I don't want," Friberg said, "to play the puling clergyman, but Alexander was your husband and was a man. Wouldn't a certain amount of regret be more seemly?"

"It would be fake," Marie said. "Alexander had to go."

"As do we all," Friberg said.

"True," Marie said, "but Alexander had to go now. Death is bad, but it was better that Alexander go. Otherwise there were worse things coming. But that, as I say, is past. Let us face the future."

"Which, I gather," Friberg said, "consists in lolling about with painted boys between calls to your broker or bank."

"Not altogether," Marie said. "Oh, I've learned a lot. You remember before I was casting around. But I didn't have anything near the freedom and resources I've got now. And then Alexander's thing started getting wound up and I thought I could be clever and ride that in the right direction but I learned I couldn't. I learned if something is that bad intrinsically you can't be clever and ride it, you lose control or you destroy it. Oh, I've learned some things. And now I'll have time and scope. I don't know where I'll go, but I'll go."

"It hardly seems fair," Friberg said. "Here am I, a mature man of incomparable qualities doomed to serf away for my bread. And here are you, a chicken-headed little fluff of a girl-child, free from the need for odious toil, free to follow the lightest littlest whim of your dollar covered heart."

"Remember," Marie said, "you once told me that civilization was made possible when the earth toilers produced enough surplus to support a class which could use its head instead of its back?"

"Possibly," Friberg said.

"Well, consider yourself in the glorious position of the surplus producing tiller," Marie said. "Me, I'm civilization."

"I hope so," Friberg said. "Marie, I hope so."

"Boy, so do I," Marie said.

Lydia and Kennan were at the apartment when Marie got there. She told them about the meeting with the lawyers and smiled at them.

"Congratulations," Kennan said, "hearty congratulations. You manage to do right at the starting gate what it takes most American women forty years to do, kill off your husband and be a rich bitch on the proceeds. Wonderful."

"Thank you," Marie said.

"Oh God, you're a monster," Kennan said. "Look, Lydia honey, do you mind if I talk with her alone a minute?"

"Sure," Lydia said, getting up. "I myself think it's fine. Perfectly fine. Real congratulations, honey." She left the room.

"Strange," Marie said, "you'd think she'd be envious. After all, she was the bait."

"Shut up," Kennan said. "For once in your life, shut up. Listen. Now this miserable farce is done. 1 don't like the way it was done but it's done. Now you can marry me. You got that? You marry me now."

"I don't think so," Marie said. "But thanks a lot."

"I'm not asking what you think," Kennan said. "I'm telling you what. I've had enough of your pushing me around, God damn it, now I'm pushing."

"I mean the thanks," Marie said, "I really do. But I don't think so."

"Don't you, now," Kennan said. "You don't, eh. Now listen to a little of your own sweet methods get used on you. You marry me or else I go to those lawyers or Alexander's sister or whoever I have to and tell them it wasn't really a marriage, you blackmailed him into it and it wasn't consummated and it isn't valid and then all this blood money you're chortling over will disappear and then where are you? Then you're standing out in the middle of the street with a hole in your slip and the cold wind whistling through it. And all your plans to remake the world whistling away on that wind. You understand me? It isn't a question of choice. You don't have any question of choice. Now, that's settled."

"Francis," Marie said, "Francis. Don't be silly." Kennan opened his eyes very wide at her, then sat down. "Look," Marie said. "I'm not twenty-one, yet. It's too early. I know that everybody gets married these days practically before they're out of high school, but no. I'm not ready yet. I want to bounce some before I do. Here, there. Bounce around. Learn more. Learn more, for one reason, so I can be a better mother to my kids than mine was. Bounce around so I won't think I've missed things and make you a lousy wife. I'm sorry, Francis, but not yet."

"My threat," Kennan said. "What about my threat?"

"Silly," Marie said. "You wouldn't do it in the first place and you can't prove it in the second place and I'd deny it in the third place and you wouldn't do it anyway. I'm sorry, but not yet."

"Not yet," Kennan said. "Talking of ages. I'm thirty-six. I'm tired of bouncing. I'd say I'd wait until you're ready, but I don't want to wait. I want to get married now."

"Lydia," Marie said.

"Lydia?" Kennan said.

"She's ready," Marie said.

"But," Kennan said.

Marie shouted, "Hey, Lydia, Lydia, Lydia."

Footsteps in the hall and Lydia came in, saying, "God's sake, what's the big noise?"

"Ask her," Marie said.

"Lydia," Kennan said, then turned to Marie. "You can't do this with people," he said.

"Sure I can," Marie said. "Ask her."

"Lydia," Kennan said, "will you marry me?"

Lydia thought for a moment. "Is it okay with you?" she asked Marie.

"I think it's wonderful," Marie said.

"I'd like to," Lydia said.

"Wonderful," Marie said. "Let's have a drink on it."

"God, you're a monster," Kennan said.

Marie looked disturbed for a moment. "I know," she said.